Merit: To be worthy of; deserve. Something that deserves or justifies a reward or commendation.

Meritism: An economical structure using productivity as the measure of currency. Compensation is based on an individual's productivity leveled against their emotional quotient and intelligence quotient, measured by factual data, free from emotional bias, prejudice, and subjectivity.

Meritocracy: Governance or the holding of power by people selected on the basis of their ability.

Luke Medina

By Martin Medina and Luke Medina

Edited by Dianne L. Sloan

Cover Artwork by Mia Medina Mueller

Readers:

Stephanie Dickinson, Tom Conley, Cathy Medina, Tina Medina,

Terri Medina, Kristin Wahl, Shawn Wingard

Jim Bush (author of Halloween Candy I and II)

Mercedes Guy (author of What It Took)

Lucia J. Johnson (author of Glimpses of Life)

Amerita.us

facebook.com/Amerita.novel/

Martin.T.Medina@gmail.com

Luke.T.Medina@gmail.com

Printed in the U.S.A.

AMERITA

Monday

December 4, 2051

Apprehension

Rain is pounding outside Luke's Dodge Charger. He disengages auto-navigate and carefully swerves around the early morning traffic.

He has been following their trail for a month, non-stop, and the garage is almost in sight. Luke turns off the siren and visualizes the upcoming encounter with the targets. His electric muscle car is stealthy. The only sound is coming from the tires rolling through puddles on the asphalt. He pulls up to the building and parks beneath a devilish-red glowing sign, *Machete's Car Repair*.

Stepping out of his cruiser, Luke takes off his slim-fitting, Kevlar-lined, black jacket and unties his black tie, leaving both draped over the driver's seat. Then he tosses his mirrored shades onto the dashboard.

Luke grabs the bar on the bottom of the garage door and pulls. "Damn it, locked," he mumbles under his breath. Taking a step back, he pulls out his handgun and shoots where the lock should be on the other side. He pulls again and the door slides up.

He yells to the three mechanics hunched over the tables of computers, circuit boards, 3-D printers, and half-finished counterfeit M-Ns, "Why the hell was the door locked? I wasted a good bullet on that."

He pauses for a moment, wondering if leaving his protective suit-jacket in the car was a good trade-off for better fighting mobility.

"Who the hell are you?" asks a burly man with the name 'Joe' embroidered on his mechanic's suit.

"I'm here for the M-Ns. How are they coming? I've got cash. Are they ready yet or what?" Luke impatiently replies.

"Listen buddy, I don't know who you are or what you want, but you really need to back off," the man warns.

Luke casually walks over to a powered-down computer. In the dark reflection of the monitor, Luke catches sight of one of the mechanics charging him with a monkey wrench. Luke dodges to the side and spins with a round-house kick, smashing the mechanic's head through the computer.

The other mechanics pick up objects to use as weapons—one grabs a two-by-four and the other grabs a sledgehammer. The one with the two-by-four swings wildly, attempting to destroy the evidence.

Luke picks up a 3-D printer and throws it, smashing the man with the two-by-four in the back of the head, knocking him out cold.

The man with the sledgehammer dashes at Luke and takes a swing at his legs. Luke jumps over the weapon and Superman punches the last conscious mechanic in the face. As the man stumbles back, Luke sees that his nose is crooked and bent.

With blood spraying from his mouth, the mechanic shouts his surrender, "Okay. You win."

The backseat of Luke's black Charger is a tight fit for the three criminals. "Don't bleed on my ride," Luke warns. The criminal sitting on the passenger side attempts to spit blood in Luke's direction, but Luke slams the back door shut with a roundhouse kick, smashing the criminal's nose into the inside of the window, right where his bloody spit landed.

The bulletproof glass prevents all sound from escaping his vehicle, but Luke easily reads the bloody man's lips. He acquired the skill of lipreading in school as an elective, taken in an attempt to figure out the last words his father spoke to him. He rewatched his father's final Merit Review hundreds of times, but he's never been able to decipher those last words.

Through the soundproof glass, all three criminals are pleading to not be exiled. Luke knows exactly what they are saying and taunts them further by mouthing, "WHAT?" and cupping his hand around his ear.

Before Luke can walk around to the driver's seat, his backup arrives. Merit Agency Investigators Murphy and Hopwood step out of their compact car. "Yo, Medina. What the hell, dude? Why didn't you wait for us?" Hopwood asks.

"Needed the challenge," Luke replies. "Can you guys do me a favor? I want to get to my Merit Review early. I'm scheduled for 07:30. Can we swap cars and you take them in for processing?"

The forensics van arrives and Agent Morgan quickly exits the vehicle. "Medina, nice work! Did you find any M-Ns?"

Murphy answers for Luke, "Yep, we sure did. 'We' as in 'Luke,' that is."

Agent Morgan jokes, "So Luke didn't wait for backup again? Typical." He strolls over to the rear passenger's seat, peers into the window through the smeared spit and blood, inches away from the criminal, and yells through the bulletproof glass, "You guys are screwed. We've got your counterfeit M-Ns. Hope you enjoy exile!" The criminal, now with a broken nose, head-butts the glass, sending a wave of fear through Morgan's spine as he jumps back and stumbles to the ground.

Murphy, Hopwood, and Luke start laughing uncontrollably. Hopwood notices the position of his vehicle, "Hey, Morgan, I think we caught that on our dash-cam! That's going to make a great fail video. I'll let you know when the clip is up on YouTube!"

"Thanks, guys. I've got to get going. Take good care of my Charger," Luke orders as he walks toward their Prius. "Careful, she goes 0 to 60 in 2.3 seconds," Luke warns. He jumps into the car and drives away before Hopwood and Murphy can object to taking the criminals in for processing.

Merit Review

Upon arrival for a Merit Review and prior to entering the County's Merit Agency lobby, citizens are greeted by a Merit Agency greeter. In a ceremonial manner, the greeter disengages the citizen's personal Merit Number display, also known as the M-N. The illuminated holographic number, ranging from 1 to 10 and glowing above the back of the dominant hand, fades until it is no longer visible.

The greeter offers encouragement to the citizen with the phrase, "Good day, fellow citizen. Your new year begins today." There is no variation in the way this phrase is delivered. The uniform greeting is a reminder, prior to the Merit Review, that every citizen has equal opportunity to make meaningful contributions to the community. Merit Agency greeters practice the greeting hundreds of times during their training to ensure every citizen, regardless of their current Merit Number, receives the exact same encouraging and optimistic hospitality. Greeters who have difficulty offering an unbiased welcome to citizens with low Merit Numbers are reassigned before their training is even complete.

The greeter then hands the citizen a printed copy of his or her Vocation Summary and Productivity Calculation and welcomes the citizen into the lobby.

The lobby of the Merit Agency welcomes citizens with complimentary fruit, naturally flavored spring water, and leather recliners for a relaxing stay. The recliners are comfortably broken in and the leather is weathered but clean and well maintained. The atmosphere is designed to alleviate anxiety; however, anxiety is often extremely elevated and the comforts do little to diminish a citizen's apprehension over the annual review. A citizen's Merit

Number and vocation for the entire upcoming year hinges on the outcome of the Merit Review.

All Merit Reviews are broadcast live. They are available for viewing at the Merit Agency office, on a dedicated television channel, and on the Merit Agency website. On the website, reviews from every County are available for live viewing, and archived reviews are also available so citizens can access reviews they may not have been able to watch live.

Many citizens watch reviews live during the day, and others prefer to listen to them during their morning and afternoon commutes. The Amerita Governance determined that accountability through full disclosure of all reviews to all citizens bolsters commitment to Meritism.

Luke's Merit Review is scheduled for 07:30. The room assigned for his review is the third lobby past the main entrance. He arrives 30 minutes early. The Merit Agency greeter welcomes Luke with a warm, positive, encouraging, very standard, and predictable, "Good day, fellow citizen. Your new year begins today."

Luke replies, "Good morning. My name is Luke. I hope you don't mind that I'm early."

The greeter glances at her tablet, taps Luke's name, and notes his early arrival. "Thank you for your promptness, Luke. Please enjoy a beverage. We are running on schedule." She hands Luke his Vocation Summary and Productivity Calculation, then gestures with her left arm extended and palm of her hand open motioning toward the lobby.

Familiar with Merit Review etiquette, Luke keeps his hands at his side, nods, and replies, "Thank you." As he crosses the threshold, the number 8 glowing on the back of his left hand quickly fades. He picks an apple from the fruit basket and settles into the leather recliner directly in front of the monitor, just in time to watch the conclusion of the 06:30 Merit Review happening in the adjacent review room. Luke enjoys observing reviews of his fellow citizens and predicting the outcomes.

Although the Merit Number displays are disengaged prior to entering the lobby, a citizen's conduct, attitude, and clothing are often reliable indicators of his or her current Merit Number.

The gentleman being reviewed is wearing generic black sneakers, dark blue denim pants, and a solid gray sweatshirt. His arms are crossed tightly around his chest, and his head is tilted slightly down as if a feeling of shame dominates his mood. His face displays a frown, and no eye contact is made with the Merit Agency administrator.

Similar to the greeters who are expected to welcome all citizens with unwavering similarity, administrators are expected to maintain emotional neutrality and not express their feelings in words, tone, or attitude. With perfect impassive demeanor, the administrator asks, "Do you have any questions?" The demoralized citizen answers with silence.

Following one minute of silence, the administrator concludes the review with the standard sentence, "And thank you for your contributions."

Luke has been on the receiving end of that standard concluding phrase several times since completing Discovery School and notes the disheartened appearance of the citizen. He mumbles under his breath, "Probably a 1 or a 2."

The citizen exits the review room, head hung low and avoiding eye contact with the other citizens who are anxiously anticipating their reviews. There is no hiding the illuminated holographic number sharpening into view on the back of his hand as he passes by. Luke sees his prediction is correct, a 2.

Luke's rumblings were louder than intended. The gentleman sitting in the next recliner comments to Luke, "Well, that's too bad. Poor guy is down a point. I walked in with him from the parking lot and saw his M-N 3. I wanted to offer him words of encouragement, but he didn't even reply when I said, 'Good morning.' I know I shouldn't feel badly about having a good M-N. We all have equal opportunity, right? Low productivity is a choice, I guess, right? I like to think Meritism works, but I still feel badly anytime someone's M-N drops."

Turning to face the man, Luke attempts to respond, but his new acquaintance continues chatting, "My name is Jonathan." He reached out to shake Luke's hand, but withdraws slightly, warning, "Sorry, I just finished my night shift and my hands are still a bit grimy. I don't have the most glamorous vocation, but I don't mind. Someone has to work sanitation!" Jonathan's smile resonates a positive attitude.

"Hi, friend. My name is Luke. Pleased to meet you." Luke overextends his hand to reach and shake Jonathan's grimy hand. "No worries, there's hand sanitizer next to the apples." Luke returns the smile and they both chuckle.

"Wow! You are a Merit Agency Investigator! I just noticed the badge on your shoulder. I hope I didn't offend you with anything I said," Jonathan apologies apprehensively.

"Hey, no offense taken at all. Part of my job is to question the Merit System and ensure the legitimacy of all Merit Numbers," Luke replies. "I'm always eager to hear what people think of Meritism."

"Jonathan, please join us," the Merit Agency administrator pleasantly requests. She is smiling as she speaks and directs Jonathan toward the review room.

"Hey, Luke, make sure you use some hand sanitizer. These hands touched some really gross stuff last night! I think you're up after me, friend!" Jonathan and the administrator head to the review room. Jonathan's easiness and humor help Luke relax, but only for a moment before anxiety begins to set in.

Luke's Merit Number prediction logic takes over. *Okay, no telling what his current Merit Number is based on his clothes since he's still wearing his sanitation uniform. His attitude is fantastic, and he seems to be content with his current vocation. He did mention having received a good Merit Number. But the definition of a good score is somewhat subjective. I'm going to guess he's a 7 and his Merit Number will go up this year to an 8.*

Luke positions himself in the recliner and takes a bite of the apple. While waiting for the broadcast of Jonathan's review to begin, he observes and appreciates the thriftiness of the Ameritan governance and their agencies, including the Merit Agency. The governance's principals of frugality regarding consumption and the use of resources evolved from having witnessed the frivolous expenditures and irresponsible resource allocations of the failed American government.

The recliners, stamped with Made in Amerita, a testament to quality construction and Amerita values, are visibly aged, however, still in very good working order and comfortably broken in.

The décor of the lobby is from the same time period the monitors were likely acquired, and all furnishings are still perfectly functional.

The greeter's touch-screen tablets are antiquated as well, however, also perfectly functional; touch-screen technology was replaced by retina-tracking technology around the time Luke was in his twenties.

The Ameritan flag and Jonathan's name fade from the monitor, and the Merit Agency administrator and Jonathan come into view. The two are sitting across from each other in gray metal folding chairs, separated by three feet, and perfectly centered in the middle of the review room. The tiled floor is the same gray color as the chairs; the ceiling and walls are white and void of decorations. The outline of the door, a single ventilation grate at the base of the floor next to the door, and a white loud-speaker centered on the ceiling are the only items that disturb the surfaces.

The scene displayed on the monitor is captured by a single video camera, sitting atop a tripod positioned in the corner of the room behind the administrator. The camera is peering just above the administrator's shoulder. The small red light on top of the video camera glows vibrantly in contrast to the white walls. The lens slowly zooms in and focuses on Jonathan, framing him from head to foot. His body language and facial expressions are easily discernible.

Luke notices Jonathan's smile turn to an expression of nervousness and uncertainty. Citizens frequently attempt to track and calculate their Productivity Calculation throughout the year. The amount of data required to accurately calculate a year's worth of productivity is daunting and realistically impossible to determine without direct access to the Amerita Data Bank. Uncertainty is unavoidable.

Jonathan's Merit Number earned over the past year, and in effect for the upcoming year, will be disclosed following the Amerita Pledge of Fidelity.

The scene switches to a nearby Discovery School where a seven-year-old, first-year student takes her turn to recite the pledge. Her voice is filled with enthusiasm and excitement for the honor of being chosen for the 07:00 Merit Review.

She begins, speaking each word carefully and clearly, "I pledge fidelity to the United States of Amerita, and to the Meritocracy, for which we stand, one society, under God, indivisible, with opportunity and equality for all."

The scene focuses on her bright smile for several seconds before switching back to the review.

Without hesitation, the administrator reveals Jonathan's Merit Number, "Jonathan, your Merit Number for the next year will begin at the conclusion of your Merit Review. 9. Do you wish to appeal the outcome of your Merit Number? If you chose to appeal—"

"NOPE!" Jonathan interrupts, knowing the administrator has several paragraphs of disclosures to recite prior to Jonathan's acceptance or appeal. "WOO HOO!!!" he exclaims, throwing his arms into the air.

"Jonathan, would you like to ask one question or make a statement?" the administrator asks, attempting to hide her smile.

"I'm all set. I was hoping for another 8 this year, but I'll take the 9." Jonathan is so excited he stands up and begins to lean in to hug the administrator but stops himself, remembering etiquette.

"I know we have 30 minutes for the review, but I really need to get some sleep. Last night was a recycle separation shift, and that's a lot of work. My arms are so sore from keeping up with that conveyor belt. So, I'm okay cutting our review short," Jonathan offers.

The administrator concludes the conversation. "Sure, Jonathan, that's fine. Let me point out first, however, that your productivity report shows the recycle separation shift is what pushed your score up to the 9. You scored 97% on the 'separation of recyclables' metric." She paused, then concluded with the standard phrase, "And thank you for your contributions," spoken with a hint of gratitude.

The administrator and Jonathan rise from their seats. The camera zooms out to display the review room. After they exit, the monitor displays the Ameritan flag, a close-up of Jonathan's face, and his information and new Merit Number.

Luke rises from his recliner to meet Jonathan as he enters the lobby. "I don't care how grimy your hands are, I'm going to shake your hand!"

While shaking hands, Jonathan directs Luke's attention to the back of his hand, "Hey, watch this, my M-N is starting to glow ... here it comes ... BAM! 9! Now to go get some sleep."

"Have a great day, friend. Not sure what I'm going to do for the next 20 minutes though since you cut out early!" Luke banters.

To pass the time, Luke reaches for the remote control and flips through a few channels, searching for an interesting Merit Review to observe. Each County has a channel designated for showing reviews in process. He stops on channel 1907, a broadcast from a lobby four doors further down the hallway.

The citizen is framed from head to toe on the monitor, but his face is not visible. His head is hung so low that all Luke can see is the balding on the top of his head. *That's got to be some really bad news,* Luke thinks to himself as he settles back into his recliner. The administrator is not speaking. The man is not speaking. Fifteen of the 30 minutes allotted for the review have passed.

Luke has seen this many times before. The silence is likely because the man is trying to decide if he wants to appeal the Merit Number. Five more minutes of silence pass.

The administrator breaks the silence. "We ask again, do you wish to appeal the outcome of your Merit Number?"

With head hung low, the man answers, "No." He rises from his gray metal chair and walks toward the door without looking toward the camera or the administrator. As the camera zooms out, the administrator hastily says the required phrase, "And thank you for your contributions," reciting the words before the man exits the lobby.

The monitor displays the Ameritan Flag, a close-up of the man's face, and his name, State, County, vocation, and Merit Number.

```
Citizen: Robert Dixon
State: New York
County: Wayne
Vocation: Manufacturing, Assembly
Merit Number: 2
```

Luke changes the channel back to 1903 and Jonathan's information is again displayed.

```
Citizen: Jonathan Givens
State: New York
County: Wayne
Vocation: Recycling and Composting
Merit Number: 9
```

Luke attempts to close his eyes and clear his mind, waiting for the remaining five minutes to pass before his Merit Review begins. A quick glance at his wrist band reveals a heart rate of 140 beats per minute. Any attempt to relax would be futile.

Jonathan's information fades from the monitor, and the lone image remaining on the screen is the Ameritan flag and the time, 07:30.

"Luke, please join us," the administrator calls. Other than facial features, unaltered by makeup, her appearance is indistinguishable from the greeters and other administrators in the County building. The Amerita Merit Agency has strict dress code regulations. Everyone assigned to the agency dresses in loose-fitting gray slacks and white button-down dress shirts. The garments have only one decoration, the Ameritan flag embroidered above the left shirt pocket. The administrator has long silver-gray hair pulled back into a single braid to meet regulations.

Luke briefly reflects on the use of the word *us* in the phrase, *Please join us*. He always thought the use of *us* was odd since only one reviewer conducts the review. However, Luke does understand the reasoning; *us* is used to be inclusive of any citizen who may be watching the review live. Luke envisions hundreds of early risers watching his Merit Review while they eat their toast and eggs and sip on coffee.

His focus quickly shifts to the administrator's demeanor. Deciphering facial queues and vocal fluctuations is an important skill for a Merit Agency Investigator. Unfortunately, the administrator seems to have mastered emotional neutrality. The intention of an administrator's emotional neutrality is to correspond with the philosophy of Meritism—compensation based on an individual's productivity, measured by factual data, free from emotional bias, prejudice, and subjectivity.

Luke has accurately predicted his Merit Number for the past five years in a row by noting the administrator's behaviors prior to his Merit Review commencing. The signs he looks for which indicate a favorable outcome are tiny details, including corners of the mouth tilted slightly upward, an uplifted chin, distinct eye contact, or a fluctuation in volume when reciting the predefined phrase, "{Name}, please join us." A good sign is when the "{Name}" is spoken louder than the "please join us." This year, "Luke, please join us" is spoken with perfect monotone and not a single moment of eye contact is exchanged.

Luke wipes nervous perspiration from his forehead using the napkin he had picked up with the apple, slowly rises from the recliner, and visualizes his Merit Number increasing by a point. Living in a 9~10 neighborhood would be a dream come true for his family. He briefly reviews the printout of his Vocation Summary, folds the sheet of paper neatly, and places the official document into his shirt pocket. Luke's son, Jake, asked his dad to bring the Vocation Summary and Productivity Calculation document home for him to use in an upcoming Amerita Timeology report.

The Merit Agency Investigator's primary responsibilities are investigating Merit Number fraud and conducting Merit Number appeals. The investigation process includes reviewing data collection methods.

Quantitative Measure

The quantitative measure is the number of fraud investigations and appeal cases closed during the measure year.

A fraud investigation is considered closed following judicial processing, regardless of guilty/not guilty determination.

An appeal is considered closed following a peer review of the investigation conducted by two Merit Agency Investigators. Both colleagues must be in agreement regarding closure or the appeal remains open and the assigned Merit Agency Investigator must conduct further review.

Qualitative Measure

The qualitative measure is the number of times a Merit Review appeal is approved for closure following colleague review combined with the number of times a Fraud Investigation is not appealed following judicial processing.

Days Worked

The Days Worked measure is the number of days during the measure year when vocational responsibilities were fulfilled during an eight-hour day. The maximum score for Days Worked is 240.

With an anxious gait, Luke walks toward the administrator and knows not to extend his hand for a greeting. Administrators are trained to avoid physical contact by clasping their hands behind their backs when greeting citizens for Merit Reviews. Luke laughs to himself recalling a review he witnessed two years ago when a citizen was so elated with his new Merit Number of 10 that he spontaneously jumped out of his chair and hugged the administrator. Then he imagines what the administrator's reaction would have been if Jonathan followed through with his hug a few moments ago.

Luke clasps his hands behind his back, an Ameritan custom showing respect for the administrator and in accordance with the Meritism philosophy of emotional neutrality.

She raises her left arm after perceiving there will not be any physical contact and motions Luke into the review room with the palm of her hand. He passes through the doorway into the review room, walking past the administrator. Luke quickly sits in his gray metal chair. He knows the next phrase spoken by the administrator once she is seated will be, "Luke, your Merit Number for the next year will begin at the conclusion of your Merit Review," followed by announcing his score. The administrator is trained to announce the Merit Number immediately regardless of the score being good news or bad news. There is no hesitation even if the new Merit Number is a 0, Exile.

During the moments that the administrator takes her seat and the seven-year-old Discovery School student recites the Amerita Pledge of Fidelity, Luke's anxiety takes hold and a full recollection of his father's final Merit Review plays in his mind. The memory, although from his young teen years, is as vivid as if just occurred.

Martin

The devastating phrase repeated over and over in Luke's mind. "Martin, your Merit Number for the next year will begin at the conclusion of your Merit Review. 0, Exile."

The scene continues, burned into Luke's teenage memories. A long pause followed the word "Exile." The question regarding appeal should have immediately followed the announcement of the Merit Number, but there was a pause and a look of sadness in the administrator's eyes as they had begun to well with tears. The administrator fought to regain composure and then asked Martin, "Do you wish to appeal the outcome of your Merit Number?"

Another pause and more silence ensued. Martin did not immediately respond to the question. He knew there was much more the administrator must disclose to the citizen facing exile prior to answering the question. Martin sat patiently, pondering, as the administrator again fought to gain composure before continuing. He gathered from her obvious distress that she was uneasy about the 0, Exile.

The administrator continued reciting the regulations surrounding exile. "If you choose to appeal, you, Tina, and Luke will be allowed to remain in Wayne County during the appeal investigation. Your Merit Number will be reduced to a 1, and Amerita will provide food, shelter, and transportation within the Level 1 classification. Healthcare will remain fully covered with universal benefits for your family.

"Should the investigation prove inconclusive after 90 days, a verdict of inconclusive will be granted. You will be given a Merit Number of 5 for the measure year, your job classification will be reassessed, and you will select a new vocation.

"If the investigation results in a verdict of Invalid, you will retain your prior-year's Merit Number for the upcoming measure year. All your compensations prior to the investigation will be fully restored, including your transportation, residence, and neighborhood location. The Merit Number deemed invalid will be permanently discarded from your records.

"Should the investigation result in a verdict of Valid, you and Tina will be exiled for one year. Luke will be provided for; his Discovery Schooling will continue, and he will reside within the school dormitory. If you and Tina return to an exile gate at the conclusion of your one-year exile, you will immediately have full citizen rights with a Merit Number of 1 for the following year. Luke will be returned to your care. A vocation within the classification of 'Exile Return' will be assigned for the year, after which time you may request a vocation re-evaluation. You will be permanently banned from all vocations in your current vocation category, Technology.

"If you choose not to appeal, your exile will commence immediately. Tina will retain custody of Luke. She will be granted a Merit Number of 5 and will be required to select and begin a vocation immediately. If you return to an exile gate at the conclusion of your one-year exile, you can reclaim your Ameritan citizenship and join your family.

"Martin, your answer please. You have five minutes to respond. If you do not respond within five minutes, the choice of exile will be final."

Luke's recollection shifts to the last conversation he had with his father, their customary family discussion prior to the Merit Review regarding the family member's response to exile.

"Luke, put your phone down! You will have this same discussion with your family someday. Please take this seriously," Martin demanded.

"Okay, fine. You work hard. You don't cheat. So you would appeal an exile. And look what I pulled up on Google, the latest exile statistics say one in five thousand Merit Reviews result in an exile, that's 0.02 percent. Of the approximately 40 million recognized vocational placements, that means each measure year there are eight thousand exiles. And of those, 90% are appealed and 10% percent of the appeals are successful. Oh, wait, that's not a good statistic on the appeal outcome. But Dad, you work hard and you're not cheating the system. Don't worry. Anything else we need to add to the discussion?" Luke put on his headphones and withdrew from the conversation.

Tina joined the conversation, making her thoughts known. "There goes your son, showing off his math skills again. We've been married 23 years, and I know you don't cheat on your Productivity Calculation and I know you're not lazy. The answer is simple—you would appeal. Your M-N is going to be fine. What we really need to worry about is the death threats that keep popping up on your phone."

"Shh!" Martin quieted Tina.

"What? Luke can't hear us, he's got his headphones on," she snapped. "We all know how crazed those people are whose professions are no longer needed, especially the politicians and investment bankers. They used to have it good, and now they actually have to work for a living like the rest of us."

"I probably shouldn't have told you about my involvement with the formation of the Meritism Party. All 97 of us signed first names and middle initial only to remain anonymous. There must be someone on the inside, maybe a Capitalist. Promise me you will never tell Luke about my involvement, and I promise to do what is best for our family," Martin proposed.

"Fine, as long as we can we stop having this same conversation every year," Tina agrees.

Martin jokes, "Could you imagine you out there in exile with me if we appealed and lost? Now that would be funny, well not funny really, but yeah, funny. You wouldn't last past the first morning without your coffee. Forget that, you wouldn't last the first night! As soon as you saw a spider or a snake, you would be all done."

"You are the one who wouldn't make it out there without your Internet and Wi-Fi and Netflix," Tina jabbed. "What skills could you possibly offer one of the gangs we would certainly come across? You would be totally useless without technology."

Martin gave Tina a sarcastic goodbye, "Okay, I love you, honey!"

"Love you too, Marty," Tina replied with an eye roll.

"Oh come on with the 'Marty'! You agreed with me that 'Marty' didn't look good as a signature on the manifesto. Everyone calls me Martin now," he pleaded.

"Whatever, MARTY. I'll never call you Martin," Tina countered and blew him a kiss.

Martin stepped away from the breakfast table and waved his arms to get Luke's attention, "Bye, son." He exchanges with Luke the remnants of the secret handshake they created when Luke was four. Horizontal palm slap, backhand slap, palm slap, fist-bump, fist-bump, fist-bump. Luke's eyes did not look up from his phone. Having done the handshake thousands of times since age four and finding the gesture annoying as a teenager, he grudgingly went through the motions to appease his father.

Luke and his mom moved to the couch to watch the Today Show until Martin's Merit Review scheduled start time.

The memory of his father's final Merit Review rushes back even more vividly.

Martin stared with a loving smile directly into the camera. Luke and Tina were frozen, unable to speak, staring back at the monitor.

He continued his gaze until the administrator broke the five minutes of silence. "Martin, your answ—"

"Exile," Martin answered with confidence and no sign of shame or remorse.

Tina jumped to her feet, slammed her hands into the monitor and yelled, forgetting for a moment that Martin could not hear her through the monitor, "You promised! You promised!" She tried fighting back the tears but only for a moment before they started to flow.

Luke attempted to console his mom, hugging her tightly. He didn't cry because the guilt was overwhelming; not looking up into his father's eyes when he left the breakfast table that morning haunts him to this day.

The administrator brought the Merit Review to a close asking, "Martin, would you like to ask one question or make a statement?"

Martin took the opportunity. "Yes. Why did my score drop so dramatically?"

The answer was shocking. "Martin, your qualitative score was negative, and even with the positive quantitative and days worked scores, your overall Merit Number was still below zero. The reason for the poor qualitative score is because 73 hospital deaths were found to be attributed to a poorly manufactured pharmaceutical, Nyxthonate, which was manufactured using your programmable logic controller software algorithms."

Martin's eyes dimmed. There was still a slight smile on his face as his lips moved with no sound, exaggerating the words, "I love you,

Tina. I love you, Luke." Both Tina and Luke had known exactly what those words were. Then Martin said another six-word phrase, but this time with extremely minimal movement of his lips. Neither Luke or Tina could decipher the six-word phrase.

His slight smile turned into an expression of terror knowing that exile was immediate. One year will pass before he sees his family, assuming he survives the chaos gripping the designated exile regions.

Luke snaps away from the memory as the Amerita Pledge of Fidelity concludes. The door closes and the administrator takes her seat across from him.

Amanda

Amanda made an exception to the rule, 'No television before school,' because today is their dad's Merit Number Review day. Jake's interest in the Merit Review system has flourished since entering his seventh year in Discovery School and beginning to study in great detail the historical timeline of Amerita.

"Get up here, Mom!" Jake yells. "Dad's going to be on soon."

Amanda hops off the treadmill and runs upstairs to join the kids. "Right on time as always," she cheers.

"I wish we were with him, waiting in the lobby like we always do," AJ disingenuously suggests as she walks into the living room to join her mother and brother. "I like to give him a hug when the review is done."

"You are such a suck-up, AJ," Jake accuses his sister. "At least I'll be honest. The reason I like to be there is so we can go to breakfast afterward."

Amanda attempts to have the last word, "Well neither of you two were willing to get out of bed at the crack of dawn. That's a nice show of support. AJ, you should be paying close attention to your father's Merit Review. You only have six months of Discovery School left before you are on your own."

"And how about you, Mom? We're old enough to stay home by ourselves. You could have gone with him. Nice show of support," AJ attempts to finish the argument.

Amanda tries to settle down the anxiety, "Okay, quiet, settle down. He's going to be on any minute now. We have nothing to worry about. There won't be any surprises this year. Maybe he'll even get an M-N 9 and we could move to a 9~10 neighborhood."

"Oh my god, what if he gets a 6! My senior year will be ruined. We'll have to move to a 5~6 neighborhood. And what about my clothes? Ugh, I would be so embarrassed," AJ expresses her main concerns.

"Relax, your dad has never had an M-N lower than a 7, and don't forget the two years he had an M-N 9," Amanda reassures, then realizes the spoiled comment from AJ. "You know what, AJ? I hope your dad gets a 6. You could use a reminder of how different things would be if your father didn't work hard. I know for a fact, AJ, that you're a snob to the girls at Discovery School who can't get their hair and nails done at a salon and wear fashionable clothes like you do. You know they have no control over their possessions and they live with the choices their parents make about being productive. Six months from now you will be on an even playing field with every student in your graduating class."

"Ugh, Mom," AJ tries to interject.

Amanda continues her rant, "And Emily is so nice to you, but you still somehow manage to be a snob to her. Emily tutored you in math last year, and that's the only thing that kept you from having to repeat your junior year. And you didn't even do so much as invite her to your birthday party. I'll never forget your comment when I suggested you add her to your invites, '...but Mom, she won't fit in with me and my friends. She's an M-N 3.' No AJ, she is not an M-N 3. Her parents are M-N 3s. She has all the potential and opportunity you or any of your snobbish friends have. You owe your father a huge thank you; he convinced me to not cancel your party. I was so pissed and had every intention to cancel the whole thing. And to top it off, Emily still offered to help you with math this year!"

Amanda ends the rant with a guilt ensuing comment, "Oh, whatever. You will learn your lesson in the Spring," and turns her back to AJ.

"Quiet, Dad's almost on," Jake demands while turning up the volume. "Check that out, the guy who went before Dad scored a 9."

The monitor changes from Jonathan Given's information to an Ameritan flag with Luke Medina written across the middle of the screen.

A young and very articulate boy from the local Discovery School recites the Pledge of Fidelity. The scene focuses on his smile for several seconds before switching to Luke and the administrator.

The administrator begins, "Luke, your Merit Number for the next year will begin at the conclusion of your Merit Review—"

BEEP - BEEP - BEEP

The monitor abruptly changes to a dull red background with the words, *We are experiencing technical difficulties. Please stand by* displayed in large, black font.

The alarming beep is piercing because Jake has the volume near maximum. He quickly mutes the sound, and Amanda, AJ, and Jake let out a simultaneous, "UGH!"

The "Technical Difficulties" scenario is very rare, however, not unheard of. Citizens are appreciative of the Ameritan governance's diligence and reliability, and complaints are infrequent.

Amanda has seen this interruption once before. She reassures the kids, "Probably 10 or 15 minutes. I've seen this happen before. Don't worry about being late for school; I'll give you a ride. I'm going to get back on the treadmill. AJ, stay by the monitor and give me a shout when they're back online. Jake, come downstairs with me and run through your lesson. You said last night at dinner that today is your day to help teach in History class, right?"

"Timeology, Mom! Timeology class. Nobody uses the word 'History' anymore," Jake explains. "Historians were never able to stop the bad events of our past from repeating. After Discovery School, I want to be a Timeologist. I want to teach people about the events on the timeline prior to the creation of Meritism and make sure they don't forget how things used to be, and then maybe 'History' won't repeat itself again. I'm so fascinated by the way things used to be and how they just didn't make any sense." Jake's enthusiasm and passion for the subject of Timeology brings a big smile to his mother's face.

"AJ, why can't you be more like your brother? Where is your passion?" Amanda yells back to AJ as she walks downstairs with Jake following.

"W-T-F, Mom," AJ yells back.

Jake continues, unaffected by his big sister's usual disrespect. "Today is my turn to instruct Timeology. I signed up to help present a couple times per week. This is way better than Elementary school where only the mentor gets in front of the class. I might sign up to present in Math too, but I don't know, probably I'll just sign up in Timeology for now. I don't want the other kids to think I'm trying to be a Mentor's Pet. My classmates already give me a hard time because of words I use that they don't understand."

Amanda starts a light jog with a slight incline. "So what is your topic?" she asks Jake through a few deep breaths.

"I titled today's lesson <u>Fiat Currency: Paper Will Not Feed, Clothe, or Shelter You</u>," Jake answers.

His mother reminds him, "Jake, make sure you don't speak over your classmates' heads. Not everyone spends their free time reading history, I mean Timeology, books. Okay, I'm listening. Let's hear your lesson."

"Good morning, Timeology class. My name is Jake Medina, and today I'm going talk about the economic collapse of the United States of America. I call my lesson <u>Fiat Currency: Paper Will Not Feed, Clothe, or Shelter You</u>.

"I'll begin by defining a few keywords—economy, currency, and fiat.

"Economy is the way a community manages available resources.

"To demonstrate a very simple economy, let's pretend there is a community of three families. The family of farmers grows grains and vegetables and raises chickens. The family of builders builds and repairs houses. The family of seamstresses makes clothing. The community provides food, shelter, and clothing.

"Every week, the families meet to let the other families know what their needs are for the upcoming weeks and to deliver their goods from the prior week's requests. The family of builders may need new clothes for one of their growing children. The family of farmers may need repairs to a roof of one of their barns. The family of seamstresses may be running out of eggs.

"Every family is a productive part of the community and contributes to the needs of the other families. The weekly meeting to discuss needs and deliver goods is this community's economy.

"Currency is something used as a medium of exchange. This 'something' has historically been a commodity, which is a raw material or agricultural product that has value and purpose and can be traded and stored for future use or future trading.

"To demonstrate a very simple currency, let's pretend a new family joins our make-believe community. Now there are four families. The new family provides medical assistance. The father and mother are doctors, and the children know basic first aid. But at the weekly meetings, if nobody is sick, they don't have anything to provide the community. The community comes up with the idea that as a community they will gather all the nuts in the land that have fallen from the trees. They will then divide the nuts equally among the families. Nuts are very valuable because they can be stored and consumed as a great source of protein, especially during the cold winter months when fresh vegetables are not available.

"At the weekly meeting, nobody needed medical assistance. The medical family gave the farmers 50 nuts in exchange for wheat and vegetables and gave 75 nuts to the builders to fix their roof.

"During the following week, one of the seamstress family's children was sick and the seamstress family gave the medical family 150 nuts for nursing their child back to health. The medical family didn't need any new clothes or food and their home didn't need repairs, so they stored their 150 nuts.

"Nuts are being used as a currency in the community, a medium of exchange. Nuts make a great commodity because they have value; they're a good source of nutrition.

"Now, let's talk about the word fiat. The best way I can describe the word fiat is people agree to give value to a worthless object.

"Three new families move into our make-believe community. The families provide services. The services are important, but do not produce food, shelter, or clothing or provide medical care. One family provides teaching services. One family provides art and music. One family provides cleaning services.

"When the nuts are collected, there are not enough nuts to share among all seven families. The community decides to stop using nuts and start using round stones collected from the riverbanks. There are many stones along the riverbanks; however, there are fewer round stones.

"More families move in and offer a variety of services. One family offers to be the keeper of the stones—they just invented banking.

"Families start demanding more stones in exchange for their offerings. For example, five round stones used to get you a bushel of vegetables, but now the farmer wants six round stones for the same amount of vegetables.

"Now families need more round stones to exchange. The family that is the keeper of the stones sends their kids out to find more stones.

"Eventually, there are so many round stones in circulation, that a bucket of stones is needed to trade for a bushel of vegetables. Stones are now impractical.

"Nobody is trading stones to the family that's providing art and entertainment because what they offer is not critical to survival. That family is now starving.

"Eventually, the three original families and the medical family decide to trade among themselves only and forgo using the stones as currency.

"The stones have no value.

"The families who do not provide food, shelter, clothing, or medical treatment are doomed.

"The currency we often hear about since biblical days is gold. Gold is a rare metal and can be fashioned into useful items, including coins, jewelry, and electronic components. Gold is also very rare and is considered a precious metal. The reason gold has value is because people desire to have gold in their possession.

"Up until 1971, the USA used gold as currency. Gold was impractical to carry and trade so slips of paper were used to represent an amount of gold owned by America. The slips of paper were called dollars. A dollar could be exchanged for the amount of gold the slip of paper represented. The existing Bretton Woods system of monetary management was accepted world-wide, and this system ensured international currency was backed by the tangible asset, gold, which had real-world value.

"In 1971, Richard Nixon, a former President of the Unites States of America, convinced the leaders of other countries to detach the slips of paper from gold. The dollar, a slip of paper, became simply a slip of paper, but was given value because of a decree. The slip of paper itself, the dollar, had no usable value.

"Over the next 50 years, countries literally printed more slips of paper dollars to put into the hands of the people. This is exactly the same as our imaginary community collecting more round stones.

"Two other issue facing America in the early 21st century were departing from globalization and a move toward nationalization, and trade laws imposed by America that strongly favored America's economic interests. These trade laws sparked trade wars with everyone, even America's allies. America's decision to stop cooperating with the rest of the world enraged all the other countries.

"Then one day, taking America by surprise, every country in the world turned against them and collectively deemed the dollar as worth nothing more than the slip of paper it was printed on. That, my classmates, is how the USA lost World War III in a single day with no human casualties.

"Many Timeologists, actually called Historians back then, predicted World War III would be nuclear. They were all wrong. World War III took place in a boardroom with representatives of every country, except America. In less than 24 hours, America was crippled financially and fell into chaos.

"But chaos and anarchy were short-lived, thanks to the foresight of the 97 men and women who started the Meritism Party! They are the Founders of Amerita! Their plans for a currency based on an individual's productivity, called Meritism, saved our Country."

Jake's crowd-cheering sound effects resound over the thump-thump of his mother running on the treadmill. She smiles ear-to-ear and compliments Jake, "That's wonderful, Jake! Your class will love the lesson, assuming they can keep up. You are well ahead of your years!"

"You know, Mom, someday I will uncover the truth about what happened to the 97 Amerita Founders. Some conspiracy theorists claim that underground members of the Capitalist Party had them all murdered. Others say they are all alive and well, hiding among us."

"One conspiracy theory claims the whole thing was contrived by the American government and the 97 didn't actually exist, and that's why there are only first names and last initial on the manifesto. But I say no way to that. The American government never saw World War III coming, so how could they have planned for the aftermath? They were all self-serving, rich, Career Politicians incapable of doing anything that would upset their balance of power. I believe the 97 were technically and socially savvy fathers, mothers, and mentors who cared deeply about the future of the nation's children. No way could that group of politicians have written the Meritism Manifesto and created the infrastructure needed to handle the massive amounts of computer programming and hardware needed for the Merit Number system!" Jake ranted on.

Amanda stopped him abruptly, having heard his theories many times, "Yes, Jake, I do hope you find the answers you are looking for. Just don't use so many big words when you present today, okay?"

Mission

BEEP - BEEP - BEEP

Luke's surprise at the alarm jolts him to standing. He is so focused on hearing his new Merit Number, for a moment the disorientation feels dreamlike.

The administrator stands up too, extends her hand, and introduces herself, "My name is Julie."

Luke stares, confused for several reasons. *Why did I not hear my Merit Number? Did she say my Merit Number and I didn't hear her? Why is she attempting to make physical contact? That's not supposed to happen.*

Julie takes two steps forward and gestures again for Luke to shake her hand and repeats, "My name is Julie. It's okay, Luke. You can shake my hand."

Silently, Luke looks around the room noticing first that the red light on the video camera has turned off. Then an arched doorway on the seemingly solid surface behind Julie appears and two administrators hurry into the review room, exiting from the blackness of a hidden adjacent room.

The two administrators, a man and a woman, are wearing identical loose-fitting gray slacks and white button-down dress shirts with an embroidered Ameritan flag above the shirt's left pocket.

The woman, approximately the same age as Julie, wears the same hairstyle, a single braid, and is also graying.

The man is bald and clean shaven. He addresses Luke, "Hello, Luke. Let me start by—"

"What the ... Director Ripley? What's going on, why are you here? Why are you dressed like that?" Luke interrupts. Visibly disoriented, he almost trips over the leg of his chair.

"Luke, please, this will all make sense after my explanation. The short answer is we need you to go undercover," Ripley quickly states to calm the situation.

Luke freezes. Panting, he instantly understands. "I assume the broadcast has been cut? Are all Merit Review 'Outages' fake like this one? Do you have any idea how pissed people would be if they found out some of the Merit Reviews were interrupted for secret governance ploys? What about transparency? That's the foundation of the Amerita governance! You still have people going undercover? What about spies? Do you have spies too? This is bullshit!"

Ripley attempts to diffuse the escalating confrontation. "Luke, please give me 15 minutes to explain. Okay? And don't go all Muay Thai on me. Settle down, you are one scary S.O.B. when you get fired up."

Luke, with his intimidating physique, gets right in Ripley's face and snarls, "Start talking."

Ripley begins, "As far as transparency, well we just don't have an alternative. If people knew we had planted undercover investigators, there would forever be a sense of suspicion among the working population."

"With that said, I might as well mention right now that if you take the assignment, you will need to take this secret to the grave. You will never be able to tell anyone, ever, not even Amanda. And if you are caught, the Merit Agency will deny everything."

Luke interrupts with ample sarcasm, "If we were living in America in the 2020s, you would be the worst salesman ever. I'm definitely going to say no, but go ahead and finish your pitch."

Ripley continues, "Sheriff Chamberlain came to me asking for my best investigator. He said a concerned citizen working over at Pharmavast, you know, that drug company over—"

"Yes, I know Pharmavast, over there bordering the Western NY Exile Zone," Luke snaps impatiently. "Get on with it, Ripley. My wife and kids are probably freaking out by now."

"As I was saying," Ripley picks up his pace, "Pharmavast is the target. Sheriff Chamberlain was visited by a data entry clerk from Pharmavast. Apparently, this woman had seen very suspicious chemical acquisition data over the past few months. She didn't want to say anything, but when she was accidentally included on a Pharmavast Board of Directors email, her concerns grew. She immediately knew not to mention any of this to anyone at Pharmavast and decided to bring the matter to our attention. I've got a copy. Take a look."

---Secure Transmission Confirmed 7890-1233-3FT4-D445---

-----Secure Receipt Confirmed 398U-495Y-JJJ5-1259------

To: [GROUP:New Year's Eve Employee Party Committee]
From: Chairman@Pharmavast.rx
Date: Monday, November 6, 2051 20:00 EST
Subject: New Year's Eve Employee Party

To the Pharmavast Board of Directors,

   Reminder, our kick-off committee meeting will be
this Monday, December 4, 2051. Attendance is mandatory.

   Agenda:
   1) Discuss this year's theme, "Capitalism Reborn."
   2) Vote on final formulation of the tickets to the
      party.
   3) Brainstorm distribution options for delivering
      the tickets.

   The additional materials needed for the "party" have
arrived undetected.

   Friends, I'm confident the event will exceed all
expectations and Capitalism will flourish once again.

Damien Myers
Chairman, Board of Directors
Pharmavast Inc.
Rochester, NY
Chairman@Pharmavast.rx
Dmyers@Pharmavast.rx

Luke reads the email quickly. "Oh yeah, Ripley, I totally see why you need me to go undercover. You need me to make sure they're planning a party and not planning to take over Amerita. Hmm, yeah. This is a joke, right?"

Ripley tries to diffuse the tension, "At first I thought both her and Sheriff Chamberlain were crazy-paranoid. But you know the Sheriff's record, he's as good as they come. He's been keeping a close eye on Damien Myers ever since he became head of the Capitalist Party. We also know that every board member at Pharmavast belongs to the Capitalist Party except for an older gentleman, Joshua Campbell. He's the only one left from his generation on the board and the only one not involved with the Capitalist Party. All the others despise Meritism."

"I know the conspiracy theories, all those former well-off people all want Capitalism to come back so they can amass wealth and once again spit on the working man. I've heard all this before, but come on, there's no way. 70% of the population belongs to the Meritism Party! Almost everyone else supports the Republican, Democratic, or Libertarian party," Luke argues.

"You are correct, there are only a small number of people in the Capitalist Party, but most of them have prominent positions in corporations. Think about it. What if, just what if they had something cooking? Their pharmaceutical reach is tremendous. They make 60% of all pharmaceuticals being used in the country, and 85% of the population is taking something for heart disease, blood pressure, cholesterol, diabetes, cancer, Alzheimer's, dementia, etcetera, etcetera, and you, Lusitropin, right? Keeps you from needing a heart transplant," Ripley fires back.

"Hand me that email again," Luke insists.

Luke reads the email with apprehension, taking his time, and thinking ... what if?

Ripley furthers his argument, "And listen to the rest of the information Anne brought us." Ripley pauses briefly and shakes his head, knowing he should not have mentioned her by name. "She works in the Acquisitions department, and prior to having seen this email, she discovered a serious spike in acquisition requests for two very highly regulated chemicals, D-phenylalanine and Levoamphetamine. She saw a spike in a moderately regulated pharmaceutical, Fluoride. She claims that the acquisition requests for these are more than 5,000% over last year. She also saw one more, this one she never heard of and never requisitioned before, Acetaminophenyltrexide. I think that's where her paranoia came from. Chamberlain and I have been working this case for a month now and are getting absolutely nowhere. That's where you come in."

Luke begins pacing with both hands on his head looking downward, considering. "Okay. I can see your case and Chamberlain's perspective. How long do I have to decide?"

Without hesitation or explanation Ripley exclaims, "Five minutes. You need to decide now. That's why we interrupted the broadcast."

While still pacing and avoiding eye contact, Luke reacts, "Dude! Are you frickin serious? If I agree to do this, will I get an M-N 10 when you turn the broadcast back on? I'm sure you all see how far above and beyond this request is."

A pause ensues. Ripley, Julie, and Ripley's assistant look at each other with blank expressions. Luke stops pacing and exchanges a glance with the team of three. His heart quickens knowing that he misconstrued Ripley's intentions.

"Luke," Ripley takes a deep breath and speaks gingerly, "Luke, when the broadcast resumes, Julie needs to announce that your Merit Number for the year will be a 2."

Silence fills the white room. Luke clenches his fists, paces to his chair, and kicks it over, causing a loud bang.

Ripley continues, "Just hear me out, please. Listen to the whole scenario. I'm sure you will like the ending. Actually, I'm sure you will love the ending."

Luke demands, "No way am I moving my family to dormitory housing and subjecting them to eating porridge for breakfast, lunch, and dinner six days a week. I'll tell you right there, that's a deal breaker. Conversation over!"

Ripley pulls out his phone, taps speaker-phone, and conferences in the four other Merit Agency Directors. "I told you there was no way he would go for a 2!"

Director Williams speaks, "Hello, Luke, this is Director Williams. I'm very happy to hear we are still in discussions. Thank you for hearing us out. Would you be okay with a 3? I'm not sure how far into the conversation you are, but know that we expect the assignment to last only three or four months. Any longer would be pointless because if they're planning something, we'll be too late."

Muffled chatter among the four directors is heard through the speakerphone. After a few moments, Director Williams speaks, "We are in agreement that a 3 will be fine. Keeps you out of dormitory housing. We understand your point about the housing, Luke. But there will still be lots of porridge."

Luke agrees, "Yeah, I hate porridge but we could deal with that for a few months. But why the low Merit Number? I don't get why that's necessary?"

"Can I continue, Luke?" Ripley asks impatiently.

"Ripley! Back off a little. This is so way above-and-beyond, you need to put yourself in Luke's shoes," Director Williams demands, then speaks to Luke empathetically. "Luke, we need this. Imagine what Amerita would be like if the Capitalist Party took hold. Now, Ripley, make it happen."

Ripley turns his phone off and continues, "You will be you; we can't take a chance on giving you a fake identification, those are so easily revealed. You will have received an M-N 2, I mean a 3, because of an extraordinary number of your cases being reversed following peer review. You will not appeal the score. You will choose a new vocation, working for Pharmavast. Our inside contact will assign you to the 10th floor where Damien Myers' office is located. You and your family will immediately need to move to a 3~4 neighborhood. When people at Pharmavast ask about the problems you had as an investigator, simply tell them you are burned out and slacked off and took shortcuts with your duties this past year. Regarding your vocation as a custodian, explain that you are at Pharmavast, planning to do the bare-minimum to avoid exile, and soon your wife will be taking on a vocation so you can be done working there. Nobody would ever suspect an Ameritan citizen would be agreeable to drop his Merit Number from an 8 to a 3 as part of an undercover assignment. If we dropped your Merit Number to a 6 or 5, that might raise suspicion.

"Now for the part we think you will love. When your assignment concludes, either finding conspiracy at Pharmavast or proving to us there is nothing to worry about, we'll announce that we found an issue with our Data Bank that affected your Merit Number. The reason for the 3 was because of an issue with data collection, and you were not at fault. You will be given the option to be reinstated as a Merit Review Investigator or to accept a new vocation.

"We are all very familiar with your community theater involvement. I saw *The Phantom of the Opera* over the summer and wow, you were fantastic. I'm willing to bet that given the opportunity, you would choose to take a shot at acting for your vocation. To show our immense gratitude for taking this assignment, if you say yes, we've already secured a role for you in a new D.C.

Comics movie. Don't ask how, just know that our contacts run deep, and Salvatore Miles, a movie director in Hollywood, is a friend of a friend. He's directing the new Batman movie, and he remembers you from the many community theater performances he attended when he lived in Rochester. He committed to giving you a role, no guarantee if this will be a lead role or not, but he did guarantee a speaking role with multiple scenes.

"Luke, we believe above-and-beyond assignments deserve special compensation, but in a world without currency, we are somewhat limited in the compensations we can offer. So, what do you think?"

Luke ponders, pacing again, head down. He has considered jumping vocations and giving acting a go, and Amanda has offered her support. His fear of jumping vocations has always been the consequences of failure. An unsuccessful vocation jump can quickly lead to an extremely low Merit Number. Luke's acting has always been his hobby, not his vocation.

Julie interrupts Luke's pacing, "Luke, we have to know now. The broadcast must resume before suspicions arise. Now, Luke! As soon as we are done here, head right to the second floor for vocation reassignment. Pharmavast Custodian. That's your cover."

"What! Oh come on!" Luke objects with a snicker and grin on his face. He sets his chair upright and takes a seat.

Julie picks up his queue and knows he's in. "Thank you, Luke. Broadcast resumes in 3 ... 2 ... 1 ..."

M-N

Amanda hits the stop button on the treadmill when burned calories reach 300. She thinks to herself, *300 calories, great, now I can eat a Twinkie. Remember Amanda, you cannot outrun a bad diet.*

She shouts to her kids as she walks up from the basement, "Jake, AJ, the bus will be here in five minutes. Sorry, but I thought your dad's review would be back on by now. Keep an eye on the Merit Agency website. I'm sure Dad will get his M-N at some point this morning."

Amanda reaches the top stair just as AJ and Jake are picking up their backpacks and walking out the door. She catches AJ's eye roll and look of annoyance aimed in her direction and decides to further inflame her daughter's attitude. "AJ, you know that's not regulation and you don't want detention because you will be walking home! Button up your blouse and put your hair in a ponytail."

Headed toward the living room, Amanda places her yoga mat directly in front of the monitor and begins her warm-down stretching routine. Impatiently, she glances at the broadcast every few seconds, unable to focus on the exercises. She attempts to relax in child pose when the broadcast abruptly resumes.

The administrator apologizes for the interruption. "Fellow community members, please excuse the interruption."

Amanda quickly pops up from the stretch and sits back on her heels. She immediately notices what seems to be nervousness in her husband. Luke is tapping his fingers on his leg, and she also notices slight perspiration on his forehead. Her stomach sinks. After 20 years of marriage, Amanda has become very familiar with Luke's mannerisms. He never gets nervous, never for a Merit Review, never when performing in front of a crowd, never. The thought crosses her mind that he probably never gets nervous before an underground fight either. However, if she were to hint that she knows about The Underground, he would be nervous for sure.

The administrator continues, "Luke, your Merit Number for the next year will begin at the conclusion of your Merit Review. 3. Do you wish to appeal the outcome of your Merit Number? If you choose to appeal, your Merit Number of 8 will remain for 30 days. If after 30 days your Merit Number metrics are found to be inaccurate, your Merit Number of 8 will remain for the next year. If your Merit Number metrics are found to be accurate, your Merit Number will be 1 point lower, a 2, for the following year."

Amanda is frozen, feeling nauseous, but not upset. Her gut feeling is that something isn't right. The long broadcast interruption. The nervousness. The extreme M-N drop from an 8 all the way to a 3.

She watches as Luke sits silently. He lowers his head into his hands. Minutes pass.

"We ask again, do you wish to appeal the outcome of your Merit Number?" the administrator repeats.

"No."

"Luke, would you like to ask one question or make a statement?"

Face still buried in his hands, he speaks without making eye contact with the administrator. "Okay, here it is." Suddenly Luke rises to his feet, leans toward the administrator in a threatening manner, and speaks inches from her face. "No, I don't want to appeal. I'm not taking a chance on losing the appeal and getting a 2 and having to deal with dormitory housing and porridge every day. I worked my ass off for years, and yeah, I slacked this year, I took shortcuts, and I guess I knew this was coming, and maybe I'm burned out and just need a break! You know what? Maybe I need to take on a vocation that's a little less intense for a while! Happy with that? Find yourselves another Merit Agency Investigator."

Luke turns and sends his chair flying with a violent kick. The chair bangs against the white wall, echoing loudly and scuffing the bright white paint. He storms toward the exit and hastily leaves the room.

The broadcast switches to Luke's information:

Citizen: Luke Medina
State: New York
County: Wayne
Vocation: Merit Agency Investigator, Level 8
Merit Number: 3

Amanda flops backward, lying silently on her yoga mat, imagining life in a 3~4 neighborhood. Weighing heaviest on her mind is the predictable reaction from AJ. She smiles, knowing this change could be good for AJ, hopefully changing her attitude toward her peers, especially Emily.

She laughs out loud, imagining the best what-if. *What if this is all a big mistake?* The laughter quickly stops and she vows not to question the M-N 3, because what if Luke truly is burned out and needs a break.

Discovery School

Jake turns around and peers over the front seat of the bus, glaring in AJ's direction, waiting to catch her eye. She stands up in the back seat and catches Jake's eye seconds after he looked in her direction. They look at each other, AJ's mouth wide open, paralyzed in shock, Jake looking calm and composed.

They both sit quietly for the remainder of the bus ride, staring at the Merit Agency website on their phones, showing their dad's Merit Number, M-N 3.

As the bus pulls up to the front of their Discovery School, Jake remains seated so he can meet up with his sister. "You see it too, right?" AJ asks.

"Yep. Did you catch the audio?" Jake asks. "I couldn't hear over the obnoxious kids around me. Looked to me like he actually offered an explanation for the 3. I couldn't tell though if he opted for an appeal."

AJ's eyes begin tearing up. "I had my headphones on and heard everything. I can't believe he let us down like this. He felt burned out. What the heck does that even mean? You know what happens now, right? We have to move, I lose my wardrobe, all my clothes and shoes and makeup. My 18th birthday party is going to totally suck! How could he do this to us?"

Jake sighs and pats AJ on the back. She cannot see the smile on his face or properly interpret the sarcastic gesture. Jake thinks to himself, *She's in for a rude awakening.*

They make their way into school, Jake trailing behind his older sister, AJ buttoning the top couple buttons of her school uniform blouse and pulling her hair back into a ponytail. They both walk a very slow pace. Jake mumbles to his sister, "Don't worry, nobody is going to know for a few days."

AJ turns and snaps, "Yeah, well I bet Chloe and Nora won't want me hanging out with them anymore. No way are they going to hang with me in my sweatpants. Oh wait, I could wear slacks and a long-sleeve t-shirt! Or better, if the weather is warm enough I could wear my muumuu! If I tell them ahead of time, I'm sure they will let me wear some of their clothes."

Almost to the door, straggling several feet behind the other students, Jake advises, "You better not wear their clothes, sis, can't hide the M-N 3 on your hand. Look—"

"I know, I saw it change on the bus," she replies, teeth clenched, making a shh sign, finger over lips. "Just make sure you keep your hand hidden. I don't feel like dealing with this today."

Much to AJ's dismay, Chloe and Nora are inside the doorway. They greet Jake in unison with an overly flirtatious, "Hi, Jake." Jake knows to expect their teasing, but he still likes the attention a lot. He blushes heavily, tucks his left hand into his khakis, and tries to reply, but no audible words come out. He heads to his first class, Timeology, among the sea of tan khakis with blue collared shirts and tan knee-length skirts with blue blouses.

The Wayne County Discovery Campus #7, also known as The Sunshine School, received the name because of the yellow ceramic tiles that line the hallways. The bright corridor is slightly subdued by blue lockers. The yellow and blue are thought to reflect the colors of the sky, representing the Sunshine School's motto, *The Sky is the Limit*. Large black and white photographs showing the growth of the campus over time are hung along the corridors.

Wayne County has 14 Discovery campuses. Each campus accommodates ages 6 through 18, following a classic approach of breaking up a youth's time at Discovery School into 12 years. The school year is 10 months of schooling and 2 months of summer vacation.

All classrooms have identical layouts of two semicircle rows, each row with 10 chairs and desks. The desks face a podium. Class size is limited to 20 students, facilitated by mentors and counselors. Students in grades 6 and higher take an active role in presenting daily lessons and leading group discussions.

Jake's Timeology Mentor, Mr. Garcia, calls class to attention. "Quiet down please." The classroom of 20 Discovery School students quickly shifts its attention to Mr. Garcia and silence ensues in seconds. "Thank you for all your respect, future contributors to the United States of Amerita!" Mr. Garcia cheers with enthusiasm. "Today's lesson will be led by Jake Medina, aspiring Timeologist."

Mr. Garcia steps aside from the podium as Jake rises from his seat and prepares to present his lesson. Mr. Garcia asks, "Jake, before you begin today's lesson, please tell us why you are interested in becoming a Timeologist."

Jake, left hand still in his pocket, fumbles to pull his lesson from his backpack. He awkwardly manages to retrieve his printouts, walks to the front of the class holding his papers in one hand, and thinks to himself, *This is ridiculous.* He pulls his left hand out of his pocket and holds his lesson with both hands.

Feeling no shame or embarrassment, he lets his M-N 3 show as he turns to the class and holds his speech in front of him.

Immediately, his best friend, Frederick, mumbles under his breath, "Whoa ... dude ... that sucks." Jake hears the suppressed comment coming from the front row. Frederick's grin lets Jake know that nothing between the two of them will change. Teasingly, Frederick flashes his hand and the glowing 7 toward Jake. This puts Jake at ease, and he relaxes and begins to deliver his lesson.

"Dear classmates, my name is Jake Medina, and when I complete Discovery School, I think that I would like to select Timeology for my vocation.

"The reasons I would like to be a Timeologist are because I'm very interested in the events that led to the downfall of America and the rise of Amerita and Meritism, and I would also like to be a Discovery School Mentor for future Timeologists. Most of all though, I believe studying Timeology is the best way to make sure Amerita does not collapse like America did.

"Nicholas Antonio, the famous physicist, introduced the concept of Timeology. He theorized that there are infinite points along the universal timeline stretching from the beginning of time until the end of time. However, there are only a finite number of possible events. Since the points in time are infinite and the number of possible events is finite, every event will eventually repeat. Countries will rise and countries will fall, and the reasons will repeat."

Jake presents his lesson, exactly as practiced with his mother earlier this morning.

When concluding, instead of making crowd-cheering sound effects, he holds his left hand high, showing everyone in class the glowing M-N 3 on the back of his hand, and declared, "I believe in Amerita and Meritism. My father received an M-N 3 today. I'm proud of all the cases my dad has solved as a Merit Agency Investigator, that's a tough job. He just needed a break, and that's okay by me."

Frederick jumps to his feet, exaggerating his applause. The rest of Jake's classmates clap as well, but none match Frederick's over-the-top enthusiasm.

Mr. Garcia waits for the applause to subside, then gives Frederick a scolding glare prompting him to stop clapping and take his seat. "Excellent job, Jake. I applaud your support of Meritism and the United States of Amerita. Class, any questions?"

Jake's heartbeat quickens as Wendy, his 7th grade crush, stands up to ask a question. He feels his cheeks blushing again, just like when Chloe and Nora said "Hi" to him this morning.

Wendy asks, "Since you are such a supporter of Meritism, I was wondering if you have done any research into who the author of the manifesto was, or is, or was it written by all 97 original Meritism Party members?"

Jake takes a second for an ahem, clearing his throat so he can speak. Attempting to sound extra knowledgeable, he answers Wendy's question, "Thank you for your question, Wendy. Many people theorize that either one, or everyone, from the original 97 Meritism Party members wrote the Meritism Manifesto. I believe one of the 97 is the author. The legend is that the 97 agreed to never divulge the author of the Meritism Manifesto because they felt the document should be viewed as having been able to be written by any Ameritan citizen. When asked, they would simply say 'the Authored By line is empty'. The problem with ever knowing for sure is that none of the 97 are around anymore. I do hope to solve this mystery someday, and my career as a Timeologist could help. So, to answer your question, I have no clue other than I believe one of the 97 wrote the manifesto, not all of them."

When no other students indicate they would like to ask a question, Mr. Garcia excuses Jake. "Excellent job, Jake. I'm sure you will make a fantastic Timeology Mentor."

At lunch time, Jake and Frederick move through the cafeteria together. They grab their trays and slide them down the food bar, and Jake lightheartedly comments to Frederick, "I'm going to be appreciating the lunch food a lot more once we start having to eat porridge."

Frederick offers, "I'll invite you over anytime you get sick of porridge, just let me know."

The two friends select their fruit, vegetable, and protein servings. As they pass by AJ's table full of popular girls, AJ flashes Jake a glare that sends shivers down his spine. Her right hand is out of her pocket. Jake realizes word has spread throughout school about their Merit Number drop from an M-N 8 to an M-N 3. A one or two point change is rarely noticed; however, when a Merit Number drops 5 points, word spreads fast among teenagers.

AJ shifts her focus back to her friends.

"Chloe, Nora, you guys will let me borrow your clothes when we meet up outside of school, right?" AJ asks.

"Why? I think you will look great in slacks and a long-sleeve t-shirt," Chloe meanly suggests. Nora joins in with a sneer.

AJ jumps to her feet and begins to storm away when Nora intercedes, "She's just kidding. Come on, AJ. Right, Chloe?"

Chloe admits, "Yes, I'm just kidding. Of course Nora will let you borrow some clothes!" The three friends laugh together.

AJ unintentionally dampens the mood, "You do realize that six months from now we graduate and we'll all have M-N 5s, and we'll be wearing the same clothes and eating the same food."

"Not me. I'm going to find an M-N 10 to marry right out of school," Chloe announces. Nora and AJ know she is serious.

"Ugh, six months until we have to start working. Okay, enough about that! AJ, text us tonight and let us know where you will be living," Nora requests as she leads the trio out of the cafeteria, headed to their next class.

New Vocation

After spending three hours in the vocational research library on the second floor, Luke heads across the hall to meet with a vocation counselor. He enters the lobby, and unlike the Merit Review lobby's comfortable and relaxing atmosphere, this lobby is very plain. The walls are lined with collapsible metal chairs and there are no refreshments provided. There are five private offices in the lobby, and a woman with graying hair pulled back into a ponytail is standing in front of office 3. Dressed in the familiar loose-fitting gray slacks and white button-down dress shirt, she greets Luke. She appears to have been standing at the threshold of her office door waiting for him to arrive.

"Hello, Luke. My name is Crystal, and I'll be your vocation counselor. Please come in," Crystal invites.

As Luke walks toward the counselor, he receives disapproving glares from the seven other citizens who have been waiting for their turn prior to Luke entering the lobby.

Luke enters office 3 and takes a seat next to Crystal. They both face a table with a monitor and keyboard, and a large window brightens the room. Crystal shuts the door.

"Luke, I've got to say, your reaction to receiving the Merit Number was so convincing, I was wondering if maybe the plan fell apart and you really did receive a 3," Crystal compliments with excitement. "I've seen you in a few community theater productions. My husband and I went to see *The Phantom of the Opera*, and your performance as Erik was fantastic. But what you just did in the Merit Review room was, well, wow, so convincing!

"And how did you think through the scene so quickly, like kicking the chair? The 'burned out' story fit perfectly! Knowing you will be taking a Level 4 vocation and you having an EQ/IQ of 9, your story was perfect. Ripley definitely picked the right investigator for the job."

Luke replies, "Thanks! Lots of improv acting practice I suppose. And I'm glad you enjoyed *Phantom*. Are you sure what I did in the Merit Review room was not over the top? I kinda hurt my foot when I kicked the chair, but that was a nice touch, right? Sorry if I kept you waiting. I spent a few hours in the library to avoid raising suspicion, wanted to look like I was taking my time trying to figure out what vocation to pick."

He pauses and then asks, "So you are in on the mission too? How many of you are there? I'm not sure I like the idea of a secret organization. This totally goes against the transparency the Amerita governance advocates."

Crystal discloses information that astonishes Luke. "We call ourselves The Elders. None of our plans exist on the network. Our communications are all person to person. There is no traceability. Congratulations, Luke. Welcome to The Elders. You are the youngest citizen we've ever asked to join us. However, we see no other option than to bring you in.

"You already know most of us in Wayne County: Julie, Ripley, Williams, Sheriff Chamberlain. Each County has 12 Elders and all communications are strictly limited to in-person meetings. Always greet with this secret greeting, especially since you are new, just to make sure anyone you think is an Elder is indeed an Elder.

"Extend your hand. This is the greeting that will ensure both persons belong to the Elders. Go to shake my hand and say, 'Ma'am, good morning'. I will reply, 'Sir, good morning.' Replace ma'am or sir and morning, afternoon, or evening accordingly. The reply should always match the greeting but leading with the sir or ma'am. If the reply to the greeting is correct for an Elder, then you shake hands and give two quick squeezes to the hand of the person you are greeting. If the person gives three quick squeezes back to your hand, then you know that person is an Elder."

To Luke's surprise, a moment of familiarity floods his thoughts. This is not the first secret handshake he has known. He remembers how his father continued to give him their secret handshake even when he was a teenager.

Crystal congratulates Luke, "Welcome to The Elders! Now let's get down to the task at hand."

Luke settles back in his chair and watches as Crystal begins typing his name into the Merit Agency database of vocations:

```
Name: Luke Medina
Citizen Number: 495.223.669.294
Action: Vocation Reassignment
Vocation Request #1:
```

"Crystal, how about we enter Custodian as my third choice. Anything we can do to avoid suspicion will be good," Luke suggests. "When researching in the library, I was trying to find other Level 4 vocations that would be a good fit. How about we go with Transportation Driver as #1 and Mail Delivery as #2? Then we pick Custodian as #3."

Crystal approves, "I like that idea a lot." She continues entering the data.

```
Vocation Request #1: Transportation, Driver
Vocation Request #2: Mail Delivery
Vocation Request #3: Custodian
```

She submits the entries and scrolls through the list of available vocational openings. "You haven't been through this process for a while, so let me review. Each vocational opening shows the location, level, and interview requirement. Look at these examples."

Vocational Opening	Level	Interview
Transportation, Driver (Newark NY)	4	Yes
Mail Delivery (Lyons NY)	4	Yes
Mail Delivery (Palmyra NY)	4	Yes

"We need to scroll past your first and second choices. If our Elder at the Meritism Data Bank got this right, we should find ... and ... ah, here it is, Custodian, no interview required," Crystal notes with relief. "Perfect. The Elder was instructed to keep that opening flagged as unavailable until after your Merit Review."

Vocational Opening	Level	Interview
Custodian (Rochester NY)	4	No

She explains, "When an interview is not required, the vocational assignment has a three month provisional period. During that time, neither Pharmavast or you can request a change to the assignment. So let us know if they try to get you reassigned. Pharmavast interviews most of their employees, but they're not as diligent with custodial staff. They have always kept that vocation as not requiring an interview and opting for the provisional period instead."

Luke observes as Crystal clicks on the custodial opening and brings up the details.

Vocation: Custodian
Organization: Pharmavast Pharmaceuticals
Location: Clinton Square, Rochester NY
Level: 4
Responsibilities:
    Report to the Custodial Lead who is responsible for all facilities management on the 10th floor.
    Assist with the setup of facilities for meetings, presentations, conferences, etc.

Clean, dust, and wipe furniture; sweep, mop, and vacuum floors; empty/clean wastebaskets and trash containers; replace light bulbs; refill restroom dispensers.

Clean and sanitize restrooms/bathrooms using established practices and procedures.

"And … submit." Crystal clicks the submit button and gives Luke final instructions, "Okay, Luke, you are all set. Report to Pharmavast tomorrow morning at 07:00. An Elder will be in touch. You know what to do. Good luck."

"Tomorrow? I don't even get a day off?" Luke asks jokingly. "Well I'm going to blow off the rest of the day then, hit the gym, go for a walk, treat myself to some comfort food, catch a movie. Or maybe I'll stop by The Underground and watch a fight. I'm just kidding about The Underground, probably doesn't even really exist."

Crystal is eased seeing Luke's cheerful mood.

Luke gives Crystal the secret greeting, she smiles, and he sees himself out.

Walking through the parking lot, Luke chuckles when he spots the light-blue Prius. He regrets trading cars because today would be the last day to drive the Charger, possibly for several months.

After School

AJ invites Jake to join her in the back of the bus with the Seniors where her friends console them. The conversation revolves around how they will all soon be responsible for their own Merit Numbers. Jake does not hesitate to join in the conversation with the older teenagers.

Jake over enthusiastically gives his input, "Did you know that 73% of new graduates drop to an M-N 4 after their first year? Assuming the EQ/IQ correlates accurately with potential vocational success, that leaves only one conclusion—"

AJ interrupts, "Jake, chill! Nobody wants to hear your science—"

"We're lazy!" Jake interrupts, abruptly ending the exchange.

Emily makes her way to the back of the bus to offer her thoughts. "Hey. It's not that bad, AJ. I've only known life with an M-N 3. The porridge gets old fast, but I can tell you first-hand that the claims are true, that mixture is just as nutritious as anything else you can eat. I've been eating porridge every night for dinner for 17 years and I'm as healthy and fit as anyone my age. Here," Emily hands AJ a small bottle, "I would like you to have this cinnamon shaker. Gives the porridge some flavor so it doesn't taste like wet cardboard. My mom always puts it in my backpack in case I don't like what's being served for lunch and decide to eat porridge instead. But I never use it. Anything is better than porridge."

AJ slowly and reluctantly reaches out, feeling badly about the way she has snubbed Emily over the years. "Take it, AJ. I really don't mind," Emily insists.

Her eyes get teary and she thanks Emily as she accepts the gift. "Emily, that's so nice. I don't know what to say."

As the school bus approaches their cul-de-sac and they see their two-story colonial home, AJ and Jake make their way to the front of the bus. Jake looks behind him and notices the level of obnoxiousness on the bus is a lot lower this afternoon. He attributes the subdued atmosphere to the news of their family's Merit Number drop and how such a drastic change reminds the youth that their time of entitlement will soon be over.

They exit the bus, and AJ rushes to the front door, ignoring Koda, their Golden Retriever. She barges in, sending the front door banging against the side of the house. Jake pauses to pet Koda and let Koda lick his face.

Amanda is standing in the doorway. AJ stops in her tracks and shoves the glowing M-N 3 on the back of her hand inches from her mom's face. AJ stares at her mom for a second, rolls her eyes, sighs, and storms up the stairs. Jake, still petting Koda in the front yard, hears AJ's bedroom door slam shut.

Jake teases his mom, "So, Mom, when are you going to follow through with your threat and take her bedroom door off the hinges?"

"So, Jake, did your and your sister's Merit Numbers change already?" Amanda sarcastically jests back at her son. "You should just never mind your sister. She needs a little time."

"Is Dad home?" Jake asks.

"Nope," Amanda answers, and then offers an explanation. "I'm not going to call or text him either. He needs time to cool off, and we should give him his space. I can't believe I didn't sense this was coming."

Jake holds Koda by the collar leading him inside. "Seems like Koda doesn't care about our M-N 3." He heads to the kitchen, grabs an apple from the refrigerator, and sits down at the kitchen table.

Amanda takes a seat across from her son. "Okay, Jake, I can tell you want to give me some statistics. I'm all ears."

Jake appreciates how well his mother knows him. "Okay, so I did my research during study hall. Turns out that Merit Agency

Investigators have one of the highest vocational jump ratios. On average, a Merit Agency Investigator jumps vocations after seven years. Dad lasted twelve years. That's almost double the average. I'm not surprised he was burned out.

"However, when they jump vocations, 90% of the investigators jump to a vocation of the same level. I looked up Dad's new vocation and saw he chose a Level 4, Custodian. That leads me to believe that his burnout is serious. If he was just a little burned out, I'm sure he would have chosen a vocation closer to a Level 9."

"Very insightful, Jake," Amanda compliments, then looks toward the stairs as she hears AJ's footsteps.

Jake adds, "You know, Mom, I'm actually excited for this change. I'll get to see how the other half of the population lives. This is going to be a great learning experience."

AJ walks into the kitchen, slaps both hands down on the table, and offers her thoughts. "I can hear everything. Really, Jake? A great 'learning experience'?" She continues to rant, "A custodian? Level 4? I know how the system works, Mom. Dad tested at a 9 EQ/IQ. Taking a Vocation Level 4 means the highest M-N he can get at that vocation is a 5 and that's only if he scores a Productivity Calculation of 10. Oh, but wait, why should I care? I'm on my own in six months! I guess I'll just have to suffer through this M-Frickin-Number 3 until then."

"Good to see you know your math, sis," Jake instigates.

AJ storms away, intentionally stomps up the stairs, heads to her room, and slams the door shut again.

"Jake, go get me the screwdriver. That door's coming off!" Amanda declares. Then she asks, "But first, what do you want for dinner? I'm going to call for delivery. Might as well get one last gourmet dinner. Tomorrow we'll be eating porridge."

With a big grin, Jake puts in his order, "Lobster mac and cheese please! Order Dad a steak, medium rare, and chocolate cheesecake for AJ. That might cheer her up." He heads toward the garage to grab his dad's toolbox.

Damien

Damien Myers sits at his mahogany desk, turned backward, gazing out the floor-to-ceiling windows of the corner office. Next to his desk, pointed westward, is a high-powered telescope directed toward the Exile border.

He is deep in thought, restlessly tapping his fingertips together, and mentally preparing the agenda for tonight's New Year's Eve Employee Party meeting.

The desk phone rings. He glances at the notification display and sees an incoming call from board member Ann Gonzales.

Damien taps Accept and greets Ann, "Go."

The annoyed voice on the other end of the call bluntly asks, "So you didn't want me involved in the New Year's Eve party planning? I cover most of the East coast. And you didn't think to include me? Do you have any idea how many employees I have under my supervision?"

Damien asks for clarification, "Ann, what are you talking—" but is cut off by Ann.

"Don't pretend with me, Damien. You and I have a history, or have you forgotten already? I know you better than any of your ex-wives," Ann argues. "You better start explaining. I had to hear from Rashad about tonight's meeting."

"Settle down, give me a minute. Of course you're on the committee. All board members are on the committee." Damien opens his laptop, brings up his Pharmavast calendar, and reviews the list of employees who accepted the invite to tonight's 20:00 meeting. Including himself, there are 20 Pharmavast board members, and all of them are on the New Year's Eve Employee Party Committee. "Nineteen names confirmed for today's meeting," Damien assures.

"Looks like you didn't confirm attendance. Maybe you deleted the email?" Damien suggests.

"What do you think I am, a moron?" Ann argues. "I want an answer at the meeting. Prove that you didn't intentionally exclude me. You know I've got plenty of dirt on you so don't mess with me, asshole." She hangs up on Damien.

He speaks into the disconnected call, "Only you, Ann. Only you can get away with speaking to me like that. Anyone else would be silenced."

Determined to figure out what happened to Ann's invitation, Damien starts a search on his laptop for the original message sent last month. After a few minutes of tapping his fingertips and waiting impatiently, the original message is retrieved.

He notes the send-to group, [GROUP: New Year's Eve Employee Party Committee], retrieves the group settings, and reads the names. He notices the email address `Anne.Gonzales@Pharmavast.rx` right away and breathes a sigh of relief, then begins typing a text message to Ann.

`Ann: Hey Bitch, WTF, take a look, you were invited. Must be you messed up.`

Then he aims the phone's camera at the monitor and pauses just before taking the picture. He notices with a sigh of dread, `Anne.Gonzales@Pharmavast.rx`.

Quickly opening the Pharmavast staff directory, he searches for A%Gonzales and scrolls until he discovers his mistake.

...

Ann Gonzales, Ann.Gonzales@Pharmavast.rx
Anne Gonzales, Anne.Gonzales@Pharmavast.rx

He clicks on Anne's name and reads her profile, learning that she is a data entry clerk in the Acquisitions department on the 8th floor of the building.

Damien quickly moves to the other side of his office, opens the door, and calls out to his assistant, "Tiffany, get in touch with Anne Gonzales in Acquisitions. I need her in my office now."

His assistant questions, "Is everything okay, Damien?"

He pauses for a few seconds, then answers, "Sorry, Tiff, I didn't mean to alarm you. Everything is fine. We noticed some inventory shortages I wanted to ask her about."

Tiffany suggests, "Well how about I get her manager instead? She's a data entry clerk."

"Just do what I asked," Damien snaps, then slams his office door.

He walks over to the telescope, adjusts the focus, and begins to scan the Exile border, hoping to see some violence. After several minutes of seeing nothing but stray dogs running along the fence, there is a knock on his door.

"Come in. Have a seat, Anne."

"Hello, Mr. Myers. You wanted to see me?" Anne asks timidly, looking at the floor. She walks toward the desk and takes a seat in a nearby chair.

Damien turns from his telescope and is momentarily thrown off guard by Anne's attractiveness. He walks to his desk and takes note of all Anne's mannerisms and body language. His ability to read people's emotions is a skill he has used to further his career and influence.

He takes his seat across from Anne.

With an overly calming tone, Damien relaxes the atmosphere, "Hi, Anne. You have been with us at Pharmavast for a while, right? I was looking over your profile and I see this was your first vocation out of Discovery School. Ten years later, your efficiency and productivity metrics are fantastic. I'm grateful to have you on our staff. And please call me Damien. And nice job, I see you have an M-N 9." Merit Numbers are always on the dominant hand; Damien takes a mental note that Anne's is on her right hand.

Anne obliges, noticeably more relaxed, "Thank you, Mr. Myers, I mean Damien." She looks up at Damien for the first time since walking into his office, "Is everything, okay? I was really nervous coming up here. I know about your open-door policy, but still, you are Damien Myers."

Damien explains about the email mix-up, as if the situation was inconsequential, "Nothing really, well just something stupid I did. I mistakenly added your name to an email group of mine. Your name is so close to another staff person. Her name is A-N-N, without an E, and her last name is Gonzales too."

Anne immediately looks down, avoiding eye contact with Damien and begins to fidget. Damien notices the instant change.

He begins to interrogate innocently, "By any chance, have you received any emails addressed to the group? The topic would have been about our upcoming organization's New Year's Eve Employee Party. You see, we wanted to keep the party and the theme a secret until a week before the party."

Anne looks up. Damien watches her eyes closely. As she begins to speak, her eyes drift up and to the right. "I, well, I'm not sure. I don't think I got any emails like that. I'm pretty certain I didn't because I'm sure I would have remembered something about a New Year's Eve Employee Party." She looks down again. "Mr. Myers, I mean Damien, would you like me to search my deleted items and see if I find anything?"

"No, that's fine, no big deal. But if you do come across anything like that, can we count on you to keep it a secret?" Damien requests.

"Yes, sir. Definitely," Anne promises.

"Come on, I'll walk you out," Damien stands and gestures toward the door. "Well now that you know about the party, maybe we could go together? I'll email you when the party plans are finalized and you can let me know then."

Feeling extremely fearful with the line of questioning and even more fearful of saying no to him, Anne manages to utter the word, "Okay."

Damien walks her out, arm around her waist, and she thinks to herself, *Oh crap, I hope he believes me. And what a creep! He's old enough to be my father.*

Damien returns to his office, locks the door, and approaches a painting on the wall opposite his desk, titled *Community Effort*. The historic work of art is a painting of ten laborers working on conveyor belts, all with big smiles and bright eyes, but they are painted in shades of gray. Each of the ten diligently attends to his own conveyor belt. Each laborer's hands are busily assembling something invisible. The conveyor belts have nothing on them. The ten conveyor belts converge on the right side of the painting where a family of five stands, painted in bright colors. The father and two sons are wearing black-and-white tuxedos with orange bowties, and the mother and daughter are wearing long pastel gowns. They are smiling and each one is holding a different object. The father holds a block of coal. The mother holds a cooked turkey. The two sons hold wrapped presents. The girl holds a porcelain doll. The doll is frowning, and its face is painted in shades of gray.

He takes the painting down and removes a concealed panel, revealing a small compartment. He opens the compartment and retrieves a phone.

Damien dials and waits. In his mind, he reviews the interaction with Anne. *Her dominant hand is her right hand. She looked up to her right when I asked her about the email. She was lying.*

"What?" asks the gruff voice on the other end.

"I've got someone who needs to be silenced."

Watchtower

The glowing M-N 3 is distracting, almost directly in his line of sight as he drives the Prius with his left hand on the steering wheel. Headed west on I-490 and listening to his favorite radio station, WBER, Luke decides to take a round-about-way to the city. The longer route drives along the eastern border of the Western NY Exile Zone.

Just west of the city, the Western NY Exile Zone begins to border the highway. Luke stops at the first watchtower and parks momentarily, looking out into the decrepit neighborhoods. He watches a few exiled citizens roam aimlessly in the streets. Luke repeats this ritual every time memories of his father return, as they had that morning. He vividly recalls that day when he was a young teenager, the one-year anniversary of his dad's exile ...

Tina and Luke decided to leave after dinner, headed to Western NY Exile Zone Gate 23, the location where his father walked into exile one year ago. They arrived as the sun began to set.

The watchtower stood on the Erie Canal Bridge, mid-way to the other side. Waterways were frequently used as natural exile zone borders. Chain-link fence and barbed wire extended from either side of the watchtower to the edges of the bridge preventing anyone from crossing. Three guards stood watch in the tower. One guard was armed with a tranquilizing sniper rifle, watching for any exilees approaching the watchtower. The other two guards monitored the area near their watchtower using a series of infrared cameras strategically mounted and on aerial drones.

Tina used the watchtower intercom to contact the guards, "Hello, my name is Tina Medina, and this is my son, Luke."

On the north side of the bridge, the area of the bridge in the exile zone, empty cardboard boxes and large plastic containers littered the pothole-covered road. The boxes and containers were all labeled, "Amerita - Food and Provisions."

The supervising guard anticipated her request, "You are here to see if Martin shows up tomorrow, correct? I read his name on our exile return-day listing for the week. You are a day early."

Luke chimed in bluntly, "We're technically four hours early. My dad's return can happen at midnight."

The supervising guard, with no sign of empathy, replied, "You have been cleared to park on the bridge behind the fence."

Tina and Luke returned to their car and pulled up next to the watchtower, only a few feet from the fence. They sat in silence, windows rolled down to prevent the windshield from fogging. Luke watched YouTube videos on his phone, while Tina unsuccessfully attempted to compose a social media post about their reuniting that correctly captured her feelings.

She started to cry. Luke consoled her, "What's wrong, Mom?" Luke realized this is only the second time he has seen his mother cry. The first time was one year ago when his dad's exile was announced.

"Nothing, I'm fine. I guess I'm happy because the worst year of our lives is over. But I'm so sad because so much happened this year that your dad was not here to see. He missed all your plays, seeing you in lead roles, Christmas. He didn't get to say goodbye to Oscar, and I know he loved that cat. He doesn't even know about your heart. I would have done anything to let him know Lusitropin worked and that you will probably never need a transplant." Tina wiped away her tears with a tissue. "I'm fine. He'll be here soon."

Tina and Luke continued to distract themselves with activities on their phones and eventually both fell asleep.

A few hours pass.

"EEEEE-OOOOO EEEEE-OOOOO EEEEE-OOOOO."

Tina was jolted awake by the combination of the blaring alarm and the beaming flood lights. She shook Luke, an extremely sound sleeper, until he woke. "Come on, let's get out of the car!"

Tina and Luke leapt out of the car, ran up to the chain-link fence, and peered transfixed at the shadow standing still on the far side of the bridge.

The figure sprinted toward the watchtower just as the guards turned on the blinding spotlight. Five more shadowy figures were visible, all rushing toward the watchtower and the chain-link fence separating them from Amerita.

With every step, their appearance became more and more defined. Luke noticed their clothes were riddled with spikes and padding. Most of them had baseball bats weaponized with nails and spikes.

Tina grabbed Luke's hand, "Get in the car!"

As soon as they were seated in the car, Tina turned the key. Nothing happened; the battery was dead from leaving the car on to keep their electronics powered up.

Tina and Luke watched helplessly as the barbarians rushed the gate. But they stopped at the cardboard boxes and plastic containers and ransacked the dropped shipment from Amerita, only to find there were no provisions or food remaining.

The unemphatic voice of the supervising guard boomed over the loudspeaker, "You all might as well go home. You missed this drop by about 12 hours."

The shadowy figures shouted vulgarities at the guards, immediately turned around, and left, dispersing into the darkness of the exile zone.

"Hey, Medinas, we have an arsenal up here. You have nothing to worry about," the voice over the loudspeaker sneered, "except for a dead battery!"

Tina finally realized there was no sympathy for someone returning from exile or for their families.

Not willing to leave, Tina and Luke remained with the car, ready to approach the fence when the next exilee, hopefully Martin, approached.

Tina called Transportation Services and requested a jump-start. After they arrived, Tina ran the car for a half-hour to charge the battery, then told Luke they will not rely on the car to power their electronics.

Eventually they fell asleep again. Tina was awakened by the alarm two more times before dawn, both false alarms, just stray dogs tripping the motion sensors.

The next watchtower shift arrived. One of the guards approached their car before entering the watchtower. He asked, "I assume you are here waiting for someone?"

Tina replied, "Yes, my husband, Martin Medina."

The guard emphatically assured, "Okay, Mrs. Medina, I'll keep calling around to the other watchtowers in case he shows up at a different gate."

12:00, noon arrived. No sign of Martin. Luke and Tina sat in the car, perfectly silent, not relying on the distractions provided by their phones.

18:00, dinner time arrived. No sign of Martin. Luke and Tina continued to pick away at the snacks they brought instead of leaving to get dinner.

Midnight. No sign of Martin.

03:00. Tina started the car, exchanged a look of hopelessness with her son, and drove away.

Luke snaps out of the memory. With feelings of anger and helplessness mounting, he decides to head for The Underground to work out his emotions.

The Underground

Luke approaches the city's inner-loop, gazes at the tall buildings, and notices the Pharmavast headquarters. Suddenly, the idea of cleaning toilets daily enters his mind with discontent.

He takes the exit that will bring him close to the Chinese restaurant, Zhan Dou Palace. He finds a parking spot two blocks away, just big enough to parallel park the Prius.

Luke decides to leave behind his button-down shirt, placing it on the driver's seat. The white sleeveless t-shirt he's wearing under his uniform and the Merit Agency issued black slacks and black boots do not have the immediate appearance of an Investigator. This will be an acceptable look for The Underground.

Confidently strolling along the sidewalk, he notices several people glancing at him with a slight look of contempt. Instantly, he realizes they are noticing the glowing M-N 3 on his left hand. He is not bothered.

He walks into a general store on the first corner and heads for the refrigerator to grab a couple bottles of sports drink. He selects two fruit-punch-flavored bottles and brings them to the shopkeeper. The young man behind the counter looks to be just a year or two older than AJ.

"Could I please see your hand, sir?" the shopkeeper asks politely.

Luke obliges, raising his left hand and placing the two bottles on the counter.

"I'm sorry sir, but the 3~4 shelf is at the bottom of the refrigerator," the courteous shopkeeper informs.

"My mistake," Luke admits and points to his left hand, emphasizing that he knows about the 3, "First day with an M-N 3." He returns the flavored sports drinks to the 7~8 shelf and selects two bottles of flavorless water/fructose from the 3~4 shelf.

Luke notices the store keeper's M-N, a 5. "Is this your first year out of Discovery School?" he asks.

"Yes, sir. I've only been a shopkeeper for six months now," the young adult confirms. He scans the two bottles Luke placed on the counter, removing them from the shop's inventory.

Luke's curiosity is peaked. "So tell me, what are your vocational aspirations?"

With much enthusiasm, the young shopkeeper answers, "I hope to be the proprietor of my own business, probably a general store, which is why I requested this position."

Luke tilts the counter-mounted Merit Evaluation Tablet toward himself. Opting to input the three questions as the shopkeeper looks on, Luke taps his fingerprint onto the tablet's touchscreen and selects Excellent for all three questions.

```
Business: A. Patterson's General Store
Proprietor: Albert Patterson 235.447.932.126
Staff Person: Clarence Hansen 490.445.987.123
Vocation: Shopkeeper


1. Helpful and Considerate:
        Poor       Fair       Good       Excellent


2. Cleanliness of Facility:
        Poor       Fair       Good       Excellent


3. Availability of Products:
        Poor       Fair       Good       Excellent


Patron: Luke Medina 556.985.321.409
```

The shopkeeper notes Luke's name and expresses his gratitude, "Thank you very much, Mr. Medina. I'm working my very best to maintain a good M-N."

"I understand, more than you know," Luke comments. Leaving the general store with a smirk, he encourages the young man, "Keep up the good work, Clarence."

Slowly walking along the second block, taking in what is left of the winter-day sunshine, Luke arrives at the Zhan Dou Palace. The delicious smells coming from the kitchen of the popular Chinese restaurant remind Luke that he has not had anything to eat since breakfast.

He approaches the elderly Chinese woman working behind the counter and asks, "May I please have five spring rolls with a side of ketchup?"

She replies, "Yes, you may have five spring rolls with a side of ketchup."

They exchange nods. She swings open the small half-door on the side of the counter and welcomes Luke into the back of the kitchen.

The Chinese woman hands Luke a to-go plate of rice and spring rolls, "Here, take this with you. You look hungry, and you are one of my favorites."

"Thank you, Mrs. Kuo. Nice to see you are still a 10!" Luke expresses his appreciation and respect for her Merit Number.

Mrs. Kuo blushes and jokes with Luke, "Are you flirting with me again, Luke? Watch out for Master Kuo, he is a jealous man. Oh, wait ... you are talking about my M-N 10, aren't you?"

Luke blows her a kiss and walks to the back of the kitchen, stopping in front of the basement door. After knocking three times, pausing, knocking two times, pausing, and knocking one time, the basement door opens and a whiff of dampness and cool air rush into Luke's face.

The Underground is a fight club. Luke ventures here to sharpen his Muay Thai skills.

Once inside the club, he stands with the crowd in the bleachers, hovering over the dirt-floor pit eating his meal. He finishes the delicious Chinese food and watches the fights for another hour, being sure to let his food digest before placing his name on the fight list and moving down to the pit level.

Sitting on the waiting bench, Luke sees he will face Brawling Brock, a crowd favorite. Brawling Brock is six-feet-nine-inches tall with a shaved head and a prominent scar over his left eye.

Luke has memorized Brock's every flaw, having seen him fight several times. He notices Brock clenching his lower-left ribs, a possible weak spot he can expose. At five-feet-nine inches, a full foot shorter than Brock, Luke knows all his opponent's weaknesses need to be exploited.

The bell rings and the team of medical professionals carry a bloodied man out of the ring. Luke takes a quick glance at the man on the stretcher and can tell he is going to be fine because the fighters have an unwritten code of conduct and respect the tap-out rule.

The usher escorts Luke and Brock into the chain-link octagon ring. He looks up at the crowd and a spectator yells, "Kick his ass, Brock!" Another yells, "He's a wimp, Brock! Send him home in a body bag!"

Luke wonders how people who are so pleasant and kind in the community can be so awful when put in a place below the law. Luke considers himself off duty when in The Underground, so he does not interfere, but still he struggles with The Underground's existence. His justification is that this place serves an important purpose; here he can hone his skills, the skills he uses to protect the population above.

The first-round bell dings. Luke is so caught up in thought that he doesn't see Brock going for a jab. Brock's fist hits him like a brick wall. Luke reaches for his nose and sees blood. He feels his adrenaline rising, controls his anger, and knows he cannot attack first. In order to win, he must parry with perfect counters and strikes on every attack until he gets an opening to finish Brock.

Now focused, Luke ducks under the next jab and parries Brock with a perfectly timed and executed uppercut. Brock grabs his chin and lets out a growl heard all the way in the upper rows.

After cracking his neck in an attempt to intimidate, Brock goes for a right hook and is so fast that Luke cannot dodge the fist. Luke is sent sprawling across the ring.

As Luke labors to his feet, he changes tactics and decides to infuriate Brock with banter. If mad enough, Brock can be thrown off his game and Luke can use his strength against him.

Luke heard on the bench that Brock hates when people call him by his real name, Marvin, instead of Brock. "Hey, Marvin? Are you running out of steroids? Cuz you're punching like your mother!"

Brock attempts to keep calm, but Luke can read his body language and see his fists tremble and the veins on his forehead swell. Luke anticipates a wildly thrown right hook and easily dodges to the left. The hook is thrown with so much force that Brock unbalances himself.

Luke continues taunting, "Marvin, you realize you're literally six, nine. Get it, like sixty-nine." Luke laughs loudly, knowing laughter in the ring toward an opponent is the ultimate insult.

"SHUT UP, YOU LITTLE PRICK!" Brock shouts uncontrollably.

Luke realizes that he definitely touched a nerve with the laughter and slowly backs up, positioning himself on the opposite side of the ring.

The crowd simultaneously cheers, "Ohhhh, you're dead now! Get him, Brock! Brock! Brock! Brock!"

Brock charges full speed. Luke effortlessly crouches and spins with a leg sweep, tripping up Brock and sending him face first into the chain-link fence. Brock springs to his feet, but before he can set himself, Luke delivers a massive side-kick to Brock's lower-left ribs. Luke's heightened senses pick up the sound of ribs cracking. Brock falls to the ground, gasping for air.

Luke kneels over Brock, left fist raised, "Bro, tap out. We don't need to do this."

Brock reaches up and taps Luke's right shoulder.

Luke extends his hand. Brock grasps Luke's hand and allows Luke to help him up into a sitting position.

The crowd sits in silence as Brock continues to catch his breath. A spectator starts booing and throws a beer can into the ring.

Luke knows he needs to get home. Amanda is likely furious by now. He decides to make one more stop.

The doors to the bakery slide open and Luke looks over the desserts on the 7~8 shelves. He chooses a two-layer, frosted, chocolate and strawberry cake.

He asks the baker, "Excuse me, miss? Can you add the writing, 'Great Job, Jake'? My son had a big test today. I think he will appreciate the cake."

"Sure, I would be happy to. I just need to see your hand if you don't mind," she asks politely.

Luke slowly raises his left hand, having forgotten he has an M-N 3. "Sorry about that, just got the M-N 3 today. I forgot I don't have an M-N 8 anymore, just had my review today."

"That's okay, I understand. But I'll have to ask you to pick a cake from the 3~4 shelves if you don't mind," she requests.

Luke obliges agreeably. He chooses a single-layer, unfrosted, chocolate cake. The baker adds, 'Great Job, Jake.'

Cake in hand, Luke heads for his car. Four shadowy figures emerge from an alley and a fifth, leading the pack, walks up to Luke. He stands face to face with Luke and grabs him by the shirt.

"Good evening, gentlemen," Luke pleasantly declares, trying to avoid as much conflict as possible.

"I had a lot riding on that fight, Luke," the man complains.

"What did you bet? There's no money so what did you have riding on the fight?" Luke questions.

"That's none of your business, asshole," he replies.

"Well, that's a shame. I've got to get home now." Luke escapes the grip on his shirt and turns to run.

The four thugs surround him and taunt, "That's a nice cake you got there."

"The cake is for my son. Back off," Luke warns.

The gang's leader is fearless, "Aww, you think I'm afraid of an Investigator? That's right, we know who you are, Merit Agency Investigator Medina. We know you won't report us because that would place you illegally fighting at The Underground."

Luke decides to attempt talking his way out, holding up his left hand, "Guys, today isn't the day to mess with me. I just had my Merit Review and dropped from an 8 to a 3, right down there with you guys. I quit the agency and report to my new job as a custodian tomorrow. I only want to bring this cake home to my son."

"You still cost me a lot tonight!" the gang's leader growls and then backs out of the way. He gives a nod to his four thugs.

A knife is pulled. Luke kicks his foot up and lands a shot to the crotch of one of the thugs. As the thug falls to his knees, Luke grabs the man's hand and directs the knife into his thigh and gives the blade a twist.

He breaks through the encirclement, tucking the cake under his arm, and sprints for his car.

Rain starts pouring as Luke looks over his shoulder. The men are not in pursuit. He notices blood on the cardboard cake box and that the box is starting to soak up the rain.

He enters his car quickly and heads for home, driving under the speed limit to intentionally prolong his unavoidable conflict with Amanda. He dreads being limited to public transportation starting tomorrow, so even though this is not his muscle car, he cherishes the solitude of a night-time drive.

Several hours late for dinner, Luke turns onto his street, the neighborhood Amanda, AJ, Jake, and he have known for the past 18 years. He is saddened that this will be the last night his family will spend in the home, knowing likely that another family will immediately move in.

Daddy's Home

Luke drives an extra lap around the cul-de-sac, pulls into the driveway, and notices the light-blue color of the Prius is an exact match to the color of his house. This coincidence makes him laugh.

The house is surrounded by beautifully manicured landscaping and impeccably uniform blades of grass. The large picture window brightens the open-concept living room, kitchen, and dining area with the light of the setting sun. Everything in the house, including the large-screen monitor, the new appliances, and the leather furniture, will no longer be theirs.

He slowly opens the front door, sneaks into the kitchen, and places the cake on the counter next to the remains of dinner. Luke pieces together a plate of cold food for himself, lobster mac and cheese, a T-bone steak cooked just how he likes it, medium rare, and a piece of chocolate cheesecake.

Exhausted, he flops down on the leather couch next to Jake, who is playing Batman *War of Arkham* on his Play Station X. He starts to eat and apologizes, "Listen, Jake, I'm sorry about getting an M-N 3. I hope you can forgive me."

Jake accepts, "Dad, Dad, don't worry. I'm kinda excited about moving because I'll get to see what things are like at other M-N levels. AJ is the one who's mad."

Luke looks up and sees Amanda. He places his dinner on the glass coffee table and approaches to give her a hug. She stops him, "Luke, what happened to your face?" Luke turns and heads to the bathroom where he sees a little bruising and swelling around his nose.

"It's nothing, Amanda. Just had a little trouble this morning during a bust," Luke tries to convince her.

Amanda sees right through Luke's dishonesty. "A little trouble, hmm? Is that blood on the cake box?"

Luke quickly thinks up a story, "That's just some strawberry frosting. I think that's from another cake the baker was working on."

"So, does anyone care what I think about the M-N 3?" AJ shouts from the top of the stairs.

Luke makes his way to the top of the stairs where AJ stands with her arms crossed, head tilted, looking at her father with as much disappointment as she can muster.

He reaches the top step, notices the door lying sideways in the hall off the hinges, and intentionally provokes his daughter, "Looks like you slammed your door again?"

The father and daughter stare each other down for several seconds until Luke breaks the silence, "Family meeting. Let's go, everyone to the living room, now please. Amanda and Jake, please bring whatever is left of our last good dinner to the coffee table."

Luke walks back down the staircase and AJ follows closely behind, stomping every step. Amanda and Jake sit next to each other on the couch, munching on the remaining food. AJ and Luke join; AJ sits on the other side of Amanda and snags the last piece of chocolate cheesecake, and Luke sits on the floor and tosses the T-bone to Koda. The family of four sits quietly, waiting anxiously for Luke to speak first.

"Anyone going to start?" Luke asks slightly annoyed.

All at once, Amanda, AJ, and Jake start speaking.

Amanda, "Maybe I should go to work instead ..."

Jake, "Let's talk about our housing options ..."

AJ, "This really, really, REALLY sucks ..."

Luke speaks over all of them, "One at a time! Amanda first!"

Amanda speaks, "We all understand that you are burned out, but you should have let us know, Luke. I could have gone back to my vocation, I do miss the animal shelter, and you could have taken care of things here. I'm sure we could still put in for that change."

Luke interrupts, "I know you would, Amanda. But I've got to do this, at least for a few months. I promise I will think about doing that though. You taking on a vocation and me taking care of the household could be a good change of pace for both of us." He switches his focus to AJ, "AJ?"

AJ remains silent, picking away at the cake. She simply stares back at her mom and dad, contributing nothing to the conversation other than a tremendous scowl.

Luke instigates again, "Okay, sounds like AJ is on board!"

"Mom!" AJ cries.

"Yep, sounds like AJ is onboard!" Amanda concurs. AJ starts to get up from the couch, lets out a loud sigh, and is scolded by Amanda. "Sit down, AJ! We're all in this together. Be disrespectful one more time and I'll take your phone away until you graduate!"

Amanda glares at her husband. "And you, Luke? Really? Please don't push her buttons."

Jake, sitting patiently, takes control of the conversation. "Listen up, family. I already downloaded and printed a copy of the M-N 3 Possession Selection form. Let's just fill out the main points together, then Mom and Dad can fill out the rest of the form, okay?"

Amanda shows her support of Jake's mature outlook, "Okay, Jake, thanks for that and please walk us through the questions."

"All right," Jake starts with a stunning sense of enthusiasm, "I've already filled out the form, but we can print another if you don't like my selections.

"Neighborhood. We have to move to a 3~4 neighborhood, and I'm thinking we choose the Village Park area. That's near downtown but on the other side of the canal. Since this is in the same town, we can stay in the same Discovery School.

"Housing. I think we should choose an apartment instead of a pre-fab house. Those pre-fab houses aren't even close to as nice as this house, and they're all packed so close together in those parks. I think that would bother us a lot after being in this house for so long. An apartment would be a cool change, and we can get into a 3~4 apartment building in Village Gardens. I found an available one in the 3~4 neighborhood with three bedrooms. The apartment is 800 square feet, on the second floor, and pet-friendly! There's a transportation stop right by the front entrance. We can easily walk to any stores we need, and we can walk to church too. If we were in a pre-fab house, we would have a long walk to the closest transportation stop. Because we won't have our car, we should stay close to the places we go to a lot.

"Food. I say we choose our two porridge meals to always be breakfast and lunch since AJ and I will be at school for lunch anyway. Dinner is the biggest meal, so let's not do porridge ever for dinner. That one is an easy choice."

Amanda, Luke, and AJ stare in awe at Jake and his thoroughness. A minute passes and Jake asks, "Well?"

"No objections from me," Amanda answers. "You kids will get out of having to eat porridge for lunch since you will be at school, but I can deal with porridge for breakfast and lunch I suppose." Amanda smiles with an overly dramatic look of self-sacrifice.

"I'm fine with those choices too," Luke adds.

AJ clutches her phone tightly and snaps, "Whatever, Jake. I don't care anymore. Village Gardens is a dump." She storms away and heads to her bedroom before Amanda can take her phone.

"AJ, we have cake! We could all use more comfort food," Luke shouts upstairs to AJ's room, knowing that without the door on the hinges, she will definitely hear him. Amanda smacks Luke on the shoulder for instigating again.

"Cake?" Jake asks. "What's the occasion?"

Luke explains, "I stopped for a dessert for you, Jake. I know how hard you studied for that algebra test today. I'm betting test anxiety didn't get the best of you."

"I did okay, I think. My Timeologist presentation went great though!" Jake shares, "Thanks, Dad! Okay if I take a piece to my room, Mom?"

"Fine. I guess any mess in your room tonight isn't a big deal since Housing will be cleaning tomorrow for the lucky family that gets this place," Amanda obliges.

Jake hands his mom the M-N 3 Possession Selection Form. "Here, you can fill out the rest. All that's left are questions about clothing sizes and estimated transportation needs. Then make sure you go online and submit the form so we can get that apartment before anyone else requests the same one. I'll be in my room." Jake heads to the kitchen to get a piece of cake.

Amanda and Luke review the Possession Selection Form and complete the remaining questions. Aware that the kids could still hear their voices, Amanda whispers, "I know something's up, Luke. You don't have to tell me what's going on, but you better come clean with me when you sort things out."

Luke gently puts his hands on Amanda's cheeks, leans in and kisses her lightly on the lips, and assures her with a whisper, "Everything is fine." He pauses after the sentence, maintains close eye contact with his wife, nods, and flashed a slightly crooked smile.

Amanda stares back into his eyes, transfixed momentarily. She holds his hands and returns the nod. She gives him a hug and suggests, "You should review this section with the kids so they know what personal items they can keep. They have not been through this process before. Grab a couple empty totes from the basement and bring them up to their rooms, please."

"AJ, here's a tote," Luke calmly tells his daughter.

AJ quickly interrupts, "Fine, just put the tote on my floor. You don't need to go over the list with me. I already searched and found out that basically I can't take anything with me. Not even any clothes. Whatever I wear to school tomorrow, I have to turn in when I get home and put on my sweat pants and long sleeve t-shirt. Oh my god, Dad, I'm going to die!"

Luke sits on the edge of AJ's bed and puts an arm around her shoulder. To his surprise, she does not push him away, but instead leans into his shoulder and cries. He expresses sympathy and tries to reassure her, "AJ, I have never let you down, right?"

AJ manages to speak through her tears, "No, Daddy, you've never let us down. I'm sorry. I'll be alright."

"I know you will be," Luke comforts. Before heading to Jake's room, he reminds AJ, "Make sure you pack all the journals. We both put a lot of work into those. Next time you get mad at me, go read some passages I wrote when you were a toddler. The ones about us having tea parties are priceless. Remember when you used to make me wear a tiara?"

AJ smiles briefly.

"I suppose you don't need this list either?" Luke asks Jake.

"Nope, I'm all set, already packed too, trophies, Legos, action figures, all set." Jake tells his dad with a smile. "I'm going to miss my Play Station X, but I'll still be able to get an older model to use for now. Some of those older games are still pretty good. Don't forget Christmas is coming, Dad. The new Play Station X2 is out!"

Luke, smiling back, realizes Jake's positive attitude is genuine, "You really are looking forward to this move, aren't you?" Then he snickers and hints to Jake, "And yes, Jake, I think I might have read something about the new regulations regarding Christmas gifts."

He places the empty tote next to Jake's bed, turns slowly in a circle, and looks to see if Jake forgot to pack anything.

Luke notices Jake's two favorite posters are still hanging, "What about the Meritism Manifesto poster? And I still don't get the significance of that Snake Plissken poster."

"I'll take them down tomorrow. My room looks too plain without them," Jake answers, then asks, "You still haven't watched *Escape from New York*, have you? Snake Plissken is the action hero in that movie."

Luke answers, "No, Jake, I haven't."

"Well, Dad, let me tell you why I like that poster so much. The movie is from 1981 and predicted that in 1997 Manhattan Island would be one big prison. Well, guess what? That exact thing happened, only 25 years after 1997. But the cool thing is that it's a perfect example of life imitating art.

"With Sci-Fi movies and books, the future of society and technology is often fictionalized very inaccurately. Take *Back to the Future*, for example. In 1989, that movie predicted flat-screen monitors and flying cars by 2015. They got the flat-screen monitors correct, but flying cars? Really? We still don't have those. That would require a gravity defying technology.

"Imagine if someone in 2016 wrote a book about Meritism in the year 2051 and included things like flying cars and telepathic brain implants for communicating instead of using phones and servant robots and colonization of Mars and ..."

Luke knows Jake enjoys demonstrating his knowledge of Ameritan Timeology as much as Sci-Fi, so he interrupts and offers a challenge to get him off his Sci-Fi rant, "Let's hear you recite the Meritism Manifesto, by heart. Are you up for the challenge?"

Jake accepts the challenge and recites the manifesto word for word, even the signature line. "Authored By: _____ ... and that line is left empty! Someday I'll figure out who authored the manifesto. That's the only clue the 97 would ever give about the true author. They all said the same thing, 'the Authored By line is empty'. Many people believe all 97 are the authors, but they left the signature line empty to represent that any Ameritan citizen could have written the manifesto. My gut feeling is that just one of them was the original author." Jake pauses for a breath, then finishes his thoughts, "Empty, intentionally. Hmm... sorry, Dad, didn't mean to get on a rant."

Luke recites the same good night phrase Jake has heard almost every night of his life, "Good night, son. I love you, you're wonderful, you make me proud. Now get a good night's sleep and don't stay up too late."

Meritism Manifesto

We, the working women and men of our beautiful and plentiful land, declare in one voice to revoke all credence to economical systems based on subjective monetary representations of individual Merit.

We, the contributors of food, shelter, clothing, sanitation, education, healthcare, technology, art, and sport, declare our vocations as necessary for advancing society. Vocations that do not contribute to the advancing of society are deemed not worthy of recognition.

We, the laborers, believe the productivity of every valid vocation is objectively and accurately measurable.

We, the parents and mentors of future generations, believe in equal education, equal nutrition, equal healthcare, and equal opportunity for all.

We, the champions of equal prosperity for equal effort, believe all persons are gifted with talents and the ability to contribute meaningfully to society.

We believe every individual has the right to choose how much or how little he or she contributes.

The more an individual contributes, the more he or she shall be rewarded.

The less an individual contributes, the less he or she shall be rewarded.

If an individual contributes nothing, the individual shall have no place in the community.

We, the people of the new Meritocracy, declare objective recognition of Merit for all.

Authored By: _____

**We pledge our unwavering support
to the Meritism Party:**

Mathew W., Lowell P., Guadalupe C., Lana C., Jodi B.,
Kenny H., Marlene C., Archie H., Yolanda W., Jeff I.,
Bill C., Geneva P., Martha G., Elvira L., Lindsay R.,
Gwendolyn S., Lydia H., Nicholas H., Ronnie B., Carlos H.,
Olga N., Peggy M., Mario K., Brandy W., Wilma L., Billie H.,
Jon H., Michele S., Robin S., Charlene R., Maxine C.,
Crystal M., Abel F., Brooke P., Doreen F., Jackie G.,
Anne H., Merle W., Marian H., Erik R., Homer M.,
Salvatore M., Valerie V., Kent G., Moses Q., Jaime C.,
Dawn P., Ricardo K., Jan K., Alfred B., Jessie D., Ken C.,
Megan L., Marc H., Isabel P., Kate H., Winston L.,
Hubert S., Annette F., Kellie D., Ramiro M., Shirley P.,
Gerardo C., Nina T., Lyle M., Joseph G., Dianne W.,
Elizabeth E., Martin T., Cesar S., Katie P., Gladys W.,
Damien M., Mary H., Sylvia C., Cornelius D., Leroy W.,
Ora A., Bennie C., Ed J., Irving M., Ann C., Bridget B.,
Loretta S., Alejandro L., Eva P., Sherri H., Brittany M.,
Jeremiah S., Edna C., Rogelio F., Ramon G., Roderick M.,
Brent G., Bryan S., Ian D., Claude S.

Party Planning

The room is silent. The 20 chairs lining the oval conference table are filled with professionally dressed business women and men, the Pharmavast board members. Damien Myers sits at the end of the table, closest to the floor-to-ceiling windows. The setting sun behind him creates a glow around his profile.

All personal electronic devices sit in front of their owners, powered off. The only electronic device powered up is a paper-thin, five-inch round silver disk with a single button and a small red light. Damien taps the button, the light turns green, and he announces, "Thank you all for attending. We can speak now."

 Ann breaks her silence immediately, "What the hell, Damien? Is this some kind of lame team building exercise? I thought the note on the conference room door was a joke, <u>CRITICAL: TURN OFF ALL ELECTRONICS AND REMAIN SILENT WHEN ENTERING THE CONFERENCE ROOM</u>. I mean, come on, what do you think we are, a bunch of children?"

Damien picks up the silver disk and speaks loudly above the grumblings, "This my friends is an EMPuG, an Electromagnetic Pulse Generator. Any electronic signals within 50 feet will have total disruption, and any electronic devices within 25 feet that are left powered up will be irreversibly destroyed. Any video or audio recording devices will have been rendered useless. Our meeting is now confidential."

Board member Michael Patterson is angered, "Are you kidding me? My phone's now a paperweight?" He pulls his phone from his pocket, presses the display button, and nothing appears on the screen. "Oh my god. Come on, man. This is stupid. What's going on? I thought we were here to talk about a party? Why couldn't we just do this over Skype?"

"You were warned, Mike. The sign was right on the door," Damien scolds. "Anyone else leave their electronics on?" he asks. Nobody replies.

Damien slowly walks around the conference table as he addresses the board, "This meeting is highly confidential, as I am sure you all realize by now. Do you like the theme of our New Year's Eve Employee Party? Capitalism Reborn!"

He stops next to Joshua Campbell's chair. "Well, all of you probably like the theme, except one person. Go ahead, Mr. Campbell, sir. Please share with everyone why you probably don't like our theme, Capitalism Reborn."

Joshua Campbell, the most senior board member and 25 years Damien's senior, nervously clears his throat. He sits boldly and small beads of sweat appear on his forehead.

"What's wrong, Mr. Campbell, sir? Are you feeling okay?" Damien asks with a total lack of empathy and concern, emphasizing 'sir' in a sarcastic and disrespectful tone. "You look a little pale."

"I'm fine, you little prick. Yes, I belong to the Meritism Party, and I'm well aware that you're all active in the Capitalist Party. You were all too young and stupid during the days of extreme income inequality to fully comprehend the suffering so many had to endure. That was a time when a man could work 60 hours per week and barely afford to feed his family and keep a roof over their heads. A time when an ingrate like Damien here would inherit his father's business and live in the lap of luxury while most people working for him would have barely enough to live on. Yes, I proudly support the Meritism Party and you all should too. Men and women should be rewarded based on their merit. But I see things clearly now. Damien has poisoned your minds with greed, preaching about the power and esteem that goes along with being a One-Percenter, where those around you grovel for just a sliver of the pie.

"A One-Percenter? In case you don't know what a One-Percenter is, let me tell you." Joshua Campbell rises from his seat and continues, his face turning beet red, sweat dripping from his brow. "I was a One-Percenter in the 2020s just like most of your parents. One percent of the country's population owned 99% of the wealth, the money. Everyone else was groveling and scheming just to pay for necessities like food, housing, and healthcare.

"We controlled the politicians, the wars, the resources.

"When World War III concluded, I was fortunate to be with Pharmavast because Damien Senior, Chairman of the Board at the time, believed in Meritism. He positioned Pharmavast to be ready for Meritism.

"But when he died in the car 'accident'," Joshua raises his hands high, emphasizing the word accident around finger-quotes, "and this little pissant Damien Junior was somehow voted into the Chairman position … Why, Damien? Why the scheming? Why did you join the Capitalist Party? You could have continued the good work your father started."

Joshua starts to get teary-eyed, walks over to where Damien is standing, places his hand on Damien's cheek, and reminisces, "You were like a son to me. I promised your father I would look after you."

Damien, emotionally unaffected by Joshua's words, reaches up and grabs Joshua's fingers, and forcefully bends them backward, and in a single motion, jams the elderly man's arm backward and slams him face-down onto the conference table.

Pressing the elderly man's face harder and harder into the table, Damien works to further reel in the other board members. "I remember the 2020s. I remember like it was yesterday. My father built an empire. We had mansions, sports cars, vacation homes, and millions of dollars in the bank. He worked his whole life to build his wealth. Then almost overnight, everything he worked for, that by

92

the way was going to be mine someday, vanished. Next thing we knew, everything we had built—"

Joshua, with the side of his face forcefully driven into the conference table, manages to mutter loud enough for all to hear, "Everything your FATHER built! You were partying at school and then goofing off in the pretend job your father handed to you because he felt obligated. We all know that M-N 10 on your hand is only possible because of the work your Father started—"

"Quiet, old man." Damien moves his hand slightly downward from Joshua's face and inconspicuously drives his thumb into Joshua's carotid artery, cutting off half the blood flow to his brain. "Anyone going to come help poor Mr. Campbell?"

All the others watch without pity, seemingly unsurprised, as if they expected this to occur.

"Look around, Mr. Campbell. Nobody is going to help you. The same thing happened to them when they were my age. THEY DID NOT GET WHAT THEY WERE ENTITLED TO!

"I still can't figure out why you stuck around so long? You could have jumped to an easy vocation to finish out your golden years. Oh wait, I remember, you promised my father you would keep an eye on me. I guess that didn't work out so well.

"All of us were destined to inherit riches and power until ..." Damien pauses briefly, then in a mocking and derogatory manner utters, "Meritism" as he releases his grip on Joshua's neck and pinned arm.

Joshua, unconscious, falls to the floor.

Millhouse Smee, board member and Damien's right hand, asks without concern, "Is he okay? Is he still breathing?"

Ann chimes in, also without concern, and asks, "We should probably call the ambulance. Do you think that would be a good idea?"

The banter continues among all the board members, "Why yes, Ann, that would be a great idea. Should we take a vote or maybe take a break then vote? How about first we vote to see if we should take a break." Cynical laughter fills the conference room.

Damien carefully observes the body language of every board member, determined to discover if anyone appears to oppose his direction. To his relief, nobody seems agitated, and everyone partakes in the banter to forego calling medical assistance to aid Joshua.

The cheers begin. "We're all with you, Damien! The time for Capitalism has returned! Down with Meritism! Let's take back what is rightfully ours!"

Millhouse and Michael walk to where Joshua is lying unconscious on the floor. With no sense of urgency or gentleness, they drag him to his chair and prop him up. "Looks like he's breathing," Millhouse shares with a sense of disappointment.

Joshua slumps forward and his forehead smashes on the conference table. He continues to lie in that position, unconscious.

"Well, okay then, let's begin our meeting," Damien declares.

Damien welcomes the attendees, "Welcome, Capitalists. Thank you for making the effort to attend in person. I know many of you have traveled long distances. Our confidentiality is imperative."

Ann asks the first question, "Why so secretive? We're talking about a New Year's Eve party. I don't understand. I don't think anyone understands, Damien."

Changing topics, Damien asks, "Ann, tell us all about how your life changed when Meritism began."

She openly shares her story, "Well, okay. Much like Damien and all of you, my parents had millions of dollars banked, owned mansions, had a personal jet, and we vacationed whenever and wherever we wanted. My Ivy League education was paid for, and I was destined for a life of luxury. My plan was to follow in my father's footsteps, taking over his investment company. Well, we all know what happened to investment banking. Everything I was supposed to inherit vanished overnight. My Finance and Economics degree was useless, so I had to start all over. I chose re-education and worked my ass off for a Chemical Engineering degree. Then one day, out of the blue, Damien contacts me. He says there's an opening on the Pharmavast Board of Directors and here I am today. You have my allegiance forever, Damien."

Applause echoes in the conference room. Ann cheerfully stands and takes a bow.

Damien calls on his next testimonial, "Michael, how about you? What's your story? And I'm really sorry about the phone."

Michael shares his story, "Well, my father was a lobbyist. I can tell by the looks on your faces that most of you have no idea what a lobbyist is. Basically, he made money by influencing lawmakers on behalf of large corporations to make decisions that would benefit these corporations. Sounds silly, I know, but he made millions. I had everything just waiting there for me to inherit. Houses, cars, money, power. Then overnight, all gone. I was lucky to have had a Master's in Business Administration from an Ivy League school. When Meritism was declared in our great State of Texas, I took a vocation in supply chain management at Green Pharmaceuticals. Then one day, out of the blue, Damien calls, and here I am. Damien, I'm sensing a pattern here."

Damien discloses, "Yes, there is a pattern, Michael. You are all here because my story is like yours. We were the privileged of our generation, and everything we were owed was stripped out of our hands!

"How can anyone call that fair? Our parents work their whole lives to accumulate wealth with the intent for that wealth to carry over to us, their children. Then out of nowhere, all the wealth and privilege is stripped away and the government decides 'Hard Work' is all anyone needs to do to enjoy wealth, to take possession of what used to be ours. What about initiative and risk-taking and intelligence and planning and strategy? What about Capitalism and the freedom to operate our business without government interference? Our responsibility, my friends, is to BRING BACK CAPITALISM! ARE YOU WITH ME?"

In unison, all the board members, except the unconscious Joshua, jump to their feet with rousing applause.

As the applause subsides and everyone takes their seat again, Damien begins to explain his plan.

"You are here because you were screwed out of your entitlement. You were handpicked because you are all highly intelligent and emotionally adept. Just in case you don't know, everyone here had scored a 9 or 10 on their EQ/IQ Test.

"Rule number 1, there is no plan. Rule number 2, there is no plan. Rule number 3, absolutely no communication other than in-person communication. This rule will be the most difficult; we'll have a lot of travel. The reason for rule number 3 is obvious I hope. Nothing on the Internet is secure no matter how good you think security may be.

"The only documentation, ever, is the notes taken by Millhouse, using pen and paper. After the meeting, the notes will be placed in the Pharmavast vault. The reason for archiving meeting minutes is so we can resolve any future disagreements regarding what has been discussed."

Ashley Haynes, Chief Operations Officer for the Northeastern region, interrupts impatiently, "Damien, what the heck is going on? This isn't a party planning meeting, right?"

"Ashley, I'm so happy you have caught on, we've only been here for a half-hour already," Damien answers with a derogatory tone. "Yes, there's a New Year's Eve party, and no, there's no theme to the party. The party is simply a holiday party for our employees. The party, however, for us, will be the launching of our new future. The email was just to get you all here. You don't really think I would suggest the theme, 'Capitalism Reborn.' What do you think I am, an idiot?" Damien circles the conference table, giving Joshua a shake on the shoulder with a laugh, "Wake up, old man!" Joshua still does not move.

"The plan. Eyes forward," Damien confirms everyone is making eye contact with him before revealing the formula. He writes on the wall-mounted white board, "15% D-Phenylalanine, 15% Levoamphetamine, 50% Acetaminophenyltrexide, 20% Fluoride."

Damien circles the conference table again, noting the confusion among the board members.

"Millhouse and I have spent countless hours in the lab and have perfected the formula and ratios. We call our discovery, D-EERg. For those of you who may not know, I do have two doctorate degrees, one in chemistry and one in pharmacology," Damien states arrogantly. "Watch and learn."

Damien retrieves a vintage movie projector from behind his desk, film already loaded. He sets the antique on the conference table, turns the projection light on, and a video appears on the far wall. "Bet none of you have seen anything like this before. Hack-proof, not on network, and not effected by my EMPuG."

The video begins showing seven chimpanzees eating from the same bin of bananas, insects, and nuts. The vastness of the projection makes the animals appear life-size.

Damien begins to narrate, "Chimps simply eating food, right? Now pay attention and watch closely. Each ten-second segment is seven days apart. Every seven days we introduced additional levels of D-EERg into their water. Observe their devolving harmony.

"In the beginning, we see they are all eating from the bin. Pay special attention to the chimp that's missing a leg."

One of the board members interrupts, "Why is it missing a leg?" she asks with compassion.

Damien turns away from the monitor and toward the conference table, uncertain of who interrupted his narration and answers with annoyance as if everyone interrupted, "Why do you think it's missing a leg? Nothing we have done here is without purpose. No more interruptions!"

"Now look, after seven days, they're not eating from the bin anymore. They walk up to the bin, collect what they're going to eat, and place their collected food away from each other. Even the chimp with the missing leg is able to collect enough food to eat.

"Here we are at day 14. The chimps are gathering everything they can and go back for more until the bin is empty. Notice here that Limpy Chimpy," Damien laughs over the nickname, "doesn't have nearly as much food as the others. And the others don't care. They all sit near their piles of food protecting their gains from others.

"Okay, you get the idea, fast-forward to day 35."

A simultaneous gasp from all viewers brings the reaction Damien was hoping for.

"That's right, poor Limpy Chimpy. He's lost a lot of weight and can hardly move enough to collect any food at all. Notice that the larger chimps have significantly more food in their piles and all chimps refuse to share, violently protecting their gains.

"I'll spare you the suspense. Limpy Chimpy is dead on day 42. Conclusions anyone?" Damien asks of his board members. "Anyone?"

Roger White, the board member from the Mid-Atlantic division, answers with confidence, "It's obvious. The more dominant chimps gathered more and empathy disappeared." Roger adds with disturbing laughter, "Poor Limpy Chimpy."

Damien continues preaching to his hand-picked audience. They listen intently, gaining confidence in his plan.

"Disrupt the harmony! Create the drive for self-ambition and a legitimate risk-reward society, reap what you sow, call it what you will, total freedom to choose our own destiny, and no need to worry about spreading things evenly among the haves and have-nots!" Damien concludes and asks, "Now, does anyone have questions?"

Miriam Chandler, the board member representing the Mid-West division, inquires once the applause subsides, "But those are chimps. What proof is there that this will work on people?"

"Ah yes, Miriam," Damien thanks her for the question. "The Western NY Exile Zone. Pharmavast supplies the mineral enhancements to the water that Amerita drops at the exile gates. Well, let's just say that we have a new formulation for the mineral enhancements and it now includes D-EERg.

"In the Western NY Exile Zone, there happened to be a large number of pockets of exilees who have banded together to help protect and care for each other. This seemed to be a new trend, as if they learned their lesson and decided to try working together, like a community or something. After only ten weeks of D-EERg added to their water supply, not even a glimmer of a community remained. Gangs led by the physically dominant quickly took hold of every area inside the zone."

Damien takes a deep breath and pauses. The room is silent. He slams both hands down on the table and begins speaking with the unwavering determination and dominance of a newly empowered dictator, "Four weeks! Yes, that's fast, but I believe we can do this. I know we can do this. Remember how quickly Capitalism fell and Meritism rose? Does anyone remember? Seemed like our parents' fortunes disappeared overnight. Meritism will fall quickly, chaos will ensue, people will join the Capitalist Party, and all will be right in our country again!

"I have hand-picked all of you, except, well, guess who I didn't pick?" Damien mocks as he strolls past Joshua.

Settling into his speech and bringing the tone down slightly, he compliments his board members, "All 18 of you are extremely qualified to be on our Board of Directors based on years of service, EQ/IQ scores, and accomplishments. More importantly, you also have special skills sets that we need to make this 'New Year's Eve Employee Party' a success without help from anyone else but the people in this very room.

"Look next to you. Look across from you. These are the faces that will bring back Capitalism. Meritism started with 97. We only need the 19 right here in this room.

"What else do we have in common? We're all avid Capitalists Party Members with influence within the party. Our people will listen to us."

Damien sees the captivated looks in the eyes of his colleagues and knows they are all hooked on his every word. Everyone is sitting up straight and following him as he continues to walk around the table, making individual eye contact with each member.

He explains the skills sets, "Six Pharmavast regions in the country, each region with a single production facility. Each region is represented at this table by three individuals—a technology genius, a pharmaceutical chemist genius, and an operations genius. Our region, the Northeastern region, has five—myself; Millhouse, my technical wizard; Miriam, my doctor of alchemy; Ashley, my operations and manufacturing guru; and Joshua, my father's best friend who has no business being here." Damien walks up to the still unconscious Joshua and slams his hands on the conference table right next to his head and yells, as if trying to rouse him, "No business AT ALL!"

Damien continues, explaining the vicious plan in great detail, and delegates the chemistry, technology, and operational tasks to the team.

He reiterates the mandatory in-person attendance required for the next four meetings and that no excuses will be accepted.

Damien takes one more lap around the conference table, looking for any indication of second thoughts in his board's mannerisms, sees none, and smiles.

He concludes his lecture, "Tear it down, Miriam. Tear it down. That, my dear, is the first step in any great revolution."

The applause continues for several minutes. Damien pats everyone on the back except for Ann. He spins her chair around and gives her a big hug. "Thanks for being here, Ann."

She replies, "I wouldn't miss this for the world!"

"Okay, settle down, settle down," Damien requests with a chuckle. "I'll see you all here next Monday, 16:00. Thanks again for making the trip. I'm confident everyone understands the importance of our secrecy. And remember, do not write anything down, do not engage in any electronic communications regarding the 'New Year's Eve Employee Party.' There should be no reason for writing down or composing any communication. Face to face only with the exception of the notes Millhouse has taken, which I'll keep in the vault." He reassures, "Good old paper and pen! Hack-free!"

Rashad Shultz, Information Technology security specialist and board member representing the West Coast division, is offended, "I'm right here, Damien. Uh, hello, we have the best security record of any corporation. No hacks from China or Russia since I took on the Chief Information Officer role. And the vault is real? I thought that was a myth. You are joking, right?"

Angered at the questioning of his authority, he berates the young CIO, "Rashad. Rashad. How would you know if someone hacked our information? You wouldn't know. And don't forget who initiated the trend back to hard-wired networking. That was me. I made your job so easy, you should be thanking me for that 10 on your hand."

Damien goes off on a tangent, demonstrating his technical knowledge, "For those of you who don't know, all six manufacturing lines are self-contained, using hard-wired network cabling. Nowhere on any manufacturing line is there a Wi-Fi transmitter. All PLCs are programmed on-location. Nowhere, absolutely nowhere, do Pharmavast pharmaceutical formulations exist other than on one of the six self-contained manufacturing lines or in the vault.

"Rashad, the vault isn't a myth. The purpose of the vault is to provide a single point of information that could be used to reconstruct Pharmavast and all the pharmaceuticals we produce should a catastrophic event occur. This, my friends, is what I call Information Containment."

Damien walks behind Joshua's chair and asks the unconscious man, "What do you think, Joshua? Sounds fantastic, eh?" He pulls a syringe from the pocket of his pale orange suit jacket and injects Joshua in the back of his neck. Joshua convulses for a few seconds, his face turns blue, then he is motionless. "Oh no, looks like our Joshua had a heart attack."

Nobody winces. Nobody except Ashley Haynes. Damien takes notice.

Tuesday
December 5, 2051

Moving Day

"Let's go, kids!" Amanda yells up to Jake and AJ. "The bus will be here in a few minutes."

Jake bounces down the stairs full of energy, wearing his school backpack over both shoulders and carrying the large tote. "I'm ready, and here are my things." He places the tote near his mother's feet and reminds her, "Make sure they get all my Legos too. Hopefully the Super Glue will hold and they won't fall apart during the move."

AJ stands at the top of the stairs and flings her backpack all the way to the 1st floor, making a crashing sound that causes Luke to exit the kitchen in a panic. She picks up her tote and carries her personal belongings down the stairs and places the tote next to Jake's.

As she turns to retrieve her backpack, Luke can't help himself and comments, "Good morning, AJ. You look really nice today. I love that outfit. Is something different today?"

"Shut up, Dad," AJ mumbles under her breath, but loud enough for Amanda to clearly hear.

"Shut up, Dad?" Amanda repeats with a giggle. "That's the best you can come up with?" She lets out another exaggerated giggle.

AJ counters as she storms out of the front door with her backpack slung over one shoulder, "UGH! Come on, Dad, this is the same school uniform I have to wear every day. That's the best you could come up with?" She heads to the end of the driveway to catch the bus. Jake follows closely behind.

Amanda shouts to the kids, "We got into Village Gardens apartments, so you will take the same bus after school. I'll text you the apartment number later today."

"Luke, you have to get going too. Don't you have to drop of your car at the office first?" Amanda asks.

Luke heads for the front door, kisses Amanda on the cheek, and replies, "Yeah, yeah, I'm going. And what are you doing today?"

Amanda gives Luke her full schedule in more detail than he expected. "Well, first I have to sit around and wait for the movers to show up. Then I have to help them pack all the things we can keep into the moving van. That should take all of 15 minutes. Then I'll take one last dip in the hot tub. Then I'll head over to Transportation and drop off my convertible that I'm going to miss so much but will probably take the long way there and enjoy one last drive. Then I have to figure out which bus will get me to the hospital because I'm on the volunteer schedule today. I'll spend time with the kids on the oncology wing trying to brighten their day. And then I'll need to figure out which bus stops by the apartment."

Luke slowly backs toward the front door trying to get out of the conversation.

"Hey, I'm not done yet," Amanda reels Luke back in and finishes her activities for the day. "And once I get to the apartment, I need to start unpacking and check out the available M-N 3 grocery options and go get some groceries." She gives Luke an eye roll and sends him on his way. "Just go already. I'll be fine."

Luke heads for the Prius and puts a lot of effort into an extra happy goodbye that comes out sounding sarcastic, "Bye, honey. I'll see you after work."

Amanda slams the door behind him, waits a second, then opens the door and returns her own overly happy and intentionally sarcastic goodbye, "Bye, honey. Have a nice day! Love you!"

Jake takes the first available seat on the bus, two rows behind the driver. He pulls out an algebra book from his backpack and reviews the lessons covered on yesterday's test, trying to get a sense of how he did.

AJ heads for the back of the bus where the other Discovery School seniors are sitting. She notices there is not much chatter this morning and everyone seems to be avoiding eye contact with her.

She changes direction and walks to Jake's seat and insists, "Move over." He obliges and does not ask why.

As the bus approaches the center of town, the driver pulls into the Village Gardens parking lot where 12 classmates are waiting to board the bus.

For the first time ever, AJ pays attention to the students boarding the bus. She is curious to know what peers will be living in the apartment complex with her. She suddenly realizes that she has no friends who live in 1~2 or 3~4 neighborhoods and feels a sense of guilt, recognizing that maybe she really is snobbish.

"Oh my god, Emily! Hi!" AJ surprises herself with the amount of enthusiasm she feels when noticing Emily walk onto the bus.

Emily responds with a bit of surprise at AJ's excitement, "Hi, AJ. What's up?"

AJ looks confused and quickly reads the situation. She realizes Emily would assume she knew this is where she lives since they have been riding the same bus for many years. "Hey ... umm ... sit here," AJ offers as she points to the seat next to Jake. "Hey, I was just excited to tell you that, well, at the end of the day, Jake and I will be getting off at this stop with you."

"No way, that's so cool," Emily replies, very happy about the news. "So you are living in Village Gardens? That's great. Well, I mean that must suck, right? It's such a big change. I'm sorry."

AJ easily reads that Emily is uncomfortable with her own response and is uncertain how to welcome AJ to the new neighborhood. "Hey, don't be sorry. It's like whatever now. In six months, all us seniors are going to have an M-N 5 anyway."

Amanda helps the movers pack her family's sentimental possessions, enjoys one last dip in the hot tub, and gets dressed for her volunteer shift at the hospital.

After an intentionally long drive to the transportation hub, Amanda drops off her convertible and asks the information desk to direct her to the regional transportation bus that has stops at Strong Memorial Hospital.

She takes a seat near the front between two M-N 4s who are reading newspapers. A considerate young man offers Amanda the local news section. She politely waves off the offer, folds her hands on her lap, and finds the ride surprisingly relaxing.

The bus pulls into the hospital entrance circle. Amanda, along with the other passengers, sits patiently as the driver helps a mother wheel her young child off the bus using the ramp.

Amanda is one of the first to step off the bus and follows behind the mother wheeling her son. The mother and son each have an M-N 2 glowing on the back of their hands.

As the mother and son enter through the large sliding glass doors, a pleasantly smiling woman asks, "Patient, correct?" The mother and child both nod. The greeter waves a wand over their hands and their M-N 2s change to a simple smiley face. The greeter welcomes them, "Good morning and best wishes for quick healing."

Amanda answers the question before the greeter needs to ask, "Good morning. I'm a volunteer headed to the pediatric oncology floor."

The greeter offers her thanks, "That's so wonderful, thank you very much." The greeter does not wave the wand over Amanda's hand and she enters the hospital with her M-N 3.

10th Floor

Luke takes the long way to the Merit Agency Investigator's office building, enjoying the drive, even though he is not driving the Charger. He returns the Prius, then stops into the office briefly to say goodbye to his friends. Nobody is surprised about Luke's Merit Review because word spread fast about yesterday's events.

As he walks along the first-floor hallway, shaking hands and giving hugs, he notices that nobody is giving him condescending looks. He is very glad that his friends and colleagues offer encouraging words and express that they can empathize with being burned out. He is elated to realize his acting skills are so good that they all believed his story.

The final two colleagues Luke encounters are Murphy and Hopwood. They wait by the entrance way for him to leave.

Murphy starts the conversation, "We love the car, Medina, thanks for letting us take it for a spin." He shakes Luke's hand with genuine appreciation. "Thanks for all the good work. Think we'll see you back soon?"

"I'll be back," Luke promises. "I need to take care of some things first."

They exchange nods and Luke heads to the bus stop.

Luke walks onto the regional transportation bus and asks the driver, "This stops by Clinton Square, right?" The driver nods and welcomes Luke on board.

"Good morning, sir. Why the bus today?" the driver asks the passenger boarding behind Luke.

Luke, curious about the question, turns around and notices the M-N 9 on the back of the hand of the man behind him.

The man with the M-N 9 answers the bus driver's curiosity, "My car wouldn't start this morning and nobody showed up in time for me to get to my vocation, so I thought I would take the bus instead. It's good, this will help me appreciate possessing a vehicle."

Luke takes a seat in the middle of the crowded bus next to a man who is a bit older than him. He is reading the morning newspaper and he also has an M-N 3.

The man with the M-N 9 attracts glances from almost every passenger, all of them with M-N 4s and lower, curious why he is riding regional transportation. He continues down the aisle and takes a seat on the other side of Luke, retrieves a newspaper from his backpack, and begins reading as the bus departs the parking lot. He turns his head toward Luke with a friendly greeting, "Sir, good morning."

Luke nods his head and mumbles, "Umm hum" without turning toward the man, hoping to be left alone for his ride.

The friendly man hands the Sports section to Luke and strongly insists, "Sir, good morning. Here, read the Sports section. On page 4a, there's a fantastic article about the Buffalo Bills and the great season they're having."

Luke, a bit put off by the man's pushiness, takes the Sports section only because the man continues to hold the paper in front of his face. Suddenly he remembers the covert Elder greeting protocol. He turns to the man, replies, "Sir, good morning," and extends his hand. When the man with the M-N 9 grasps Luke's hand, Luke gives two quick pulses. The man gives three quick pulses.

Luke flips the newspaper to page 4a, and now very curious, looks for an article about the Buffalo Bills. Toward the bottom-left corner is a white piece of paper taped below a Buffalo Bills title. The handwritten text on the white piece of paper reads:

Good morning, Luke

I am an Elder. Don't look surprised.

This will be our only mode of communication. An Elder will be on the bus every Monday morning starting next week, and he or she will make contact with you.

Tape your notes to the Sports section, and place the newspaper between you and the Elder. The Elder will place his or her newspaper on top of yours, notes taped to the Sports section as well. You pick up the Elder's newspaper; he or she will pick up your newspaper.

I am about to place a pen between the seats, next to your leg. Take this pen with you and use it to write your notes. The ink from this pen will evaporate within 60 minutes, so time your notes accordingly.

Keep the paper given to you by the Elder on your possession at all times until the ink has evaporated. Then dispose of the newspaper and the note into separate trash receptacles.

Thank you for your service.

Luke does his best to appear unsurprised. He reaches next to his leg and feels the pen waiting to be picked up and inconspicuously slides the writing device into his pocket.

He reads the note three more times before folding up the newspaper and securely zipping the communication into an inside jacket pocket.

The Elder and Luke sit silently, refraining from exchanging glances or words, until they reach Clinton Square. Luke gives the Elder a nod and exits the bus with a few other passengers.

The bus stop is one block from the Pharmavast building. Halfway down the block, Luke approaches St. Joseph's Church, a Catholic Church built from large stones and adorned with beautifully colorful stained glass. As he steps onto the sidewalk in front of the church, he glances at the M-N 3 on the back of his left hand, anticipating the disappearance of the brightly glowing number.

He smiles as it disappears.

Another 40 yards down the sidewalk, he steps off church property and watches as the number reappears.

The sidewalk changes from concrete to cobblestone as Luke arrives at the Pharmavast building's front entrance. He stands at the entrance for a moment, looking up to the 10th floor. He is amazed at the all-glass exterior of the stunning work of architecture.

Letting out an audible sigh, Luke contemplates his decision but knows turning back is not an option.

A young doorman dressed in a suit and tie greets Luke, "Good morning, sir. May I see your ID?"

Luke hands the doorman his Citizenship ID without saying a word. He decides at that moment to play the part of a disgruntled citizen who feels strongly that he was wronged, so he wears his best angry face.

The doorman scans the ID with his tablet and Luke's picture and vocation assignment with Pharmavast appear. He cautiously informs Luke, "You're all set, Mr. Medina. Mr. Tammarin will be on the 10th floor waiting to show you around."

Luke gathers every ounce of discontent he can fabricate and replies to the doorman while forcefully snatching his ID, "Recognize me tomorrow so I don't have to stop at the door." As he walks away, he continues to stare down the young man who is visibly shaken. Luke thinks to himself, *Maybe that was a little over the top. I'll make that up to him someday.*

The elevator ride to the 10th floor was slow, stopping on almost every floor. Luke was the last person on the elevator when the doors opened to the most elaborately decorated and expensively furnished office floor Luke has ever seen. His first thoughts are of the deep contrasts between the frugality of the Merit Agency where he was at this time yesterday and the overindulgence of the Pharmavast executive floor where he stands 24 hours later.

Marble tiles line the hallways. Granite sets on top of all the counters and tables. Unblemished leather and suede cover all the furniture. Natural sunlight from endless windows and large skylights fills the 12-foot-high hallways.

In contrast to the highly polished marble tiles on the floor, sit two identical custodial carts parked in the hallway right in front of the elevator doors, each with brooms, cleaning supplies, and a waste receptacle. Standing behind one of the carts is a very elderly man, slightly hunched over, as if the years of pushing the custodial cart have permanently reshaped his back.

As Luke exits the elevator, he is greeted by his custodial supervisor, "Hello, son. My name is Ned I. Tammarin, the I is for Irritable. But you can call me Mr. Tammarin, sir. Welcome aboard. I'm kidding about the 'sir.' I'm not kidding about the Mr. Tammarin, or the Irritable. To save time though, just call me Mr. T. Nobody ever pronounces my name correctly, and I doubt you will either."

Luke decides to forgo the disgruntled act when in the presence of Ned because he senses a humble personality under his sarcastic exterior. Ned's pale face is mostly hidden by an overgrown gray mustache and beard with a few streaks of brown. The color of his facial hair matches the color of his scraggly, thinning, curls draping around the rim of his blue mesh baseball cap. His eyes are obscured behind slightly tinted glasses. "Good morning, Mr. Tammarin, excuse me, sir, I mean Mr. T."

Luke's new supervisor interrupts him before he can get in any additional conversation. "Okay, that's enough chit-chat. Let's get down to business. Save all questions for later."

He hands Luke a cardboard box overflowing with dark blue clothing. "Go get changed. I'll wait here. The ball cap is optional. Take the rest of these clothes home. Dark blue collared work shirt and dark blue cargo pants will be your new uniform. Feel free to choose a short sleeve or one of the long sleeve shirts depending on the temperature of the day. Now hurry up. I have a lot to show you."

Ned points to the bathrooms, and Luke hustles to get changed. He returns in less than three minutes to which Ned comments, "What took you so long?" Luke barely contains his laughter, sensing that Ned has a deeply covered sense of humor that in time will be fully revealed.

"This cart is mine. See my name?" Ned points to the lettering 'Ned I. Tammarin' taped to the handle of the cart in front of him. Then he points to Luke's cart. "See the name on that cart? That's your cart." Ned takes time to point to the lettering 'Luke T. Medina' on the other cart. Luke is again on the verge of chuckling.

"Follow me with your cart, the one that says 'Luke T. Medina'," Ned instructs with a patronizing tone and noticeable smirk.

"The floorplan is simple, I'm sure you will catch on quickly. The main hallway is a square. There are four corner offices. Damien, the boss, has this office. Don't bother asking him if he needs anything other than what is on our daily worklist. If he needs anything else, he'll let you know."

They turn the first corner and Ned continues, "Between Damien's corner office and the next corner is the conference room. We're in charge of setting up for meetings and cleaning up their messes. Setup requirements will be on your daily worklist.

"This next corner office is for visiting board members to use. Most of the time this office is empty."

They turn the second corner. "The offices along both sides of this hallway are for Human Resources. These are the people who are in charge of setting the Productivity Calculations for every vocationalist at Pharmavast, not just our location.

"This corner office is a smaller conference room. The setup is always the same so we just need to keep the room clean and the refrigerator stocked with beverages and make sure the coffee is hot and fresh."

They turn the third corner and stop abruptly. "And this is our closet," Ned announces as he opens the closet door to reveal a rather spacious room. "Pretty nice, eh? This is where we store our carts and the extra supplies. We can take our breaks here too. I find this a great place to nap. I nap a lot at my age. That ladder leads to the roof. During the summer, feel free to go up there for lunch. I go up there to work on my tan." Luke can't contain his laughter and chuckles out loud. Ned just smirks and continues, "Nothing up there except the hatch to the elevator shafts.

"On this side, we have the kitchen and lounge. On this side, we have the bathrooms and the Travel Arrangements office.

"And the last corner office belongs to Joshua Campbell. He's my age and the greatest board member Pharmavast has ever known. They call him an old-timer behind his back. I'm not sure what they call me, but I'll tell you what, if I ever heard one of those young ones call me old-timer, I would take them down so fast they wouldn't know what happened. Let's knock and say hello. He's always here before me."

Ned knocks repeatedly on Joshua's wooden office door, but there's no answer. He peers through the narrow glass window bordering the door, but only one corner of the office is visible. "Looks like he left a light on. Probably has a meeting somewhere this morning. We'll stop by later so you can meet him."

They turn the last corner, "And in this hallway are the offices of Damien's assistants. You will notice they're all young and attractive women. Doesn't set right with me, but I don't ask questions. I keep my head down and just do my job. That's how I've managed to keep my M-N 9 for the past three years here.

"I started as a custodian when I was 55 and bounced around to lots of different office buildings. I'm 81 now, that's right, 81. I bet you thought I was still in my late 70s. I only have to work ten hours per week, any ten hours of my choosing. The ten hours qualify as a full week of work for me. And that my young friend is why you are here, to pick up the slack."

Luke and Ned are back to where they started, in front of the elevator. "And here we are, right where we started. A square. Easy enough, Luke?" Ned asks without allowing Luke time to answer. "Welcome aboard."

The elevator dings, the doors open, and Damien Myers steps onto the polished marble floor. He is wearing his usual attire, a slim-fitting suit jacket and slacks. Today, an orange tie, perfectly draped over a white collared dress shirt, completes his look.

With fake enthusiasm, Damien walks up to Luke and extends his hand. Luke immediately shifts his demeanor to disgruntled, removing any trace of happiness from his face, which was difficult because he really enjoyed the last hour with Ned.

Damien and Luke shake hands. Luke does not speak first. Damien breaks the awkward silence, "You must be Luke Medina."

Ned points to the lettering on Luke's custodial cart. Damien finds no humor in his gesture.

"I'm Damien Myers. I did my homework and read up on your career as a Merit Agent. Very impressive work, Luke. I'm sure you understand my surprise when I found out you would be here with us. When I received notification that this position was filled, I was able to see your other choices as well and noticed that we were third on your list. Unfortunately, we're stuck with each other for at least three months. So, what happened at the agency? Too much for you to handle? Well this should be just your speed then," Damien taunts. He stops speaking, waiting for Luke to pick up the conversation.

Luke sighs, then plays the part of the disgruntled vocationalist, "Tons of stress. Hated the people I worked with. I wanted out for a while. Finally got to the point where I just had enough."

Damien looks at Luke with contempt, "Yes, I see you wanted out. Nice M-N 3 on your hand, guess you really didn't do much this past year." Then he raises his coffee cup and flaunts the M-N 10 on the back of his right hand, holding the glowing number directly in Luke's line of site for several seconds. He takes one sip of his coffee, then purposely drops the almost full ceramic cup on the marble floor. Fragments and splashes extend for several feet. "Crap, some got on my shoes. Mr. T, how about we let Luke get started right away with cleaning up his first mess."

Luke looks at Ned and nods, "I got this."

"Oh yeah, and after this mess is cleaned up, you should go meet Joshua Campbell," Damien suggests. "He might be running late though. We had a late-night board meeting and he said he was going to stay for a little while after and finish up some work."

Gathering every ounce of self-control, Luke removes a roll of paper towels from beneath the personalized handlebar of his custodial cart. He bends down and begins cleaning the spill. He watches Damien walk away, tapping his fingertips together, without an apology or a thank you. The groveling is almost too much to take. However, Luke knows the importance of remaining in character.

"Meet me in the men's restroom when you are done here and I'll show you how to clean bathrooms," Ned instructs. He glances in Damien's direction and shakes his head with disapproval, making sure Luke notices the gesture.

"Good job, Luke," Ned compliments, "the men's and women's restrooms look fantastic. I'm heading out for the day, my two hours are done. Make sure you head over to Joshua Campbell's office to meet him. He should be there by now. If he's not in, let yourself in and empty his wastebasket." Ned jingles his sizable key-ring and pulls an identical set from his custodial cart. "Here, you will need to hold onto these. I have no idea which key is for which lock. Guess you will have to figure that out the hard way."

Ned heads for the custodial storeroom to drop off his cart, "See you tomorrow, Luke."

Reviewing the task list attached to the clipboard, Luke sees that he is ahead of schedule and decides to go meet Joshua.

Luke greets a young woman who is exiting into the hallway from the glass doorway of Damien's administrative assistant's office. "Good morning."

The bubbly, blond, tall, blue-eyed woman who looks to be only a few years older than AJ cheerfully returns Luke's gesture, "Hi! I'm Amber. Welcome to the 10th floor."

Luke thanks her for the welcome and turns to continue down the hallway toward Joshua's office.

Amber continues chatting, oblivious to Luke's attempt to conclude the conversation. Giving in, Luke turns and politely listens to Amber declare, "On the 10th floor we have lots of fun. We're really low-key here, first names only, except for Mr. T and Mr. Campbell. Mr. T hates when we call him anything but Mr. T. And we all like to say Mr. Campbell instead of Joshua because, well, he's a lot older than us, like Mr. T. He always asks us to call him Joshua, but we still like to call him Mr. Campbell. I'm Damien's personal travel assistant. He's so nice. I book all his travel, and lots of times he lets me join him, especially during the winter months when he has to travel to Florida or Texas."

Amber tries to begin her next sentence, but Luke successfully interjects, "Great meeting you too, Amber." He turns and immediately begins to push his cart.

Amber heads for the elevators, "Stop by and I'll introduce you to the other girls on the floor. Bye, Luke."

Without slowing his pace, Luke turns to acknowledge Amber's genuine friendliness, "Okay. Nice meeting you." As she stands waiting for the elevator, Luke notices that she is tall because of her extremely high heels, she has an M-N 10, she is holding a designer purse, and her skirt is really, really short.

His thoughts pause on a few things as he stands in front of Joshua Campbell's door, not knocking yet, and noticing there are still no lights on in the office except for the same dim floor lamp in the corner that was on this morning. First, he tries to recall ever seeing anyone as young as Amber with an M-N 10. Then he pictures Amanda's feet and her perfect toes and is glad he frequently thanks her for not destroying her feet by wearing non-sensible shoes like the ones Amber had on.

For a moment, he reflects on the unexpected pleasantness of this morning's routine. He realizes this was, by far, the most stress-free work morning in over decade.

Knock-knock, no answer.
Knock-knock, no answer.

Luke fumbles with his key ring for five minutes before finding the correct key. He walks backward through the door, pulling the cart behind him, propping the door open with his hip.

The cart bangs against the auto-closing door a couple times before Luke and the cart are in the office. The auto-closing door shuts quietly.

Still facing the door, Luke pulls drawers out of the custodial cart one at a time looking for wastebasket liners. "Ah, there you are," he vocalizes out loud, perfectly content with talking to himself.

He turns to look for the wastebasket, assuming the container will be next to the desk, and there is Joshua, head down on the wooden desk.

If not for the dried blood on his forehead, Luke would have thought he simply fell asleep last night while working late.

Luke's first reaction is to feel for a pulse and check his eyes. No pulse. From experience, he knows almost instantly that based on pupil dilation, body temperature, and skin color, the time of death was at least 12 hours ago.

Instinct takes over and Luke sees everything. Dried blood on Joshua Campbell's forehead. No blood on the desk. The desk is pristine, no papers, no open laptop, and the pens and pencils seem to be organized into a compulsive pattern.

Luke dials 9-1-1 from Joshua's office phone immediately to avoid suspicions. He speaks to the 9-1-1 operator while at the same time foraging for evidence.

"9-1-1, what's your emergency?" the operator asks.

In the time taken for the phone to be answered and the standard question to be asked, Luke scrapes a small sample of dried blood into one plastic wastebasket liner and places a few strands of hair into the other and shoves them into his pocket.

From experience, Luke knows the information 9-1-1 will need, "White male in his 80s, unconscious, maybe dead, I couldn't feel a pulse. He's on the 10th floor of the Pharmavast building at Clinton Square. His name is Joshua Campbell."

While giving the pertinent information, Luke pulls out his phone and starts snapping photos without further disturbing the position of the dead body. He was just about to put the phone back into his pocket when he notices what looks like a bug bite on the back of Joshua's neck. Unlike a normal bug bite, there is a very slight appearance of bruising. Luke snaps one last picture of the suspicious mark and sets his phone on top of the custodial card.

"Okay, help is on the way. What is your name?" the operator asks.

Having often dialed 9-1-1 while on the job over the past 12 years, many of the operators know Luke. He offers only his first name to avoid any unnecessary conversation or questioning. "Luke. I'm going to start CPR." Then he hangs up abruptly.

Luke darts into the hallway, acting as though he has no suspicions from the lack of blood on the undisturbed desk, the bruising on the back of Joshua's neck, or the elapsed 12 hours since time of death.

Amber is exiting the elevator, returning to the 10th floor. "Amber, Help! Something is wrong with Mr. Campbell. I called 9-1-1.

Have someone from your office go down to the lobby and wait for the ambulance and show them the way to his office. Then locate Damien and have him get over here. I'm going to continue CPR on Mr. Campbell."

Amber shuffle-runs in her high heels to the administrative assistant's office, almost catching one heel in the floor-gap of the elevator threshold, "Oh my god, okay, oh my god. I'll get the AED too."

Luke returns to the office, nauseous at the thought of performing CPR on a body that has been dead for 12 hours. He lays Joshua on the ground, elevating his feet. He places his hands in chest-compression positioning and waits for someone to enter the office before beginning CPR.

A few minutes pass. Damien bursts into the office with the AED.

Luke fakes having concluded a few mouth-to-mouth breaths and moves to chest compressions, but stops and removes Joshua's suit jacket and shirt instead, preparing for the use of the AED.

Amber looks on, impressed with the fluidity with which Luke is able to attach the four AED patches to Joshua's chest and presses the green "GO" button.

Luke acts as if he does not know what the computerized voice will say next. A very robotic female voice speaks, "No shockable rhythm detected."

"Try it again," Amber pleads.

Damien looks on.

Luke presses the green "GO" button a second time.

"No shockable rhythm detected."

The EMTs arrive, entering the office just in time to hear the message from the AED.

The EMTs conclude their paperwork. Joshua Campbell is deemed to have suffered a massive heart attack. Time of death is placed at 23:45, Monday, December 4, 2051.

The two rookie agents from the Protect and Serve Agency conclude that, based on the EMT report, no suspicious activity took place. Joshua fell face-first onto his desk after suffering a massive heart attack. A laceration to his forehead was left untreated and continued to bleed following the heart attack. This occurred following a Pharmavast Board meeting and Joshua's decision to work late.

The coroner wheels the body bag toward the door.

Damien slouches in an office chair on the other side of Joshua's desk, holding his head in his hands, speaking to Amber, "He was my father's best friend. He was like a father to me."

For a moment, Luke feels for Damien, wondering if maybe he is not an asshole. That thought quickly fades, however, with Damien's next words.

Amber continues to rub Damien's hunched shoulders. Damien obviously welcomes the consoling gesture. Then he quietly, almost in a whisper, asks Amber, "Will you stop by tonight? I think having someone keep me company would be helpful. The divorce has not been easy and being alone in that house is tough right now."

Luke's ability to read lips proves to be useful. He is able to decipher their conversation.

Amber is hesitant with her answer and speaks nervously, also in a quiet, almost whisper, "I don't know, Damien. Maybe we could just go get something to eat this evening and you can tell me all about your friendship with Mr. Campbell?"

Luke stealthily watches Amber and Damien. He moves toward the exit to stop the auto-closing door with his cart for the EMTs and coroner to exit.

He catches Damien's glare at Amber, a chilling look of disapproval suddenly void of all emotion related to the death of a man who was supposedly like a father to him.

Amber's words do not match her body language. Luke picks up on her posture change, shallow breathing, and most obviously, he notices her begin to nervously bite at a nail, "Okay, Damien. Text me when you get home and I'll stop by."

The EMTs, coroner, and body bag exit the office and Amber leaves ahead of Damien.

As Damien passes by Luke, his eyes shift to Luke's phone sitting on top of the custodial cart. The photo application is open with camera lens bringing the ceiling into view.

Back at his office, door locked, Damien rushes to open his laptop. Wading through various screens of the Pharmavast portal, he pulls up call records from Joshua Campbell's desk phone. He selects 12/5/2051, scrolls to the end of the records, and notes a call to 9-1-1 made at 11:32.

Having confirmed the call to 9-1-1 was made from the desk phone, Damien grows suspicious of what Luke may have been doing with his phone if not using it to call 9-1-1. He hurries to the *Community Effort* painting, slides the artwork to the side, and retrieves the phone from the hidden compartment.

The voice on the other end of the call asks, "What?"

"Keep an eye on Luke Medina, the new guy on the 10th floor," Damien orders.

Apartment

"AJ, this is our stop," Jake and Emily yell from the front of the bus, backpacks slung over one shoulder and ready to exit.

"AJ!" Jake yells a second time. He then looks at Emily and comments with disapproval, "She's in the back with her 'Popular' friends, too busy talking about their 'Popular' stuff."

"AJ!" Jake yells one last time.

AJ looks up and quickly gathers her backpack, "Later guys, I guess this is my new stop."

Shawn, one of AJ's least favorite peers in her circle of friends, boastfully holds up the back of his hand showing off the M-N 9 and shouts loudly enough for everyone to hear, "Have fun at Village Garbage, AJ!" He follows the insult with forced laughter.

AJ turns around, looks around at her friends gathered in the back of the bus, realizes nobody is standing up for her, and flashes her middle finger at Shawn. She runs off the bus and bursts into tears.

Emily puts her arm around AJ and offers comforting words, "Hey, don't worry about them. They just don't get it. They all live in this fantasy world where just because their parents have high M-Ns, they think they're better than everyone else and that following in their parent's footsteps is some sort of entitlement. Remember, AJ, we're all on our own in six months. Them too. Every single one of them."

AJ sniffles and accepts Emily's comforting arm.

Jake attempts to add to Emily's conforming words with factual statements, "And AJ, check this out," he pulls out a printed copy of the M-N Handbook. "I printed this a couple years ago and have been carrying these pages in my backpack ever since. This copy isn't official like the one you guys will get to sign, but all the rules are right here. Check this out, bet you guys didn't know this. So you graduate, get your vocation, your M-N 5, and your clothes and housing. Lots of those 'Privileged' kids end up visiting their parents' home frequently because they miss the material goods they once had. But they can't drive their parent's car, can't wear clothes not allowed for an M-N 5, can't go on vacations not allowed for an M-N 5. Basically they can't use or participate in anything their parents have earned. I read that many families drop their vacations to a Level 5 so their graduates can join them, but a common practice is to leave their kids behind after a few years if they're not putting forth the effort to contribute at the same level.

"As for food, we all know they can stop by their parents' for a better meal, no way to really stop that, but it works itself out anyway because their parents' allotment of food is no longer at a level to support their graduate. Eating at their parents' house on a regular basis just doesn't happen."

"Really?" AJ genuinely inquires, "Why do you know all this?"

"Really, sis? Have you not noticed yet? I've been doing my research for a few years now because I don't want to mess up my opportunity when I'm your age like you're doing now," Jake criticizes and quickly realizes the insult. "Wait, I don't think that came out right."

"Oh, it came out right." AJ's tears suddenly stop. "You think I'm like my friends, don't you?"

Jake looks down, nods, and admits that AJ's response accurately conveys his feelings, "Yeah, AJ, yeah. I guess I do."

Silence takes over as the three walk toward the lobby, distance between them and the other students who also exited the bus at Village Gardens.

The walkway extends from the parking lot to the lobby and is surrounded by neatly mowed grass, trimmed along the sidewalk.

The surrounding landscape is plain. There are a few trees on either side of the walkway in front of the main entrance.

Village Gardens is a six-story building with a cement block exterior finish. The apartments all have large windows, some with balconies. The main lobby serves as a mail pickup location with no additional amenities. Four elevators and two stairwells service the tenants.

As they approach the lobby, Emily breaks the silence, "You guys probably don't have key fobs yet. Is your mom or dad here already?"

"Good question," AJ realizes. "I'll text my mom."

Emily uses her fob to open the sliding glass entrance door and waves for AJ and Jake to come in. She offers, "I'll hang here with you guys and if you can't get into your apartment yet, you're welcome to wait in our apartment."

"Hang on, I just got a text from my mom." AJ shares the text, "Sorry about that kids, I'm still at the hospital. Probably another hour or two before Dad or I will be there."

"Okay then, come up to our apartment and have your mom text you when she or your dad gets here. Tell her you will be in apartment 220," Emily suggests.

The three friends take the stairwell to the second floor. As they exit the stairwell to Emily's floor, AJ's phone beeps. She reads the text, "Okay, I'll just knock on their door when I get there, we're in apartment 221, right across the hall. I have to pick up Koda at the kennel first so I may be later. Your dad isn't going to be back until late, he said something about an accident at his new job."

A genuine smile comes to AJ's distraught face and she shares her excitement, "Emily, we're neighbors! That's cool, right?"

Emily is equally cheerful, "Yeah cool, and helping you in math will be a lot easier now!"

With appreciation AJ jokes, "Not anymore! I aced my final, remember? Maybe I'll tutor you."

Jake is the first to hear the guitar and beautiful female singing voice coming from down the hallway. "Wow, what a voice."

"That's my mom singing and my dad playing the guitar. Hope you like their style of music. Sounds like they're still in their 'Folk Punk' phase," Emily informs and blushes with slight embarrassment. "I keep asking them to shut the door, but they claim since the neighbors don't complain that must mean they enjoy the music."

The music gets louder as they walk down the beige-painted concrete flooring of the hallway, passing industrial doorways. They arrive at the open door to apartment 220. Emily bursts in, AJ and Jake follow timidly. Emily shuts the door behind them and pleads, "Please keep the door shut. You don't know for sure if people like your music or if they're just too nice to complain."

Emily's parents simultaneously stop singing and playing. They look at Emily, both staring at her with pouty faces. Her father fakes wiping a tear from his eye, then they begin singing and playing even louder.

Emily stands with her arms crossed, scornfully staring down her parents while AJ and Jake smile at her parents' antics. Jake whispers to AJ, barely loud enough to be heard over the music, "And you thought you were the only teenage girl whose parents purposely antagonize her. Nice to know you're not alone?"

When the song concludes, Emily's mom gives an overly enthusiastic, "Hi, honey! How was your day?" knowing well that there will be no response.

Emily's dad walks over to Jake and extends his arm for a handshake, "Hi, young man. My name is Ward Mills and this lovely singing beauty is my wife, June.

Jake instantly breaks out in laughter. AJ smacks him on the arm. "Jake, what the—"

"Oh my god, I'm so sorry, Mr. Mills. I never knew your first names. I only knew Emily Mills. I'm so sorry for laughing. The thing is that I'm a fan of old TV shows, the ones that used to be in black and white. And there was this one show—"

Ward Mills interrupts, "You know *Leave It To Beaver*? We escape the humor befallen us by our given names 99.999% of the time. I can't believe you know that show! Emily, who is this genius of useful information?"

Emily slowly unfolds her arms and answers her father with a slightly improved attitude, "Meet our new neighbors, AJ, that's short for Amanda Junior, and this genius of extremely useful information and master of everything Meritism is Jake. Their parents will be here later this evening. They're moving in across the hall!"

"Well, come on in! June, do we have any porridge cookies left? Jake, come with me, let me show you around." Ward leads Jake around his apartment, and June sits with the two girls at the metal kitchen table.

"Over here we have June's art gallery. She does all these oil paintings herself. Since she created them, we'll always be able to bring them with us if we ever move." Ward extends his hand toward the two walls bordering the kitchen table and recites the titles and themes of all 23 paintings. Barely any concrete wall shows from behind the closely aligned works of art. June blushes.

Ward motions toward the outside corner of the living room, "And this is our music studio. We have collected our instruments over the years after taking lots and lots of lessons. Our instructors attest to our practice and efforts and are able to acquire top-of-the line instruments for us."

Jake is smitten by the black five-piece drum set. "Can I stop by and try out the drums?" Jake asks.

Ward is excited with Jake's enthusiasm, "Of course! Stop by anytime. I would love to give you lessons."

Leading Jake to the other corner of the living area, Ward points to his favorite section of the home, "And this is our library! Emily likes fantasy books, stories about knights and castles and sorcery. I like Sci-Fi and deep space adventures. And these are June's favorites, biographies."

Jake catches sight of a familiar book out of the corner of his eye, *Luke, I Am Your Daddy*. "No … way …." He pulls the book from the lower shelf. "No way! You have a copy of *Luke, I Am Your Daddy*!"

June walks over to the library, overhearing their conversation, "Jake, that's a pretty obscure book, a friend gave me her copy many years ago. You know the book?"

"Uh, yeah. The Luke in the book is my dad, and the book was written by my grandfather," Jake tells June.

She bursts out laughing. "Good one, Jake. You really had me for a second there."

AJ confirms her brother's claim, "He's serious. That book is all about my dad when he was a little kid."

Jake hands the book to Ward. He looks it over and declares, "I'm going to have to read that one, and I'm going to start today!"

"You have never read any book from my biography collection before, Ward," June points out with a friendly smile. "That's an amazing coincidence."

Ward comments, "Coincidence? Hmm … is anything ever really a coincidence? I believe coincidences are simply the aggregation of choices us humans make that sometimes converge in unsuspecting ways."

Ward gives Jake a pat on the shoulder, "Well, Jake, that's the tour!"

Jake takes another look around and notices an 18-inch monitor on a shelf next to the stacks of books. He almost did not notice the monitor because of the many board games stacked in front.

"Oh wait, one more thing, Ward," June points out, standing in the kitchen next to the refrigerator. "This is our collection of refrigerator magnets. We have one from each State, all 50 of them. We've visited each one in person!" 50 refrigerator magnets, shaped like the 50 States, cover a large section of the refrigerator, arranged with geographic accuracy.

Jake thinks to himself that somehow the Mills family has managed to make the 800-square-foot, three-bedroom apartment feel enormous.

The slamming industrial door leading to the 2nd floor echoes in the concrete hallway. Amanda's first impression of her new apartment building is a prison cell, something she has only seen in movies. She hears her daughter's laughter coming from behind a door half-way down the hall and she shakes her head silently, not knowing what to make of the conflicting sounds, eerie echoing door slam and her daughter's laughter that she rarely hears anymore.

She swipes her new key fob over the deadbolt lock of door 221. Amanda smiles at the light-hearted conversation she hears coming from her new neighbor's apartment, even though she can't quite understand the muted words through the heavy steel door.

The deadbolt to her apartment unlocks easily and Amanda peaks in. Koda is sniffing at the crack of light coming from under the Mill's door, his leash tugging on Amanda's arm. He starts scratching on the steel, prompting June to open the door.

Before June can speak, Koda starts barking and AJ and Jake rush to welcome their mom and dog.

AJ greets her mom warmly, "Hey, Mom. This is Mr. and Mrs. Mills."

Amanda stays in the hallway keeping Koda from charging through the threshold. "Finally, we meet! Let me just tell you how wonderful of a daughter you have. Emily was so helpful tutoring AJ over the summer."

Amanda and June continue to exchange pleasantries. June offers her new neighbor a plate of porridge cookies with the strong scent of cinnamon.

"Cinnamon, I love cinnamon," Amanda expresses her gratitude. "Thank you so much. Come on kids, let's go check out our apartment."

Jake reminds Mr. Mills that he will be by for a drum lesson.

AJ asks Emily to wait for her in the morning so they can walk to the bus stop together.

"Hey, AJ," Emily asks as AJ and Jake exit the Mill's apartment, "want to hang out Friday evening? Go to the Varsity basketball game or something?"

"Definitely, that would be cool," AJ agrees, smiling.

Nervous about seeing the differences from their previous house, the three walk into their new apartment slowly. The vertical blinds are all open, and the white walls and white ceiling reflect the ample light coming from the western-facing windows. All the furniture is various shades of brown, and most of the floors are covered with laminate designed to look like hardwood flooring. Tan ceramic tiles cover the floor of the kitchen.

The kitchen is to the right of the entrance, and to the left is a closet for coats and shoes. Straight ahead of the entrance is a single large space for both the dining area and the living area. To the right of the living area, a hallway leads to three bedrooms and one bathroom.

The furnishings are already in place: refrigerator, stove, dining table and chairs, couch, recliner, 18-inch monitor on a small table, beds, dressers.

A stack of unassembled shelving sits in the hallway along with nine neatly stacked large plastic totes.

A private balcony extends from the far side of the living area. On the balcony, a small table and two chairs face the setting sun.

Jake does not hesitate to state the obvious, "Sure looks plain compared to Emily's apartment."

AJ adds a positive comment that surprises both her brother and her mother, "I think this is kinda cute."

Jake and Amanda turn and stare at AJ, looking at her with extreme surprise.

AJ, annoyed with their reaction, shouts, "What?"

"What? Nothing, honey," Amanda says attempting to disguise her surprise and turns toward the kitchen. Jake laughs under his breath.

AJ picks up the tote labeled with her name and storms down the hall to get away from her mother. She slams her new bedroom door, and the effect is minimal since the interior doors are hollow and flimsy. Amanda notices the attempted rampage and laughs at the swish noise knowing AJ expected a loud bang.

Amanda shouts out a string of commands to the kids, "Unpack your totes and get your rooms all set. Let me know what you want for dinner and I'll call for delivery. There are M-N 3 dinner menus on the kitchen table, so take a look."

"While we're waiting for dinner, try on your clothes. You don't have to try on your school uniforms, they will be the same. But you should have a new set of clothes in your closets and drawers.

"Let me know how many shelves you would like, and I'll ask your dad to put them together tonight."

"Honey, I'm home!" Luke shouts lightheartedly as he bursts through the door. Jake thinks to himself how his father's attempt at humor sounded like something Ward probably says every time he enters his apartment.

The kids stare at their father, not breaking a smile. Amanda, annoyed at Luke's late arrival, advises, "You better grab some mashed potatoes and a slice of meatloaf before dinner is cold. Oh wait, too late."

Koda jumps up, paws landing on Luke's stomach. "Well at least someone is happy to see me."

"Don't ask. We're fine," Amanda says, predicting Luke's next question. "We're all just a little bummed with the M-N 3 dinners. Not much selection and not much flavor."

AJ grabs a menu, flips to the back page, points to a comparison chart and sarcastically informs, "Says right here in the nutritional chart, the M-N 3 dinner has the exact nutrition as any higher M-N dinner! Doesn't say anything about flavor!" She tosses the menu across the table almost landing on the mashed potatoes Luke is dishing onto his plate. She storms off to her bedroom and attempts another failed door slam.

Amanda and Luke exchange glances, both now smiling thanks to the light and flimsy interior doors. Amanda tosses Luke a glare that he understands perfectly, *Do not antagonize her.*

Jake, not catching the humor in AJ's sarcastic analysis of the menu offers his opinion, "Yes, equally nutritious. But I'll bet we don't eat as much. I won't be eating just for the taste anymore. Did you notice that I didn't have seconds tonight? Maybe I'll finally lose my baby fat and start to grow taller."

Amanda reassures her son, "You're not chubby, Jake. And don't be in a rush to grow up. Soon enough you will be an adult with aching joints wishing you were a kid again."

Jake excuses himself and heads to his room, "I'll be in my room hanging up my posters and unpacking."

"Welcome home, honey. Like what I've done with the place?" Amanda asks without expecting an answer. "How was your first day?" she asks.

Luke offers only an abridged version, "Well, one of the older board members passed away, and guess who found him dead in his office? Yep, me. At the end of the day, Human Resources called everyone to a mandatory meeting where they spent a couple hours consoling and talking about Joshua Campbell's years of work at Pharmavast and his accomplishments. Then his closest friends stood up and told stories about their time spent with him." Luke looks sadly at Amanda, intentionally soliciting as much sympathy as possible, "And that's why I'm late."

Amanda rises from her chair and sits on Luke's lap and gives him a loving hug. "Sorry for giving you a hard time about being late."

Thursday
December 7, 2051

First Date

"Yes, I follow. Won't be a problem," Damien assures his contact. He ends the call, powers down the phone, slides the *Community Effort* painting to the side, and places the phone back into the hidden compartment.

Damien takes one last look at his laptop, further stalking Anne Gonzales' social media pages. He reconfirms she is single and notices that she enjoys live music. Based on her Discovery School graduation date, she is 12 years younger. He concludes she is not too young to be interested in dating him.

He closes his laptop and walks to the other side of the office, unlocks the door, and enters the small reception area. He sits comfortably on the corner of Tiffany's desk, positioning himself at an angle where he can glance down toward her low-buttoned blouse.

Tiffany immediately stands up, holding a pile of papers to give the perception that she was just about to walk away from her desk. Damien knows he makes her uncomfortable and does not change his behavior.

Damien leans in toward her and asks, "Hey, Tiff, can you please call down to Anne Gonzales? Tell her that I need to meet with her before she heads out for the day. Could you do that now, please? People will be heading home soon. Can you believe how soon the sun is setting now? We come to work in the dark and go home in the dark."

"Sure, I'll knock on your door when she arrives," Tiffany offers, hoping Damien will excuse himself and return to his office.

He remains seated on the corner of her desk, glancing downward as she sits and retrieves Anne's number from the Pharmavast portal.

"Hi, Anne, do you have time to stop by Damien's office before heading home?" Tiffany asks over the phone.

Damien sits patiently waiting for the response.

"She'll be up in about 15 minutes," Tiffany says, then picks up the pile of papers and stands, ready to walk over to the copier. "I'll let you know when she's here."

"Thanks, Tiff. I'm really glad to have you working with us on the 10th floor," Damien compliments, gawking noticeably at her long legs, then heads for his office.

Tiffany forces a smile and offers her thanks. She thinks to herself that she regrets accepting the promotion and wishes the rumors she heard prior to accepting the position were not true. Further, she vows to start wearing flats, slacks, and sweaters, instead of trying to fit in by wearing high heels and short skirts, in hopes of reassignment to a different floor.

Damien greets Anne cheerfully, "Hi, Anne. Come on in."

Tiffany holds the door open for Anne and whispers to her as she walks in, "I love your outfit."

Anne senses the genuineness of her compliment and smiles, unsure why her flats, slacks, and sweater drew such notice from another woman.

Damien excuses his administrative assistant, "Thanks, Tiff. You can head out for the day. See you tomorrow." Then he walks from the floor-to-ceiling window to greet Anne with a handshake and intentionally leaves the door partially open. He turns to confirm Tiffany is leaving for the day and glances up at the security audio/video camera in the reception area, assured that the open door will allow the audio of his conversation with Anne to be recorded.

"Please have a seat," Damien insists, gesturing to the couch in the corner of the office opposite his desk. Anne takes a seat on the couch, crossing her legs, appearing very unsettled. Damien sits across from her in an arm chair.

Without looking up, Anne asks, "What can I help you with?" just as her phone begins to ring. She apologizes for the interruption and takes the call. "Okay... great, thanks.

"Sorry about that. Millhouse from Information Tech said he would be calling before the end of the day. They needed my laptop for some upgrade or something. He wants me to stop by and pick it up on my way out today. Sorry. What can I do for you?"

Damien replies, acting bashful, "Well, you see, umm, okay, this is kinda weird."

Anne relaxes, sensing her being called to Damien's office is not work related. She looks up at the seemingly bashful man sitting across from her.

He shyly asks, "Okay. I was just wondering if you wanted to join me at the Canalside Café after work? Tonight is Open Mic night, which I really enjoy, and just wanted to know if you would like to meet me over there after work, say at 19:00, have some dinner, listen to some live music, not too late. I'm thinking just a couple hours. I have an early day tomorrow."

Anne giggles quietly, forgetting about all the rumors she has heard about Damien over the past decade and forgetting about the high proportion of young, attractive women who work on the 10th floor. She replies, "I don't know, Damien. I really appreciate the offer but—"

Damien interrupts with an apology, "I'm sorry. You probably have a boyfriend. I don't see a ring on your finger, that's the only reason I thought I would ask."

He watches her body language, hoping for a shift in posture and a positive response. Instead she slouches and looks down.

Damien pressures her further and loses the bashfulness, "Are you sure? I'm just looking for an opportunity to get to know you. Ten years and only two floors below and we have never had an opportunity to chat. You don't have a boyfriend or a fiancé, do you?"

Anne senses his demeanor changing and becomes uncomfortable with his advance. She thinks to herself, *I'm glad I don't dress trampy like the women on this floor*, and realizes the rumors she momentarily discounted now seem to have some truth.

Feeling apprehensive about saying no to the head of the company for which she would like to continue working and resolving that the dinner-date will only last a couple hours, she changes her mind, "Well, okay. And no, I don't have a boyfriend or a fiancé, and honestly, I'm not really looking for a relationship." She surprises herself with the believability of the *not really looking for a relationship* white lie she delivers.

"Okay, perfect," Damien agrees. "Just two coworkers getting to know each other. I'll meet you there at 19:00?"

"Sure. Sounds good." Anne confirms, sounding relaxed and assured that Damien understands the dinner date is casual.

Luke presses the elevator down button, ready to go home for the day, and glances up at the clock noting the time, 17:15. He thinks to himself, *What a wonderful change, working a regular schedule and arriving home in time for dinner.*

He turns at the sound of footsteps approaching and sees a young woman, conservatively dressed, exiting from Damien's office.

Entering the elevator, Luke holds the door-open button for the young woman, forgets his pleasant thoughts of working a regular shift, and puts on his disgruntled attitude.

Anne offers a pleasant greeting, "Good afternoon."

Luke does not turn in her direction, only returning a grunt and a nod.

The patrons at the Canalside Café fill half the tables and randomly placed sofas, an average-size crowd for a Thursday evening. The M-Ns on the hands of the patrons range from M-N 7 to M-N 10, the designated M-N range for the café.

The musicians waiting to play for the crowd have M-Ns ranging from M-N 3 to M-N 6. Musicians with low M-Ns but abundant talent still garner much respect. They are viewed as having sacrificed material gain for pursuit of their passion. As musicians gain popularity and citizens attend their concerts and listen to their music, they often make the vocation jump to Arts and Entertainment - Music.

The vocation jump to 'Arts and Entertainment' is understood to be extremely risky. Quality and Quantity metrics are measured by concert and event attendance and bytes of audio streaming. A musician's M-N is heavily dependent on his or her fan base.

Damien and Anne sit at a round table away from the open-mic stage where the volume is low enough for conversation.

Anne listens to Damien talk positively about his accomplishments and negatively about everything else, including women. She is having a difficult time engaging in conversation with the chauvinist.

Damien continues with small talk, "What's your opinion on husband and wife splitting 40 hours into two 20-hour vocations? Call me old-fashioned, but once kids enter your life, my feeling is the father should make the 40-hour vocation commitment and the mother take care of the household. I just don't see how anyone can excel at a vocation working 20 hours, especially a woman. Her maternal instinct to be at home with the kids would be a huge distraction."

"Well, someday when I'm a mother, I think splitting the 40 hours into two 20-hour vocations would—" Anne is interrupted as if she had never joined the conversation.

"And you know what else? I never understood the draw a person would have to forgo a big beautiful house, wonderful culinary delights, personal transportation, and vacations just to play music," Damien rants.

Anne counters softly, "Looks like this is the last number of the night. We should get going after this one, almost 21:00 already." She shifts uncomfortably in her chair and musters another white lie, "Can you believe how fast the time flew by?"

"This ought to be good," Damien comments insultingly toward the middle-aged couple getting set on the stage. "M-N 3s. They're probably just here to see how the other half lives."

Anne sits silently, nodding and avoiding eye contact with Damien. She knows anything coming out of her mouth at this point is highly likely to offend her arrogant companion.

"Hi, folks! I'm Ward, and this is my beautiful wife, June! And we're going to play our favorite Folk Punk numbers for you tonight!"

As the music winds down and the two make their way to the exit of the café, the hostess politely hands Damien a Merit Evaluation Tablet.

```
Business: Canalside Café Proprietor: Margot Barnett
420.953.256.668
Staff Person: Kari Robbie 794.431.562.665
Vocation: Hostess/Barista


1. Helpful and Considerate
       Poor      Fair      Good      Excellent
```

2. Food and Beverage
        Poor   Fair   Good   Excellent

3. Cleanliness of Facility
        Poor   Fair   Good   Excellent

Without thought, Damien taps Fair, Fair, Fair, and passes the tablet to Anne.

Having watched over Damien's shoulder and accurately predicting his feedback, Anne taps Excellent, Excellent, Excellent and hands the tablet to Kari with a big smile and expresses her gratitude, "Thank you, Kari. I enjoyed the music and beverages very much."

"I'll walk you to your car," Damien offers.

"Sure," Anne replies. She walks briskly in an effort to escape Damien's hedonistic, narcissistic, misogynistic small-talk.

They reach Anne's two-seat luxury coup and Damien makes a request, "Hey, Anne, would you mind running me an inventory analysis from last quarter? I need to present the report to the Governance Fraud, Waste, and Abuse Agency auditors first thing in the morning. You know how they are. If we're late on our reporting, they will send in auditors who will bog us down for weeks. Everyone's productivity metrics will suffer. I totally forgot to send the request to Acquisitions this morning. You can do this from home and email the report to me, right? I don't want you to have to go into the office this late at night."

Anne obliges, "Sure, no problem. I picked up my laptop on the way out today, so yes, I can take care of that from home."

She quickly scoots into her car avoiding any chance of Damien attempting to give her a kiss.

They exchange smiles through the frosty window and Anne heads home.

The parking valet greets Anne and opens her car door as she pulls up to the entrance of the upscale apartment complex, "Good evening, Miss Gonzales."

She makes her way through the lobby, exchanges greetings with her neighbors, and takes the stairs to her third-floor apartment.

She pours herself a glass of red wine, hoping to forget the night's events.

Sitting on the leather couch, watching the increasing snowfall out her picture window, she flips open her laptop, presses the power button, and plans to take care of Damien's request.

No power.

She plugs the laptop in, hoping the issue is a dead battery.

Still no power.

"Ugh," she sighs out loud, knowing that without a Pharmavast-issued laptop, the only other option is to go into the office.

She contemplates arriving early but knows that if there are issues with the report generation that Damien could be left in an unfortunate situation with the auditors.

Leaving the glass of wine, she calls the parking valet, apologizes for the inconvenience, and asks to have her car brought to the entrance.

Anne decides to park under the portico of the Pharmavast entrance. She notices that only a single set of tire tracks exit from under the covering into the inch of snowfall. She concludes that leaving her car parked here should not cause a problem for anyone and she'll avoid having to scrape snow off her windshield when she leaves.

Upon entering, she is greeted by the night watchman, Willy, a man about her age, sitting behind a circular reception counter. An

M-N 7 glows on the back of his right hand. Anne has noticed Willy is always jubilant when greeting her, and sometimes flirtatious.

"Miss Gonzales! What the heck are you doing here? My watch says 22:53 and the snow is coming down pretty good now. Let me guess, you are here to ask me to join you for a cup of coffee?" Willy teases.

Anne thinks Willy is very nice, but she is convinced he is not her type. She thinks to herself as she approaches Willy, *He's so nice, but I don't know, maybe if he was taller, oh my god, I'm so shallow. No, that's not it. Maybe if he was more confident. Like Damien? Oh GOD no. Willy is kinda cute. Maybe I'll ask him to join me for a cup of coffee. I don't know. I'll think about it while I'm upstairs.*

She explains her unexpected arrival, "Sorry, not tonight, Willy. I have some reports to run. Damien needs them first thing in the morning. And my laptop isn't working and I just got it back from Info Tech. Looks like I was not the only one who had to drive here tonight. Okay if I leave my car there?"

"No problem, Miss Gonzales," Willy assures. "I think the last person, other than me, has left for the night."

"Probably someone else having laptop problems," Anne suggests.

Willy, hoping to extend his conversation as much as possible, continues, "Nope, not a laptop issue. But a Damien issue. Someone was here to work on the 10th floor heat. I guess Damien found his office was a bit cold, probably from all those huge windows he has, right? I would think the 10th floor would be nice and warm being the top floor. Heat rises, right?"

Anne smiles pleasantly, slowly inching in the direction of the elevators, trying to hint at concluding the conversation without being rude.

Willy goes on, "Would you like me to escort you to your office? This building can get kinda creepy at night. I'm used to the creepiness though. Kinda grows on you, right?"

Anne successfully interjects, "Yes, right you are. Definitely a bit creepy, but I'll be fine. I appreciate the offer though."

As Anne continues toward the elevator, Willy keeps chatting, "Just call down if you need anything. When you're ready to leave, I'll walk you to your car. Need to be safe. Oh, wait, I can see your car from here. Forgot you parked right in front. Call me if you need anything. And the lights won't come on after midnight, so I'll head up there with my flashlight if you're not done by then."

Anne calls to Willy loudly as the elevator doors close, "Thanks, Willy. I'll call if I need anything."

The doors open on the 8th floor to a pitch-black hallway. Anne extends her arm into the darkness hoping to trip a sensor. She hesitates, then takes a timid step out of the elevator and lets out a chuckle when the lights turn on, laughing at her own skittishness.

The sound of her footsteps echoes loudly in the silence. She can see her reflection in the glass window at the far end of the hallway.

Anne swipes her identification card at the entrance to the Acquisitions office, pushes the door open, and steps into the darkness again, timidly and with hesitation. She glances behind her, thinking she heard another set of footsteps in the hallway, then steps into the office. The lights turn on and she chuckles again.

"Okay, that was weird," she comments out loud to herself.

Walking through a few rows of cubicles, she reaches her workspace, takes off her jacket, and powers up her desktop computer.

"Sure, the desktop works fine," she comments out loud again.

After several minutes of booting up and entering the correct sequence of credentials, Anne accesses the reporting portal. She sets the inventory analysis reports to run specifying last quarter's data as instructed by Damien.

Having run these reports many times, she knows there is going to be between 30 and 45 minutes of waiting before she can confirm that the data extraction was successful. To pass the time, she reaches down to her purse to retrieve her phone when suddenly the lights go out. Only the glowing monitor provides light among the many rows of cubicles.

"What the fu—!" she exclaims, stopping herself from saying what she feels is a vulgar word, even if there is nobody around to hear. She freezes, convinced she heard footsteps, and turns slowly noticing a slight shadow on the back of a cubicle across the aisle.

Anne realizes quickly that it's her shadow, giggles out loud, stands, and waves her arms hoping the lights turn on. The lights turn on at the second wave of her arms.

She accesses her phone and begins reading through her favorite social media sites. She first checks for messages on the Christian singles site and pouts at the lack of communications coming her way. Then she checks the site where she interacts with family and friends and there are two notifications waiting, two friend requests.

"No fu... frigging way!" she shouts loudly, knowing nobody can hear her. "Damien AND Willy?" She taps to accept Willy's friend request and swipes Damien's invitation to the Maybe Later folder. "Much later," she mutters to herself. "And maybe we'll have that coffee, Willy, and I'm going to make sure Damien hears about our date through the grapevine of hussies who work on his floor."

"Oh, COME ON!" The lights go out again. Anne checks the time on her phone, 23:57, and notices she has been surfing her social media sites for the past half-hour. She hears a sharp clank, sounding like a metal object hit another metal object, quickly turns in the direction of the sound and theorizes that the noise just came from the heating vent. Maintenance was doing work on the heating, she remembers.

She realizes the lights will not be coming back on after another three minutes, quickly exits out of her social media sites, and refreshes the display on the monitor. A chime sound indicates that the reports have been successfully generated. Anne emails the reports to Damien, logs out, powers down the PC, gathers her purse, and puts on her winter jacket.

Fumbling with her phone, she manages to find the flashlight application just in time. The lights are not coming back on now, she realizes, and counts on the small flash bulb of her phone to light the way. She waves her arms hoping to get lucky, but the overhead lights remain off.

She pauses momentarily, trying to make no noise, so she can hear if there are any other noises. The 8th floor is perfectly silent.

Anne scurries out of her office and down the hall, almost running, feeling goosebumps because she knows everything behind her is in darkness. Her footsteps echo loudly.

The glowing up and down buttons of the elevator are easy to find in the blackened hallway.

She pushes the down button repeatedly for several seconds, thinking to herself that she knows the elevator will not arrive any faster.

What feels like an eternity passes, then "Ding."

She jumps backward into the bright elevator, keeping the darkness at bay in front of her.

The elevator doors shut.

She breathes a sigh of relief, then giggles out loud again.

Willy abruptly puts down his phone realizing the time is now Midnight and Anne is not back yet. He regrets losing track of time, but very happy Anne accepted his friend request, and convinces himself that, before she leaves, he will ask her if she would like to join him on a date.

He picks up his industrial flashlight and rushes to the elevators, presses the Up button and—

KA-BAM!

He is thrown to the other side of the hallway from the rush of air and debris sent flying out of the elevator shaft, landing back-first against a glass case.

Friday
December 9, 2051

Clandestine

The public transportation bus stops by the side of the road instead of pulling into the parking circle under the Pharmavast portico. Luke looks out the window and notices yellow caution tape surrounding a white two-door coupe. The parking circle is blocked by two ambulances, a Fire and Rescue truck, and a Protect and Serve investigation van. Luke exits the bus from the curb.

As he makes his way to the lobby, a stretcher passes going in the other direction. The head of the stretcher is propped up at a 45-degree angle, carrying Willy. Luke exchanges a nod with the night watchman as he is pushed toward the ambulance. Looking closely at the patient's face as he passes, Luke can tell by the drowsiness of his eyes that he likely suffered a concussion. The many lacerations on his face indicate that there has been a bad accident.

Luke enters the lobby and approaches three security guards blocking the walkway to the elevators. They point him to the signage instructing all employees to temporarily use the stairwell. He pauses and peers between the guards and can see the mangled elevator doors, the demolished glass case, and debris strewn across the floor. His perfect eyesight brings into focus the spattering of blood on the shards of glass still clinging to the case.

He sees four firemen with heavy demolition equipment sitting on the ground looking defeated.

"Step aside," the guards demand of Luke and the other two bystanders.

The ambulance crew pushes the second stretcher through the debris, wheels catching on shards of metal. This stretcher is laying flat, and the body is fully covered with a black sheet. Luke backs out of the way as Damien comes sprinting into the lobby from outside.

Damien runs to the stretcher and pulls back the portion of the sheet covering the victim's face.

Luke clearly sees both Damien's and the victim's faces. He instantly recognizes Anne, the woman who exited Damien's office and joined him in the elevator at the end of the day yesterday.

Then Luke closely watches Damien's every move. Damien's fists are not clenched, he is not trembling, and he shows no signs of restlessness. Although Damien's surprise and words are a perfect fit for the situation, there is no fluttering in his speech.

"Oh my god, Anne, no! No." Damien screams, "Is she? Is she?" he begins to ask the EMTs.

"We're very sorry, sir," the lead EMT consoles Damien as he puts one hand on his shoulder and pulls the black covering back over Anne's face with his other hand. They continue wheeling Anne's lifeless body to the waiting ambulance.

Damien drops his head, begins tapping his fingertips together, and follows the stretcher to the ambulance. Luke expected to see Damien cover his mouth with a hand, or cover his face with both hands, or bring his hands to the top of his head. Instead, Luke notices a likely unconscious tell of Damien's; he is tapping his fingertips together. Luke sees right through the ruse.

Luke quickly looks away, but not before he has a split second of eye contact with Damien.

Feeling grateful that he is fit, Luke easily reaches the top floor using the stairwell.

Ned is in the hallway drinking his morning coffee. "Good morning, Luke. Good thing I got here early. It took me awhile to get up the steps."

"Hey, Mr. T, what happened? Do they know yet?" Luke asks his supervisor.

"I was the second one here this morning and got to hear everything first-hand. Raymond, he's the maintenance supervisor on the 1st floor, was the first one in the building this morning. He found Willy, still unconscious, lying in a pile of glass across from elevator 1 and immediately called 9-1-1.

"I showed up shortly after the Fire and Rescue crew freed Anne's body from the elevator. I heard them talking about how the cable crashed right through the ceiling of the elevator and almost cut that poor girl in half. That elevator doesn't go down to parking, which is why it exploded out into the lobby, sending Willy flying.

"She was such a nice girl. I talked with her a few times at mass on Sundays. She went to my church and sang in the choir too. And she worked in Acquisitions, Luke. Acquisitions," Ned concludes, emphasizing the word *Acquisitions*.

Luke finds Ned's emphasis of the word Acquisitions to be odd, not fitting with the rest of the conversation. Immediately though, that bit of information sends thoughts spiraling in Luke's mind. *Anne, that was the name Ripley mentioned. Said she works in Acquisitions. Never said her last name for fear of endangering her. That has to be her though. Saw her coming out of Damien's office. What was she doing in Damien's office? What about Joshua Campbell? Was Damien actually distraught at Joshua's death? What about the elevator? There are two elevators she could have used from the 8th floor. What if she used the other one? Why was she here late at night?*

"Wow, bad luck that she didn't take the other elevator," Luke realizes, sharing his thought with Ned.

Luke and Ned review the morning worklist. Luke offers to take cleaning the men's and women's restrooms knowing Ned will appreciate the gesture. He also knows he can get away with a quick superficial cleaning of the men's restroom and leave the 'Cleaning in

152

Progress' sign posted at the entrance of the women's restroom while he takes a quick look at the top of the elevator shaft from the roof.

"Sure you're all set with the conference room setups?" Luke confirms with Ned.

"Yep, all set," he answers and pushes his custodial cart down the hall.

Luke scrambles through the men's restroom, superficially wiping down the toilet seats and counters. He holds down the deodorizer spray nozzle for several seconds, walking back and forth from one end of the bathroom to the other. He laughs to himself, knowing that he is cleaning the same way he cleans at home when Amanda asks for his help.

After the three-minute restroom cleaning, he takes a quick walk down the hall to confirm that Ned is in the conference room working on the morning setup. He returns and pushes his custodial cart into the women's restroom and snags a few items to make a forensic kit: two plastic bags, utility knife, flashlight, and duct tape. Then he blocks the doorway with the yellow 'Cleaning in Progress' a-frame sign and waits for an opening when the hallways are vacant.

A few minutes pass and all is clear. Luke scoots over to the custodial storeroom, leaving the sign and the cart behind to make it look as if he is in the middle of cleaning.

He locks himself in the storeroom and climbs the metal rung ladder leading to the hatch. Unable to turn the handle to the open position, he climbs down, retrieves a rubber mallet, climbs back up, and gives the handle a few whacks. The latch swings to the open position.

Luke climbs another rung and rams his shoulder into the latch, trying to break the metal door free from the ice and snow. He almost loses his footing when the latch bursts open, sending ice and snow falling onto his face. The snowfall on the roof cushions the noise of the hatch as it crashes to rest in the open position. Bright sunshine fills the dimly lit custodial storeroom.

The first thing he notices when looking out onto the roof is an inconsistency in the snowfall levels leading to the two elevator shaft hatches. There are no visible footprints; however, if someone had attempted to mask footprints, the inconsistency of the snowfall levels would make sense.

He gently brushes away the snow from what he thinks may be a path someone attempted to hide, and the very bottom layer of snow shows a footprint. Having worked investigations in Western NY for many years, he has become familiar with the way snow packs tightly under a footprint. Next he notices that the amount of snowfall accumulated on the hatch of elevator 1 is a lot more than the accumulation on the hatch of elevator 2.

He concludes that both elevators were tampered with, and after Anne took elevator 1, the tampering was removed from elevator 2. Luke thinks to himself, *So much for having taken the other elevator. She had no chance.*

Knowing his theory is still pure speculation, he investigates elevator 1. Luke cautiously lifts the hatch only a couple of inches, just enough to confirm nobody is in the shaft inspecting the accident, not surprised at the ease with which it opens. The shaft is pitch-black; no light is shining upward.

He lifts the hatch all the way up and crawls in, stepping securely onto the catwalk that extends diagonally across the shaft. Seeing the incoming sunlight fill the shaft, he quickly closes the hatch and turns on his flashlight.

Luke walks to the middle of the catwalk where he can closely examine the cable and pulley system. Surprisingly, there are no shredded cables dangling. What he sees instead is that the steel rods holding the pulley system in place have sheared. The pulley system was compromised, which means the main cable as well as the safety backup cable were both rendered ineffective, sending the elevator car and cables plummeting to the 1st floor.

Using his homemade forensic kit, he scrapes into the first plastic bag what appears to be charred metal from the warped remnants of the steel rods that had been supporting the pulley system. He stuffs the plastic bag into his back pocket.

Then he unwraps a few feet of the duct tape and runs the sticky side along what remains of the pulley system, across the surrounding metal of the catwalk, and any area that may be in proximity of an explosive charge.

"Ka-BAM, Ka-BAM," the sound resounds up the shaft, amplified by the echo.

Luke swiftly stuffs the duct tape into the plastic bag and into his other back pocket, then turns off his flashlight. He freezes, laying prone on the catwalk, holding his breath.

"Ka-BAM." Light floods from the 1st floor as the elevator doors are pulled off their tracks and crash inward into the elevator.

"You can't see anything from down here. I told you, we need to go up to the roof," an impatient and annoyed man yells. Luke can tell by the bright yellow overcoat, glowing through the dark from eight floors down, that the Fire and Rescue department is beginning its investigation.

The men disappear from view, and a few seconds later he hears the elevator shaft on the other side of the cement blocks engage. *Crap! They'll be up here any minute*, Luke thinks to himself.

Luke jumps to his feet and scrambles to exit through the hatch. Standing on the rooftop, he looks around at the obvious signs of tampering, evident by the disturbed snowfall. He figures he has less than 60 seconds to come up with a plan. Hide. No. Dash to the women's restroom, too risky, could be seen. Hide, possibly, maybe, but will still look like someone was up here.

He decides to hide, despite nowhere to hide on the flat rooftop. There is a closet in the storage room for storing paper goods. He envisions curling up into a ball at the bottom of the closet, then dashes for the metal rung ladder leading down from the rooftop.

Luke locks the door to the storeroom from the inside to buy a little extra time, then hustles to the paper goods storage closet and sees the doors are locked. Looking at the massive ring of keys, he knows there is no way he will find the right key in time.

He hears voices coming down the hall.

"Right this way, gentlemen," Luke hears Ned guiding the Fire and Rescue personnel to his location.

Luke stands frozen, nothing he can do but try and fabricate a story. He hears Ned fumbling with his key ring.

"Sorry, but the door is locked. I'll find the key eventually," Ned now speaking loudly and crisp, "Luke must have hit the lock by accident when I asked him to go up to the roof and sweep the snow and break up the ice because we figured you guys would need access to the elevator hatches."

Luke looks around and spots a push broom, grabs the broom, and runs up the ladder. He quietly pushes open the hatch, laying the heavy door lightly on the roof to not make any noise, and exits to the bright rooftop carrying the broom.

He begins sweeping off all the snow from the hatch leading to elevator 1.

"Almost done up there?" Ned yells, standing on the first run of the ladder.

"Yes, sir. Snow is just about cleared," Luke replies. Perspiration is beading on his forehead, but not from exertion.

Luke climbs down the ladder, rests the push broom against the wall, and exits the storage room with Ned, making room for the two Fire and Rescue Investigators to make their way to the rooftop.

Damien is standing in the hallway, arms crossed, silent. As Luke passes Damien on his way to finish up the women's restroom, Damien notes Luke's helpfulness, "Thank you for taking care of the snow, Luke."

Luke turns to Damien for a split second of eye contact, acknowledges with a nod, then looks away again, head down, avoiding further conversation.

The squint in Damien's eyes and the monotone, emotionless mention of thanks don't sit well with Luke. He is now concerned whether Ned's intervention was convincing.

Ned calls out to Luke from the hallway, "Hurry up in there, will ya? And I'm headed out for the day."

Luke looks out from the women's restroom and nods, "See you Monday, Mr. T. Have a nice weekend."

Ned replies with a subtle wink and a remarkably accurate mimicking of Damien's earlier gratitude, "Thanks for taking care of the snow, Luke." Then he looks behind to confirm nobody is around and quietly admits to Luke, "I knew you would be the curious type. But don't be too curious, could get you in trouble."

Luke spends the remainder of his Friday checking off items on his worklist and contemplating a few questions.

Is Ned helping me or is my imagination running wild?

Is Damien really up to something or is he just a dickhead?

Why are all the women on this floor so frickin hot?

Possession Enforcement

"And that was my day," Luke concludes. "Not bad for a first week at work, eh?"

"Oh my god, Luke. What if you had taken that elevator? Oh my god," Amanda frets. "So what did they say caused the accident? And that poor girl."

"I overheard the Fire and Rescue Investigators saying something about bad bearings and metal overheating, or something like that. I guess they knew pretty quickly what happened," Luke explains.

Knock-knock … Knock-knock ….

"Forget your key, AJ?" Amanda calls out toward the door.

Knock-knock ….

"Coming," Amanda yells as she gets up from her seat next to Luke on the couch. She looks over at Luke and asks in a hushed voice, "Who could that be this late at night?"

She looks through the peephole and gasps, "What the—?"

Luke rushes to the door and stands over Amanda's shoulder as she quickly unlatches the chain, unlocks the deadbolt, and opens the door.

AJ is standing between two Possession Enforcement Officers who are dressed in dark blue uniforms. AJ's head is hung low, not looking at her parents. She is wearing her M-N 3 issued clothes, plain dark blue denim jeans and a tan, long-sleeve, collarless cotton shirt.

Amanda initially thinks the two officers are Protection and Serve Officers. Luke knows the difference immediately. These two officers are not armed with Tasers and handguns.

"Hello, ma'am. I'm Officer Jackson, and this is Officer Anderson," states the older of the two officers.

Luke puts his arm around Amanda's shoulder and takes the lead in the conversation. "Hello, gentlemen. Come on in."

Officer Jackson explains, "Hello, sir. This is really awkward, so I apologize if I seem nervous. We know you as Agent Medina and have looked up to you for years, and we hope to see you back on the force really soon, sir. Here is my card." Officer Jackson hands Luke his contact information. "Feel free to call me if you want to discuss this further. I know you know what's going on, and we're confident that AJ can fill you in on the details.

"Unfortunately, the incident occurred at the school basketball game, so we'll have to include this in the weekly violations section of the newspapers. Believe me, sir, if there was any way we could keep this between us—"

"Hey, don't worry, I totally understand. I started out as a Possession Enforcement Officer. I've been there. You guys are doing a great job. Keep up the good work. I know this is one of the most thankless vocations," Luke empathizes.

"Thank you very much, sir. Good night, ma'am." Officer Anderson concludes the conversation as the two exit the apartment, "Thank you very much for your cooperation, young lady. We appreciate that you came with us without making a scene."

"Amanda, sit!" Her mother shouts uncontrollably, but AJ continues to her room. She uses two hands and all her might to slam the door but fails to make any slamming sound. The doorknob rattles, loosened from the force. Amanda walks to AJ's bedroom and yells through the door, "AJ! Amanda Junior!! You have ten minutes to settle down and join your father and me at the dining room table."

Amanda briskly walks to the dining room table, takes a seat, and yells at Luke, "Sit!"

Luke sits immediately, fearing the glare Amanda just flashed him.

Amanda glances at the clock on the stove every ten seconds, anxiously waiting for ten minutes to pass.

As if AJ was timing her ten minutes, she slowly opens her bedroom door just as Amanda is inhaling, preparing to yell again.

Luke sits patiently, hands folded, resting in front of him on the table.

Amanda sits anxiously, fidgeting, arms crossed.

AJ slowly walks to the dining room table, pulls out a seat next to her father, sits, and makes eye contact with her parents for the first time since the officers escorted her home.

During the silence, Jake walks out of his room and lounges on the couch, attempting to stay incognito so he can listen in on the conversation.

AJ breaks the silence, "Does Jake really have to be out here?" AJ questions.

Amanda and Luke do not answer, but continue to sit silently. AJ knows this is her queue to tell her side of the story.

"Ugh … fine." AJ attempts an abridged version of the night's events, "I went to the game, wore some clothes I'm not 'supposed' to wear, and got in trouble."

Amanda and Luke do not flinch and remain silent.

"FINE! You want the whole story? Here it is!" Amanda begins her detailed version, "I didn't take the bus to the game. Nora and Chloe picked me up."

Amanda interrupts, "Nora and Chloe. Okay, great. I know where this is going."

AJ gets angered at her mother's disapproval, "You never liked them, Mom. I get that …."

Before an argument breaks out, Luke intervenes, "Amanda, AJ, let's just continue with the rest of the story."

"Oh wait a second, Luke. Did you know our precious daughter had already told Emily she would go to the game with her? June mentioned that today when I saw her in the hall, and she also mentioned how much Emily was looking forward to hanging out with our precious daughter. But no! She went with those two prissy princesses who think they're entitled to that number on their hand. Yeah, that's right, they have a rude awakening coming this spring when they're out on their own," Amanda argues.

"Fine, Mom. Fine. Okay, I get it. You know how much this M-N 3 on my hand sucks? Let me spell it out for you," AJ continues.

"Chloe and Nora picked me up, and I had already told Emily in school today that I had promised I would go with them. Yes, that was a lie.

"I asked them to bring a change of clothes that I could wear to the game. Yes, I know that's not accepted, I know. You don't have to tell me.

"I changed in the car on the way over, put on Chloe's jeans, and Nora's button-down teal blouse. Oh my god, I miss those clothes.

"Don't you understand? I just didn't want to look like ... you know ... an M-N 3. Sorry, Dad.

"At half-time, this kid Shawn, I hate that asshole, texted me in to Possession Enforcement. I know it was him because he kept turning around and laughing at me when those two officers walked toward our section of the bleachers.

"And I swear I saw him show Chloe and Nora the text on his phone when they thought I wasn't looking.

"The officers were nice, I'll give them that. They walked right up to me in front of the whole school though, the WHOLE SCHOOL!

"I knew what they wanted. And so did everyone else. They pretended not to notice what was going on, but they all saw. I know they did.

"So I walked out, escorted in front of everyone by the two officers. Nora and Chloe didn't even own up to possessing the clothes when they were asked …."

AJ breaks down, walks over to her mother and sits on her lap, and begins to cry on her shoulder.

Amanda, convinced her daughter is genuinely sorry, comforts AJ with a hug.

Through her tears, AJ continues, "The officers asked Nora and Chloe if they knew who gave me the clothes because I was sitting between them. They said they had no idea. I think they set me up, Mom."

AJ continues to cry on her mother's shoulder for several minutes before Amanda asks, "Who wants some comfort food?"

Jake makes his way to the dining room table and pats AJ on the shoulder. "Let's see. We have some porridge! We could try and make some cinnamon porridge cookies. AJ has a cinnamon shaker."

The family spends the remainder of their Friday evening making several attempts to bake edible porridge cookies. Some are too burnt. Some are too soggy. Some have too much cinnamon, and some have too little.

Jake counts "1-2-3-Eat" to coordinate a simultaneous tasting each time a new batch is ready.

The family of four laughs together more this evening than any other time Amanda can recall since AJ started her teen years.

Monday
December 11, 2051

Blood and Residue

"Bye, babe," Luke kisses Amanda goodbye as he heads for the door.

"Why are you leaving early? Can't you go in a little late? The kids get on the bus soon. We didn't get to spend any 'quality' time together last week," Amanda whispers flirtatiously to Luke, pulling him close to her.

"I really can't. I promised my supervisor I would be there early today. He said something about lots of meetings to set up for today," Luke replies, knowing his answer is a bit of a white lie, but also knows he needs to buy a little extra time to write his note for his Elder contact.

Amanda sees him out with a pout on her face.

When he reaches the bus stop, he begins writing his note with the specially issued pen, timing the writing carefully, knowing that the ink will be visible for only 60 minutes.

Bag 1, blood sample, Joshua Campbell, check for suspicious toxins

Bag 2, residue from elevator shaft 1, check for explosives

Luke grabs a newspaper from the news stand adjacent to the benches of the bus stop. He opens to the Sports section and tapes his note over an article about the health benefits of cross country skiing. He also tapes the two plastic bags just below the handwritten note and flattens them out.

The bus arrives and Luke boards, sitting all the way in the back, along the driver's side, with open seats next to him on either side. An older woman dressed in a feminine business suit sits next to him. They sit silently until the first bus stop.

As additional passengers board, she introduces herself, "Sir, good morning."

Luke acknowledges, "Ma'am, good morning." He extends his hand. They shake covertly. Luke indiscriminately squeezes her hand twice in quick succession, hoping that does not seem odd to her if he does not receive the expected response.

She squeezes his hand three times in quick succession.

Luke places his newspaper between them. The Elder places her newspaper on top of Luke's. They sit silently as the passengers continue to board.

Once all passengers board and the bus departs, Luke picks up the top newspaper. Attempting to act casual, he holds the newspaper for several seconds as he glances around the bus.

He notices a man sitting across from him, someone he has not seen on the bus before. Also catching his eye is the man's M-N. Luke knows instantly that the M-N is counterfeit. Having worked numerous counterfeit investigations, fake M-Ns jump right out at him. The shade of green is not correct. The difference is incredibly subtle, but Luke's perfect eyesight and training spot the difference.

Luke fights the temptation to approach the man, knowing the engagement could arouse suspicion. He imagines pulling out an M-N Verifier, a phone-sized electronic tool he used to carry, that when held over a citizen's M-N hologram, will display the validity of the M-N implant under the skin on the back of the hand.

Also striking are the man's clothing. Luke assumes the man is on his way to work, but Luke can't determine what possible vocation his apparel would be appropriate for; heavily worn black cowboy boots, shiny and not dirty from mud or salt, loose-fitting black leather pants, black trench coat, long hair sticking out from under a black, flat-brimmed cowboy hat. The only vocation Luke can think of, for a person dressed like this man, is a rancher, but he is headed for the city. Luke laughs to himself, *Maybe he's a male stripper,* then instantly feels guilty for making fun of the man.

Luke very casually opens the Elder's newspaper, crosses his legs, and flips one section at a time until he reaches the Sports section. Taped to the bottom-left corner is a handwritten note:

Security camera footage from Thursday. We were unable to find anything conclusive. Please review closely and see if you find anything helpful.
You will find these credentials useful:
Username - Pharmavast_admin_2051
Password - 9h@rm@c0n!@#

Taped below the note is a mini-disk.

Luke continues to casually read the paper, enjoying the article about how the Buffalo Bills have clinched a spot in the post-season playoffs, but he is anxious to view the footage on the mini-disk. As for the username and password, he knows the time has come to implement his technical skills.

The man in the flat-brimmed cowboy hat is facing his direction, but his head is tipped just enough that Luke cannot determine if the man is peering at him from under the brim of his hat. The temptation to question his M-N comes back, but he resists and decides not to engage the stranger.

Luke and the Elder exit the bus at the same stop and walk off in different directions.

As Luke heads for the Pharmavast entrance, he can't help but to think about how Ned covered for him on Friday. *I've got to know*, he wonders.

Luke takes elevator 2 up to the 10th floor, drops off his coat in the custodial storeroom, and pulls out his cart. As he backs into the hallway, he bumps into Ned's cart.

Luke greets Ned, "Sir, good morning," hoping desperately he responds with the same covert greeting.

"Sir, good morning," Ned replies. But before Luke can extend his hand for a shake, Ned jokes, "Sir? What's up with that? No Mr. T today, son?" He continues laughing while handing Luke the worklist for the day.

Luke hides his disappointment. He was hopeful that Ned was an Elder, but deep down he knew his imagination was getting the best of him.

Throughout the day, Luke finds time to view segments of the video on the mini-disk by inserting the disk into his phone. He isolates three segments of particular interest and notes the time stamps, 12-9-2051 16:45, 12-9-2051 20:37, and 12-9-2051 20:53.

The last item on his worklist for the day, cleaning the women's restroom, is complete. He takes his time and cleans with extra diligence to make up for last Friday.

Luke glances at his watch and then his checklist and is happy to see his work is done early. Instead of leaving for the day, he spends the remaining time reviewing the security camera footage in the custodial storeroom.

He sits comfortably on a wooden stool in the corner, an earpiece in one ear, watching and listening attentively focused.

The first segment he isolates is from a camera positioned in the hallway of the 10th floor. Cameras are not positioned in any offices, just hallways and the main lobby. He drags the scrollbar to 16:45, about 15 minutes before he entered the elevator with Anne after witnessing her exiting Damien's office.

The video images are not revealing since they don't capture inside Damien's office, just a small section of the area at the entrance to his office where his administrative assistant, Tiffany, sits.

He listens carefully to the audio.

Damien: "Hey, Tiff, call this maintenance company. Here's the number. Tell them the 10th floor is cold and to please check out the heating unit. Seems to have been cold all day. Don't you think?"

Tiffany: "Yes, now that you mention, it does seem a bit chilly."

Damien: "Oh Tiff, I think you are correct. Your, umm, you know, your 'blouse' is agreeing, definitely you're feeling a chill. Maybe we shouldn't get the heating fixed."

Silent pause.

Damien: "I'm just kidding. You know me, just kidding. Do make the call, please."

Luke thinks to himself, *What a frickin dickhead!*

Then he fast-forwards until Anne enters Damien's office. Luke listens to the conversation, cringing with every word out of Damien's mouth. He replays one segment several times:

Damien: "Are you sure? I'm just looking for an opportunity to get to know you. Ten years and only two floors below, and we have never had an opportunity to chat. You don't have a boyfriend or a fiancé, do you?"

Luke notices a distinct change in Damien's tone. He is not asking as much as he is demanding she join him. Very odd change from the way he began the conversation, sounding bashful and uneasy.

Oh, he's good … or am I overthinking, Luke wonders.

He moves on to the next segment, 20:37. The video caught his eye because this was the only time anyone, other than Anne, entered the building after business hours. He watches a maintenance van pull up to the entrance. A man dressed in overalls enters carrying a toolbox. He is wearing a baseball cap with the brim pulled low. Luke is not able to see the man's face but is able to discern the M-N 4 on his hand despite this copy of the video being low resolution. He zooms in on the sewn-in nametag, blurry like his M-N, and is able to make out the name, Cyrus Lance. The available audio is minimal. He hears the clack-clack-clack of hard-soled boots against the marble-tiled lobby floor, which seems odd for a maintenance man's footwear, followed by a brief exchange with the night watchman.

Willy: "Good evening. You must be here to check on the 10th floor heat?"

Maintenance man: "Yes." Nods and heads for the elevators.

Willy turns to further engage in conversation, but the maintenance man's back is already facing him.

Luke fast-forwards to find the time when the maintenance man leaves and finds that at 21:52. There is another minimal conversation.

Willy: "All set?"

Maintenance man: "Yes." He attempts to exit, but Willy intercepts his path to the door. He looks eager to converse with another person.

Willy: "So, what's up? All fixed? Were you able to figure out what was wrong?"

Maintenance man: "Yes."

Pause.

Willy: "So what can I tell Mr. Myers?"

Maintenance man: "I had to change the filters. They were clogged, blocking the airflow."

Willy: "Oh sure, that makes sense. My first career out of Discovery School was Heating-Ventilation-Air Conditioning. I changed a lot of filters. But I thought all the heating units were filter-less and used electrification instead. That's weird. Must be the unit that heats the 10th floor is an older model. Hey, whatever. My M-N dropped to a 2 during that vocation. I just couldn't do the job efficiently. My boss said I talked too much. So that's why I'm here! How about you?"

Maintenance man: "Good night." He nods politely and exits.

The next segment, 22:53, shows Anne's arrival and her conversation with Willy. Luke listens to the whole conversation and feels badly for Willy and how lonely the night watchman job must be. He notices how Willy attempts to extend conversation with Anne the same way he did with the maintenance man.

Luke replays another segment of the audio several times:

Anne: "... Damien needs them first thing in the morning. And my laptop isn't working and I just got it back from Info Tech."

He flips back to Anne's conversation with Damien and replays a possibly related segment:

Anne: "Millhouse from Information Tech called. They needed my laptop for some upgrade or something. He wants me to stop by and pick it up on my way out today."

He switches back to the video clip of the 10th floor, scrolling to 23:00, and watches Anne enter the dark hallway. He is entertained by her skittishness. He skips through the next hour of video footage until she enters the elevator.

Luke switches to 00:00 on the lobby footage and watches the horrific scene that sent Willy flying into the glass case.

Several minutes pass while he ponders the audio and video he witnessed. What is connected? Is anything connected? Was this all a coincidence?

He glances at the time on his phone, 17:00, tucks the earpiece into his pocket, puts on his jacket, and heads for the elevator.

Before he can get to the elevator, Damien stops him, "Luke, HEY LUKE."

Luke turns and nods, letting Damien know he hears him.

"Hey, come clean up the conference room," Damien commands.

Luke pauses for a moment, waiting for the word *Please*, even though he knows that word will not be spoken. He heads back to the custodial storeroom to retrieve his cart.

After finishing with the conference room, Luke waits for elevator 2 alongside Amber. He knows the wait will be long because the building is limited to one working elevator. He sees that Amber is holding a bouquet of flowers. She is crying softly, trying to hide her tears.

Preferring to stay in character and not acknowledge her obvious sadness, he keeps his eyes forward, not engaging in conversation.

Tiffany arrives at the elevator as the doors open. She puts her arm around Amber's shoulder. All three enter the elevator.

Luke stares downward, listening in on their conversation.

"I can't believe he's gone," Amber mutters through her tears. "I was supposed to bring these to him at the hospital on my way home." She cries as the elevator descends. Tiffany gives her a hug.

"I heard this morning that he was going to be fine. Then Damien told me what happened. He survives that accident then dies of a morphine overdose?" Amber weeps. "I mean, really? Those things just never happen, and he was such a nice man."

Luke glances at the name on the envelope in the bouquet of flowers: Willy.

Productivity Calculations

"You lazy bastard! Get your butt out of bed and get to work you good-for-nothing son of a bitch! What's your problem? If I knew I would be living here in Village Garbage and my husband was going to be lazy, you better believe I would have left you at the altar," the woman in the adjacent apartment yells without concern of anyone overhearing their conversation.

"I put a roof over your head, food on the table, clothes on your back. I provide plenty!" her husband argues. "Maybe I like public transportation. Maybe I like working 15 hours a week instead of 40. Maybe I like my television and mid-day beer! I'm living like a King! Except instead of a Queen, I have an ungrateful Princess."

They argue for several more minutes before their volume dies down and is no longer heard through the walls.

Luke rolls over, "Look on the bright side, honey, we don't need an alarm clock!"

Amanda gives him her glare, and they both roll out of bed. She wonders, sharing a thought with Luke, "What would this place be like if all our neighbors were like Ward and June?"

The morning schedules are all in sync today, and the family of four leaves the apartment together. Luke and Amanda walk to the transportation bus stop one block away, Luke on his way to work and Amanda on her way to a volunteer shift on the pediatric oncology floor at Strong Memorial Hospital. Jake and AJ head for the school bus stop at the front of the apartment complex.

Emily exits from her apartment at the same time.

AJ immediately acknowledges last Friday, "Hey, Em, about Friday ...."

Emily cordially stops her mid-sentence, "Hey, no worries."

The two teen girls exchange friendly smiles.

AJ boards the bus and walks directly to the back seats. She looks Nora and Chloe in the eyes and exclaims, "F-You and F-You!"

She looks at Shawn, the person she suspects was behind the confrontation with the Possession Enforcement Officers, drops her backpack, and leans into his seat, putting her face right up to his face.

"After school, asshole, you and me. The woods behind the gym, 15:00." She continues to stare him down until he turns away and cowers into his seat. "Yeah, that's right, you know, don't you? Muay Thai, Khan 10. You wouldn't have a chance. Forget meeting me after school, I know you wouldn't show up. What's the matter? You look like you're about to piss your pants? Mess with me again and I'll be waiting for you on your front lawn."

She turns back to Nora and Chloe and snidely informs them, "Birthday party is off, by the way."

AJ picks up her backpack and walks toward the front of the bus surrounded by applause and cheers. She takes a seat with Emily and asks, "My birthday is this Friday. I still get to keep my M-N 8 birthday party because the reservations were made before my dad got the M-N 3. Jake let me know of that loop hole. I have reservations for eight at Mireille's Maison de Cuisine Française in the city. I was going to take Nora, Chloe, and a few others in that clique, but I'd like very much if you and your family and me and my family went instead. What do you think?"

"Absolutely!" Emily cheers. "I love French food ... I think." They both giggle. "My parents told me that when I was little we once went to an M-N 8 restaurant with relatives, but I don't remember that at all. Oh my god, this is going to be awesome!"

Timeology Mentor, Mr. Garcia, calls class to attention. "Quiet down, please. Thank you, future contributors to the United States of Amerita, for all your respect. The first of two lessons for today will be led by Jake Medina."

Jake walks to the front of the class and stands with confidence.

"The topic of my lesson is titled Vocations of Days Past. I'll be discussing three vocations that existed before Meritism that don't exist now because they serve no useful purpose: Politicians, Financiers, and Advertisers.

"First, I would like to talk about the word 'Vocation.' Why do we use vocation instead of career?

"The definition of career is 'an occupation undertaken for a significant period of a person's life and with opportunities for progress.'

"The definition of vocation is 'a person's main occupation, especially regarded as particularly worthy and requiring great dedication.'

"Many studies have shown that undertaking the same contributions for significant periods of a person's life often leads to apathy—"

Mr. Garcia interrupts, prompting Jake to recognize when he is speaking with words that may not be recognizable by his peers, "Ahem, Jake? Apathy?"

"Thank you, Mr. Garcia. Many studies have shown that undertaking the same contributions for significant periods of a person's life often leads to lack of interest, enthusiasm, and concern. All three of these lead to lower productivity and lower M-Ns. Take my dad for example. He spent 12 years as a Merit Agency Investigator. Probably he should not have stayed in the same vocation that long. I would say that after 12 years, he could call that a career.

"First up, Politicians. That's what people used to call their Governance representatives. The words they used were Senators, Congressmen, and Assemblymen. I find it very ironic that the definition of Politician is 'a person who acts in a manipulative and devious way, typically to gain advancement within an organization.' I guess that definition is actually quite fitting.

"Many Politicians got in trouble for creating laws and approving laws that worked in their favor. And people still elected them. For example, Politicians would vote on their own salaries. Sorry ... 'Salary' is how much currency someone was given for doing a vocation, or job as they used to say. Remember last week when we talked about currency, right?" Jake's classmates all nod, confirming they paid attention last week and are absorbed in today's presentation.

He continues, "Compare that with our Governance Representatives. Their M-N is the average M-N of the people they represent minus one point. Our town, Macedon, has an average M-N of 7. That means if you took all the M-Ns in Macedon and averaged them out, the result would be 7. The Town's Governance representative, Mrs. Leslie Wright, has an M-N 6.

"If Politicians were around today, they would probably create a law that says all of them get M-N 10s regardless of the average M-N of the Town, County, or State they represent. What's up with that?

"I believe Meritism is the purest form of Meritocracy. YES, Mr. Garcia, I'll explain that word. Meritocracy, the holding of governance power by people selected on the basis of their ability and desire to serve the public interest. The M-N system for Governance Representatives ensures they have taken on the responsibility because they want to serve the people, not because they're serving their own interests.

"Wait, this gets even better. 'Career Politician.' Most Politicians made a life-long vocation, or career, of being a Politician. This led to lack of interest, enthusiasm, and concern.

"As a Politician's career advanced, they would have more and more possessions than those they represented, and they cared less and less about representing the people who elected them.

"The Meritism Handbook clearly states under the vocation of Governance Representative that no one person can hold that vocation for any more than ten years. And that doesn't mean you could do ten years as a County representative and another ten as a State representative. That means you can only do a total of ten years across all representations.

"Next up is Financier, another vocation that's obsolete, I mean, serves no real purpose. A Financier is a person who works with currency. Remember the round stones used for currency in my pretend civilization from last week? Well, a Financier would be the person in charge of holding onto the round stones and collecting them and passing them out.

"To keep with the correct terminology, we're going to use the word Money. That's what people used to call their equivalent of round stones.

"There were lots of Financiers. Two common names they went by were Investment Bankers and Stock Brokers. Here is a funny twist of fate. Lots of them used to work on Wall Street on Manhattan Island, which at the time was part of New York City. We all know what Manhattan Island is now, the biggest exile region in the whole country. And when the hovercrafts drop off the exiled, they drop them off on the rooftop of buildings that are on Wall Street!

"Basically what Financiers did was use other people's round stones, I mean money, to generate more money."

Jake looks out at his peers and can see confusion on their faces.

Frederick chimes in, "I ... don't ... get it ...."

Jake uses an example, "Okay, here's a story. Investment Banker Bob convinces citizen Sally that if she gives him 10 round stones, he will give her back 12 round stones.

"Investment Banker Bob then convinces citizen Sam that if he gives him 14 round stones that he will give him back 16 round stones.

"Sam gives Investment Banker Bob 14 round stones. Investment Banker Bob gives Sally 12, like he promised, and keeps 2 for himself.

"Then Investment Banker Bob looks for someone to give him 18 round stones so he can give Sam 16 and keep 2 for himself. Then Investment Banker Bob looks for someone to give him 22 then 26 and so on and so on.

"Bob now has hundreds of round stones for which he did NOTHING PRODUCTIVE, he didn't contribute in any way, no food, no clothing, no shelter, no medicine, no art, no entertainment, no sanitation, nothing!"

"Come on! You're joking, right?" several classmates question.

"Nope, totally serious. Right, Mr. Garcia?" Jake asks.

Mr. Garcia gives the class an affirming nod, "Yes. Believe it or not, Jake is correct. I was a young man when this was going on, and I gave a lot of the money I had to the Financiers. Then I lost it all when everything crashed around us. But enough about me, Jake, please continue."

"Another way the Financiers gathered more stones was using what was called the 'Stock Market.' Basically, the Stock Market was a way for people to own small parts of companies. When the Financiers convinced the population that certain companies were worth more, then people could trade in their ownership for more stones than they traded to first acquire the ownership.

"Crazy, right? How could a business just magically be worth more the next day? I'll tell you how. These Financiers were sneaky and very, very convincing.

"There is no Meritism replacement for Financiers since we don't have currency. Good riddance to them I say!

"And now for the most useless occupation I could find, Advertisers!

"An Advertiser was a person whose whole occupation was trying to get other people to trade their round stones for someone else's goods and services.

"For example, going back to last week. Let's say two families provided cleaning services: the Smith family and the Jones family. And let's say the Smith family had an Advertiser working for them. The Smith's Advertiser would go around to other houses and tell them how great the Smith family is at cleaning houses and how poorly the Jones family is at cleaning houses. Well, guess who got to clean more houses, and cleaning more houses meant they received more round stones. Anyone? Which family had more round stones?"

Wendy raises her hand and answers, "The Smith family, right? But didn't they get in trouble for saying bad things about the Jones family?"

"Ahem," Jake regains his composure after having his breath taken away for the few seconds when Wendy spoke directly to him. "Yes, the Smith family had more round stones. And their Advertiser could say whatever they wanted.

"My research into Advertisers talked a lot about the evil ways they talked badly about other companies and the evil ways they used to convince people to use their goods and services.

"I'll give you some examples. There was this drink called 'Cola.' Basically, it was just fizzy water with lots of sugar and some caramel flavor. That's literally all it was. The people who owned that business were some of the richest people in the country. By rich, I mean they had millions and millions of round stones.

"Confusing, right? Why would so many people trade their round stones for something that had zero nutritional value?

"Commercials! A commercial is a short story, about 30 seconds long, that plays in the middle of broadcasted shows, and on phones, and while surfing the Internet. These 30-second short stories even played on the sides of buses, on big monitors mounted on tall buildings, they were everywhere.

"A typical example of these short stories is a family picnic. Young children run around and play games. Their parents are happy and never fighting. The children play together and get along, and they're all smiling and having fun. The sun is shining and they're enjoying a summer day at a park. AND they all had bottles of cola in their hands."

Frederick chimes in again, "I ... don't... get it ... What does that have to do with cola?"

"Exactly!" Jake cheers. "That's my point! The short story said nothing about the cola! I had to dig deep to find the answer. And the answer is wicked scary," Jake has fear in his eyes as he exposes the answer. His classmates hang on his every word.

"Brainwashing."

Jake stands silently and nods his head, looking over to Mr. Garcia, who nods his head, affirming to the class that Jake is accurate in his analysis.

"When people watch happy kids and happy families having a fun picnic on a warm, sunny day, they feel happy and positive too. They're feeling happy and positive not because of the cola, but because of the story. However, the cola is the focal point, 'Cola' spelled on the side of a bottle as the bottle is tipped and poured into the smiling mouth of a child.

"People watch these short stories over and over and eventually they associate the cola with being happy and positive. They eventually think that the cola will make them happy and positive."

Jake pauses and takes a long look at his classmates before continuing, "Brainwashing. And that's not bullshit. This used to go on, for real … Sorry, Mr. Garcia." Jake catches his language slip-up. Mr. Garcia smiles and waves off the unintentional use of the word.

Jake smiles, happy to present the alternative of the current day, "And today we have no Advertising! That has been replaced with online Merit Reviews for products and Merit Evaluation Tablets for services. We all know what those are, so I don't have to go into detail.

"My parents are diligent about doing the online product reviews for the products we've used during the week. We do this as a family every Sunday evening after dinner. And my sister and I have been taught to always give a fair evaluation when we have an opportunity to complete a Merit Evaluation Tablet survey.

"We don't need advertising anymore. We are responsible for researching the products and services we choose to acquire. The reviews of other citizens are there to help us with our decisions.

"In conclusion, No Politicians or Financiers or Advertisers will ever exist in Amerita. No more lack of empathy from our representatives, no more trickery from Financiers, and no more brainwashing."

Wendy is the first student to stand and applaud. This brings a huge smile to Jake's face.

"Welcome, future Amerita contributors!" Mrs. White, the Discovery School's Vocational Guidance Counselor, repeats this phrase at the beginning of each Vocational seminar. Then she asks the opening question. "Please raise your hand if you have decided what your first vocation out of Discovery School will be."

Chloe shoots her hand high in the air before anyone else. Eleven other students raise their hands. Mrs. White comments, "12 out of 20, not bad. And yes, Chloe, we all know you plan to marry an M-N 10. I can't say that's an actual vocation, but having goals is important.

"Who would like to volunteer and lead our opening discussion?" Mrs. White asks.

AJ stands immediately, "Mrs. White, I would like to lead the opening discussion."

Mrs. White smiles, pleasantly surprised with AJ's uncharacteristic attitude, "Fantastic, AJ. Please come up to the podium. The class is yours."

As AJ makes her way to the podium, Eddie, a very obnoxious classmate, mumbles loudly and intentionally under his breath, "Ahem ... THREE ..." AJ turns in his direction and flashes him an eye roll.

Mrs. White disciplines, "Eddie, remove yourself from our classroom immediately. Stay home tomorrow and keep to your bedroom without access to any technology. Reflect all day on what your life will be like six months from now when you are dethroned from that M-N 10 your mother has tirelessly worked for and how you will adjust to your M-N 5. I will be sending your parents a follow-up as soon as class concludes. Goodbye."

With head hung low unable to pretend he does not feel shamed, Eddie slings his backpack over his shoulder and heads for the door. He does not make eye contact with any of his classmates. As he walks past the podium where AJ now stands, head still hung low, he genuinely apologizes, "Sorry, AJ."

"No worries," she answers.

Mrs. White retreats to her desk. The class settles down, and AJ begins the opening discussion.

"I just don't think the whole EQ/IQ testing thing is fair, and this is the topic I would like to discuss," AJ begins. "We just got back our EQ/IQ Pre-Testing results and I scored really high, a 9. That means I have to take a Level 9 vocation because my M-N will be penalized if I choose a vocation at a lower level. How is that fair?"

Mrs. White speaks, "AJ, that's a very good question. I'm not going to facilitate this discussion; however, before the discussion starts, I would like to take a few minutes and review the basics of EQ/IQ testing and the Merit Number system calculations. Then the discussions can begin.

"As you all know, your parents have an M-N based on a scale of 1 to 10. The higher their number, the nicer the goods and services available to you.

"AJ, if you don't mind, I'm going to use you and your EQ/IQ Pre-Test result as an example."

"Yeah, sure. Go ahead," AJ agrees.

Mrs. White continues, "Let's say AJ graduates Discovery School with an EQ/IQ of 9. She accepts a level 9 vocation, Science: Biomedics, and after her first year she achieves a Productivity Calculation of 10. Her M-N would be a 10 for the following year. If she achieves a Productivity Calculation of 5, her M-N would be a 5 for the following year.

"But this is what I think AJ is referring to. If she accepts a Level 5 vocation, for example Service: Waiter/Waitress and achieves a Productivity Calculation of 10, her M-N for the following year would only be a 6. The calculation is really quite simple."

Mrs. White writes the formula on the board along with the examples from the discussion.

Productivity Calculation - (EQ/IQ - Vocation Level) = M-N

Biomedicine
10 - (9-9) = 10 - 0 = Merit Number 10

Waiter/Waitress
10 - (9-5) = 10 - 4 = Merit Number 6

Mrs. White returns to her desk and waves on AJ to continue the discussion.

AJ ponders for a moment and realizes she knows more than she thought, thanks to Jake's engrossment with the Merit Number system.

"Thanks, Mrs. White. I would like to add one other point I know about because my little brother is obsessed with the Merit Number system and talks about Meritism all the time. If anyone scores at least a 1 for their Productivity Calculation, regardless of their EQ/IQ - Vocation Level, they will not be exiled."

Mrs. White confirms, "You're correct, AJ. Very good." Mrs. White returns to the board and adds to the example.

Productivity Calculation - (EQ/IQ - Vocation Level) = M-N

Waiter/Waitress
10 - (9-5) = 10 - 4 = Merit Number 6
9 - (9-5) = 9 - 4 = Merit Number of 5
8 - (9-5) = 8 - 4 = Merit Number of 4
7 - (9-5) = 7 - 4 = Merit Number of 3
6 - (9-5) = 6 - 4 = Merit Number of 2
5 - (9-5) = 5 - 4 = Merit Number of 1

4 - (9-5) = 4 - 4 = Merit Number of 1

3 - (9-5) = 3 - 4 = Merit Number 1

2 - (9-5) = 2 - 4 = Merit Number 1

1 - (9-5) = 1 - 4 = Merit Number 1

Mrs. White further explains her example, "As you can see in this chart, we show all ten examples of what AJ's possible Productivity Calculation could be and the resulting Merit Number. As long as a person's Productivity Calculation is at least a 1, they would not be exiled, regardless of the Vocation Level chosen.

"And don't forget the flipside. What if a person with an EQ/IQ of 7 wants to try a Level 9 Vocation? They certainly can; however, this is discouraged and very rare for fear of scoring an extremely low Productivity Calculation. We occasionally do see people jump one or two Vocation Levels above their EQ/IQ, and sometimes they succeed and choose to stay at that higher Vocation Level.

"But their M-N doesn't benefit. The EQ/IQ - Vocation Level can never be a negative number. Here is one last chart of examples. In this case, a person with an EQ/IQ 7 choses a Level 9 vocation. AJ, please continue as I write this on the board."

Productivity Calculation - (EQ/IQ - Vocation Level) = M-N

Biomedics

10 - (7-9) = 10 - 0 = Merit Number 10

9 - (7-9) = 9 - 0 = Merit Number of 9

8 - (7-9) = 8 - 0 = Merit Number of 8

7 - (7-9) = 7 - 0 = Merit Number of 7

6 - (7-9) = 6 - 0 = Merit Number of 6

5 - (7-9) = 5 - 0 = Merit Number of 5

4 - (7-9) = 4 - 0 = Merit Number of 4

3 - (7-9) = 3 - 0 = Merit Number 3

2 - (7-9) = 2 - 0 = Merit Number 2

1 - (7-9) = 1 - 0 = Merit Number 1

AJ continues, "And I also know the theory behind the Vocation Levels. Just like M-N and Productivity Calculation, there are ten levels of vocations.

"The higher the Vocation Level, the lower the percentage of the population that is likely to have the potential to be productive at that level. The curve isn't perfect, but pretty close. I'll write out the scale," AJ explains and approaches the board.

99.9% of the population, that's almost everyone, based on Merit Review EQ/IQ testing, has the potential to achieve a Productivity Calculation 10 at a Level 1 vocation.

Mrs. White interjects, "We must always remember that 0.2% of the population does not have the ability to complete the EQ/IQ Test because of serious mental or physical limitations, and we all pitch in so Amerita can take good care of them too. Continue AJ."

90% of the population, based on Merit Review EQ/IQ testing, has the potential to achieve a Productivity Calculation 10 at a level 2 vocation

80% of the population at a Level 3 vocation

70% of the population at a Level 4 vocation

60% of the population at a Level 5 vocation

50% of the population at a Level 6 vocation

AJ turns to the class, "And this is where the percentages change a little." Before continuing writing, she pauses and thinks of Jake and all the times she pretended to ignore his lectures about the Merit System. She realizes her appreciation for her little brother.

30% of people at a Level 7 vocation

15% of people at a Level 8 vocation

5% of the population, that's 1 out of 20, based on Merit Review EQ/IQ testing, has the potential to achieve a Productivity Calculation 10 at a Level 9 vocation.

1% of the population, that's 1 out of 100, based on Merit Review EQ/IQ testing, has the potential to achieve a Productivity Calculation 10 at a Level 10 vocation.

"And this brings me back to my original question. If I choose Service: Waiter/Waitress, assuming my real EQ/IQ Test is a 9, like my EQ/IQ Pre-Test, and say Nora and Chloe test at an EQ/IQ of 1," AJ pauses and stares at her former friends, enjoying their gasps at feeling insulted.

"And Nora and Chloe choose Service: Waiter/Waitress, and we all achieve Production Calculations of 10, they will have M-N 10s and I'll have an M-N 6. How could that possibly be fair? That sucks."

The classroom sits silent, absorbing all the information. AJ stands still waiting for anyone to comment.

Derrick breaks the silence, "Well, I'll tell you what, I'm considering blowing my EQ/IQ Test, know what I mean? Intentionally doing poorly? Have you considered that option, AJ?"

"I have considered that," AJ answers truthfully. "But I guess my little brother's obsessions with Meritism have actually had an impact on me. You know they claim the EQ/IQ Test can't be faked. Jake told me that he doesn't think the real EQ/IQ Test is anything like the pre-test. But anyone who has taken the real test, when asked by someone who has not taken the real test, well they just say, 'The real test is just like the pre-test.' But I don't buy that. If they were the same, both just done with paper and pen, anyone could blow their test intentionally.

"Watch this … Excuse me, Mrs. White, what is the real EQ/IQ Test like?" AJ asks, hoping for an answer.

"The real test is just like the pre-test," Mrs. White answers, just like Jake explained to AJ, but her crooked smile and quick answer lead AJ and her classmates to believe there's more to the answer that Mrs. White, or any Ameritan citizen who had taken the EQ/IQ Test, is willing to divulge.

"Ha, you see?" AJ questions, "I KNOW there's more to the real test. I mean come on, the real test can't be just paper and pen. And if the test was not extremely reliable, then the Merit Number system wouldn't work and Amerita wouldn't be the best country in the world. "Canada's not bad, but Mexico? China? Anywhere in Asia? Russia? No way would I want to live in any of those countries. A European country, maybe if I had no other choice, but only in England, France, or Spain. The other European countries have a long way to go before their Merit Number systems are perfected."

AJ stands silent for a moment, realizing she just stated that Amerita is a great country, thanks to Meritism.

She begins to wrap up the topic, "So I did my very best on the pre-test at the beginning of the year, believing that the actual EQ/IQ Test can't be purposely blown. This way I have longer to prepare for choosing a Vocation on graduation day. And actually, next week I'm taking my real EQ/IQ Test, and oh my god, I'm so nervous.

"Of course there's always Chloe's brilliant plan. She's going to marry an M-N 10. If she doesn't sink her claws into someone before her first year out of school, she'll probably get herself exiled!" AJ further insults her former friend.

Mrs. White lets the conversation go on just long enough for AJ to get her point across, "Okay, AJ. That's enough."

"Sorry, Mrs. White," AJ apologies without sincerity. "Does anyone have other comments?" AJ is about to return to her seat when she notices, out of the corner of her eye, sitting shyly in the back row, Millie has half-raised her hand.

"Hi, Millie. Please share with us," AJ asks softly, understanding that Millie, having Down Syndrome, often feels insecure to participate. AJ walks over to Millie's desk, puts her arm around her shoulder warmly, and encourages, "What are your thoughts, Millie? I sure would like to hear what your thoughts are."

Millie looks down at her desk.

The class waits patiently for her.

After a few moments of fidgeting nervously, she picks her head up and looks out toward the class.

She begins, "Hi, class. Hi, Mrs. White. Hi, AJ. I scored a 2 on my pre-test. I thought for sure I would score a 1, but I studied really, really hard and got a 2."

Millie turns and looks up to AJ, "And I wanted to say that I think you are so lucky to be able to score a 9. And I hope you become the best scientist in the whole world. Maybe when you become a scientist I could work in your building. I can help in lots of ways. I have been looking at Level 2 vocations, and I think I would be really great at Business Management: Interoffice Mail Delivery."

AJ adds, "And I think you would be the best Interoffice Mail Delivery person in the whole world."

AJ wipes a tear from her eye, feeling so much emotion in Millie's contribution.

Millie continues, "And I want you to know that your EQ/IQ 9 is a really great gift, not a punishment."

AJ hugs Millie with both arms and whispers, "Thank you so much."

Traitor

"Please, friends, this is the time to be totally honest. If any of you are feeling squeamish or having second thoughts about moving forward, please, please speak up. I want all of us to be in this together," Damien pleads for honesty among his board members. "I do understand if you're having second thoughts."

All board members sit around the oval conference table leaning comfortably back in their seats, except Ashley. She sits forward, posture slightly slumped. "Ashley? Are you having second thoughts?" Damien asks, noticing her uneasiness.

"I'm fine, Damien. I'm on board," she quickly fires back, Damien sensing she is annoyed with his questioning. She pictures the horrific scene from last week involving Joshua Campbell and knows Damien's statements are simply a ruse to uncover any defectors.

"Okay, great! Any questions or comments?" Damien asks.

Michael Patterson shouts lightheartedly, "Like my new phone, Damien? It's powered down this time!"

"Thank you, Michael," Damien replies. "Let's start with the Pharmaceutical Chemists. Who would like to report?"

Miriam Chandler volunteers, "All good news, Damien. We conducted all our test scenarios using time-lapse technology and have confirmed that D-EERg will remain viable when diffused in a solution that includes sodium fluorosilicate. The other minerals are inconsequential to the stability of D-EERg.

"The other concern you asked us to investigate was the bioavailable half-life once ingested. Our testing concludes that D-EERg has a half-life of 24 hours. This is 12 hours longer than your initial estimates. We suggest reducing the percentage of D-EERg diffused in sodium fluorosilicate from 5% down to 2.5%. The advantage is that the supply produced will last twice as long."

Damien is very upbeat hearing the good news. "Fantastic! Millhouse, how were we so off on the half-life? Whatever. Never mind. Miriam, you and your team are the experts. We'll go with your numbers.

"Tech? How are my tech guys doing?"

Rashad shares, "Tech is all set. We built up a manufacturing line simulator using VMs on a single server that doesn't have wireless capabilities and was not networked into our system. The virus—"

Damien interrupts, "In English please, and don't call this a virus."

"Okay, sorry sir. We used a fake manufacturing line and all you have to do is plug this thingamajig," Rashad holds up a USB drive, "into the USB plug on any server that's on the manufacturing line."

Damien baits his peers and chuckles at the use of the word thingamajig, "Thingamajig, ha, ha." A few of the other board members chuckle. "What? You think that's funny? Thingamajig? What do you think I am, a child?" Damien sneers. The laughter subsides. "Continue, Rashad."

"Once the thumb drive is plugged into any of the servers on the manufacturing line, the application on the USB drive will create the necessary changes to the PLCs, excuse me, I mean appropriate changes to the sensors and nozzles, and D-EERg will be included along with sodium fluorosilicate into our mineral enhancement formula.

"I'll make the change right after the meeting to accommodate for Miriam's suggested percentage change, and we'll leave the drive with you.

"And here is the second thumb drive," Rashad slides the small device across the table to Millhouse. "Just plug this software data-scrubbing application into any networked server and the acquisitions data in all systems for D-phenylalanine, Levoamphetamine, Fluoride, and Acetaminophenyltrexide will be modified to levels that will not raise any alarms. The acquisitions are complete, correct?" Rashad asks.

Damien clarifies, "Yes, all those acquisitions are complete and received as of last week. Great job, Rashad. I'll feel a lot better knowing this data manipulation has been made. Millhouse, take care of this as soon as we're done here. Next up, Operations."

Michael takes the lead on operations, "All set on operations, Damien. All municipal water supply stations throughout all six regions have been notified by myself and the other five Chief Operations Officers that a new mineral supplement concentrate will be delivered to them beginning on January 2nd, 2052.

"Delivery routes are already planned. The new mineral supplement is scheduled to depart from the Rochester plant on December 31st and loaded onto the cargo plane. The plane departs at 00:00 on January 1st destined for the six regional distribution centers. The first stop will be Buffalo. From the distribution centers, the deliveries will be made by truck.

"Also, as you requested, we've scheduled drivers who are certified to swap out mineral supplement canisters. Our drivers will be instructed to make the swaps when they drop off the new canisters at the water supply stations, ensuring the new mineral supplement concentrate is in place."

"Very good, Michael! Thank you." Damien emphasizes his pleasure at the progress with a round of applause and a pat on the back for Michael as he continuously circles the oval conference table.

"However, we do have one problem." Damien stops behind Ashley and places his hands on her shoulders, very close to her neck. "The problem is," he quietly states and then pauses. Damien can feel Ashley trembling underneath his hands. "The problem is we have too much D-EERg! We were planning to start with a three-month supply, but since Miriam's team discovered we only need a 2.5% solution, that doubles the amount we can produce!

"Well, I guess operations has some homework for the week, folks! Operations, double the capacity of the delivery and notify all the municipal water supply stations that we underestimated our production capacity and will be delivering a six-month supply instead of a three-month supply."

Damien concludes the meeting, "Thank you for attending and we'll see you all on Monday the 18th."

"Excuse me, Damien," Rashad interrupts as his fellow board members already begin to pack up their belongings, "when do you plan to plug in the thumb drive and begin production? And are you sure this one facility can manufacture double what you were planning?"

Damien happily answers his question, "Good question, Rashad. We only needed one week to create the three-month supply, so we're actually going to start production tonight, as soon as you have our thumb drive ready, one week earlier than planned. I love when a plan comes together! Great job, team! See you all next week."

Damien struts to his seat at the head of the table, smacks the button on the EMPuG. He gives Michael two thumbs up, "Okay to turn your phone on, Michael." Michael laughs and appreciates the friendly gesture.

As the board members begin to exit the room, Damien stands in the threshold and gives them all pats on the back and good-job handshakes. He spots Luke down the hall, "Luke, HEY LUKE."

Luke turns and nods letting Damien know he hears him.

"Hey, come clean up the conference room," Damien commands.

Luke pauses for a moment, then heads back to the custodial storeroom to get his cart.

Damien heads to his office, leaving Luke to clean. He sees Ashley is still fumbling with her things, "Bye, Ash. See you next Monday."

When the room is clear, with the exception of Ashley and Luke, she greets him, "Good afternoon, sir."

Luke, taken by surprise with the phrase she used, walks over to Ashley and returns the greeting, "Ma'am, good afternoon." He extends his hand, but instead of shaking his hand, she hands him an upside-down coffee cup. He realizes her greeting was reversed, *Good afternoon, sir* instead of *Sir, good afternoon*.

Ashley subtly taps the bottom of the paper cup and while continuing to hold the cup, asks, "Would you mind throwing this out for me?" She keeps tapping the bottom, making obvious eye contact with him, as Luke's hands grasp the cup. He places the trash into the bin on his cart.

She goes on to tell Luke that she works on the 9th floor in the Operations department and has been a board member for a few years. Surprising to Luke, she also mentions that she remembers reading about his many heroic awards earned as a Merit Agency Investigator. She even mentions specific examples. Her most memorable being the Medal of Valor Luke was awarded for thwarting the hotel conspiracy that was artificially inflating productivity metrics for all their vocationalists.

Luke enjoyed the reminiscing.

As Ashley heads back to the 9th floor, she encourages Luke, "I sure do hope to read about you in the papers again someday."

Luke finishes straightening up the conference room, then pushes his custodial cart to the stairwell landing where he can access the trash chute.

He lifts the trash container from his cart and opens the trash chute. As he begins to tip the container, the writing on the bottom of Ashley's coffee cup catches his eye. Barely legible, obviously written with haste, are the words, "LOOK IN THE VAULT."

Back at his office, Damien locks his office door, slides the *Community Effort* painting to the side, and retrieves the secret phone.

To the man on the other end of the call, he orders, "Keep an eye on Ashley Haynes for me."

Friday

December 15, 2051

Hacker

Jake, Amanda, and Luke wake AJ with a song, singing loudly through her door, "Happy birthday to you. Happy birthday to you. Happy birthday, dear AJ. Happy birthday to you!"

AJ slowly opens her bedroom door and peeks out, "Good morning, guys. That was a much nicer way to wake up than the screaming from next door."

Jake hands AJ a neatly wrapped present. "We picked this out for you. Well, actually Mom picked this out for you."

AJ opens the gift right away, still standing in the threshold, "I absolutely love the outfit! Great choice, Mom. How did you know?"

"I asked Emily what she thought you would like," Amanda admits. "But you know that—"

AJ cuts off her mom politely, "Yes, I know. There are only certain times I can wear these clothes, but that's okay. Mom, thanks so much. I know you guys must have given up something of your own to get this outfit."

"Thank your brother. This was all his idea," Amanda proudly states to let her daughter know about Jake's thoughtfulness. "He suggested that we all pitch in a few articles of clothing from our own allotments to trade for a Sunday outfit for you."

AJ gives Jake a great big hug and a kiss on the forehead.

"Awe, my sister does love me!" Jake jokes lovingly. He shares his knowledge of the Meritism rules regarding clothing, "So, AJ, you can wear this outfit when attending a religious service such as Sunday Mass, or to any family event, including family reunions, weddings, funerals, birthday parties—"

AJ politely interrupts, "Got it, brother. I know I have probably never mentioned this before, but I do appreciate how much you know about Meritism. I have learned a lot from you. And don't ever ask me to admit that again. Hey, Jake, I can wear my new outfit tonight since we're celebrating my birthday, right?"

"Sure can, but the rest of us will all look out of place. That's all right, though, we don't mind."

Luke gives AJ a loving hug, and she surprises him with an affectionate response, "I love you, Dad."

"I love you too, AJ." Luke excuses himself and heads for the door.

Amanda reminds her husband, "Make sure you get home on time today. We don't want to miss our reservation."

Luke gives his wife a kiss and leaves for work.

The 10th floor is very quiet, and Ned informs Luke that most of the staff members are spending the day attending a Human Resources seminar on conduct and behavior at the workplace. Luke thinks to himself, *I hope Damien has a front row seat.*

Noon approaches with a crawl. The repetitive tasks are taking a toll on Luke's tolerance of his assignment. He replays the many dangerous and thrilling events that used to spike his adrenalin when he was a Merit Agency Investigator. He stops reminiscing and reminds himself that he is still a Merit Agency Investigator.

Luke checks the time on his phone frequently and finds that the more he checks the time, the slower time passes.

One activity he enjoys to help pass time is creating Christmas jingle parodies. He sings his latest song quietly to the tune of Jingle Bells, first making sure that nobody else is around to hear:

Sweep the halls,

Mop the halls,

Clean the sinks and toilets!

Oh how much it really sucks,

To kiss Damien's ass all day... Hey!

Noon finally arrives and Ned says farewell for the day. Luke is left with a completed worklist and a free afternoon. He decides to use the opportunity to take a nap.

Luke enters the custodial storeroom and locks the door from the inside. He fashions a bed for himself alongside the two carts by laying down a few layers of cleaning towels for a sleeping pad and stuffing a waste basket liner with crumpled paper towels for a pillow.

His thoughts spin as he lays down on his makeshift mattress.

Looking back on the past two weeks, he questions if there is a threatening conspiracy brewing at Pharmavast. Three deaths. One elderly man, two because of a faulty elevator. Not certain yet if tampering caused the elevator accident. Damien may have actually liked Anne. Coincidence that her laptop was not working and she had to come into the building? Coincidence that board member Millhouse 'fixed' her laptop? Motives? Damien could have found out Anne knew about the oddities in the drug acquisitions. But how would he have known which elevator she was going to choose on the way down and at exactly what time? No second person was seen in the video camera footage, but there definitely were footsteps leading to both roof access hatches. Board meetings every week? Makes sense if preparing for a party I suppose, but why do they all need to be here in person? And Ashley asked me to 'LOOK IN THE VAULT.' What vault? Maybe she was just doodling on her cup?

Luke fights the urge to simply acknowledge all these events as pure happenstance. The temptation to nap and just forget about everything is strong.

He snaps to a sitting position. The image of 'LOOK IN THE VAULT' written on the bottom of the coffee cup will not leave the forefront of his mind. He revisits the memory and concludes, *I'm certain that she was tapping the bottom of the cup. Certain.*

Time for some hacking he decides.

On his second day of work, he noticed several fiber-optic networking cables running through the custodial storeroom. The cables appear to run from inside the firewall, which is probably in the basement, up to the 10th floor.

He double-checks that the door is locked by giving the handle a jiggle. Then he pulls what looks like a deck of cards out of the inside pocket of his winter coat. Sitting on the floor by the back wall where the cables run up and into the ceiling, he begins to assemble the micro laptop.

Eleven components with the combined dimensions of a deck of cards slide out of the box. Nine of the components snap together and form a keyboard. The tenth component, a holographic projector, snaps onto the keyboard providing a 16-inch display. From the back of the holographic projector, a fiber-optic cable is pulled out and crimped onto one of the networking cables using the eleventh component, a fiber-to-fiber adapter.

Luke had preprogrammed the computer to bypass network discovery, and he is confident the connection will not set off any alarms once powered up.

Fingers crossed, he hopes he correctly memorized the complex username and password provided by the Elder last Monday. Memorizing hundreds of lines and multiple songs for community theater productions has always come easily, but he feels overwhelming anxiety from not being able to write down this critical username and password and having to rely on memorization.

The micro laptop boots up flawlessly, prompting for fingerprint, retina scan, or username and password. He types the username,

```
Username: Pharmavast_admin_2051
```

But before typing the password, he realizes the fifth letter from the right could be either the letter O or a zero. An invalid password will probably not set off an alarm but definitely will be logged by the Info Tech department. Luke decides to go with the zero,

```
Password: 9h@rm@c0n!@#
```

Login Successful!

During his first three years as a Merit Agency Investigator, Luke worked on Sub-Level 3, in a cubicle. His assignment was Data-Mining. He spent countless hours wading through files, database servers, and emails. His diligence and success in this area propelled his vocation.

He begins by hunting down the most recent inventory and acquisition data, looking for keywords he remembers from the discussion with Ripley, D-phenylalanine, Levoamphetamine, Fluoride, Acetaminophenyltrexide. A few minutes pass and the data begins to scroll on the holographic display. He pokes his finger at the display and watches the data scroll as if the numbers and letters were going right through his skin. He still finds this technology amazing.

Luke snaps a micro-disk into the keyboard and downloads the inventory data. Then he searches for email account files, locates Damien's and Anne's, and downloads all email activity from the past two months. The time period covers all activity since November 6, 2051, the date on the email Anne turned into the agency. Luke reflects for a moment on how grateful he is for his nearly photographic memory.

Checking the time, he sees the hours have flown by. Only 90 minutes until he would be expected to be seen leaving for the day.

He decides to squeeze in two more searches, laptop repair work orders and building schematics.

The work orders data is found quickly and a search for 'Anne Gonzales' returns no incidents since July 2051. He double-checks, searching again for her recent laptop repair, but still finds nothing.

Finally, he searches for building schematics with the goal of locating a vault. After a half-hour of scouring servers and directories, he finds a folder containing thousands of blueprints and engineering designs. He narrows the search by including the keyword 'vault' and finds a schematic drawing of a Sub-Level in the building with a modified room, but there is no indication of which Sub-Level. The date-time stamp on the file is from the year 2016. The drawing shows a 20x20-foot room with 5-foot-thick outer walls retro-fit from three storage closets. He concludes that must be the vault.

Curious about the vault's security, Luke queries for any purchases with the word *vault*. Seconds later, he finds a single invoice for a Titan 1800 from 2016, the same year as the schematic drawing. Not familiar with that model, he does a quick search using his phone and finds that the vault uses thumbprint security.

Then he hacks into the Human Resources portal using the same username and password that accessed the network. He reviews scheduling data, specifically for security personnel, and discovers the night watchman is not the only person in the building at night. There are also several other shifts scheduled for nighttime security in Sub-Levels 1 to 10.

That makes sense, the Sub-Levels are where they do all the research and manufacturing, Luke figures, but wonders *Why didn't they call Fire and Rescue the night of the elevator accident? They must have heard the crash. Are they expected to never leave their post under any circumstances? I suppose being several floors below maybe they didn't hear anything. Were they in on the sabotage, well, that is, if there was sabotage?*

Luke's thoughts drift momentarily, *I love that song Sabotage!* He reminiscences about a video he made with his dad's help when he was 12 where they used *Sabotage* for the soundtrack. The video is a fake movie trailer about a kid with the superpower to stop time; the kid's name is Justin Time. He laughs to himself thinking how useful that superpower would be right now. Then he begins to think of his dad, and that night he did not show up at the exile gate, and—

The handle to the custodial storeroom jiggles from the outside. Knock-knock. KNOCK-KNOCK-KNOCK!

Luke tears the cable and adapter from the fiber-optic network cable and slides the micro-laptop under Ned's custodial cart. He vigorously rubs his eyes to make them appear red, is about to open the door, and checks to make sure the holographic display is not showing from under the cart. He slowly opens the door, wide enough so the makeshift bedding is visible.

Damien and Luke exchange stares. Damien catches sight of the bedding. "Napping. Must be nice, Three. Learned that from Mr. T, did you? I thought he was joking when he said he was going to show you how to nap on the job. I don't care if he naps—he's like a hundred-years-old."

Luke wrangles his pride, "Sorry, sir."

"Three. Hmm. I like that. I'm going to call you Three from now on. You don't mind, right?" Damien intentionally prods.

"Whatever," Luke replies, coupled with an eye roll as effective as Amanda's.

"Before you go home, clean the men's restroom again, I saw piss on one of the toilet seats," Damien demands. "Don't forget, Three, I'm the one with the final sign off of your Productivity Calculation."

"Sorry, Damien. I'll take care of that before I head out," Luke chokes down his contempt, reminding himself that he is simply playing a role. "Have a nice weekend. See you Monday."

Damien attempts to return an apology. "Yeah, okay. You too. I'm just a bit grumpy. I hate sitting in those seminars all day long when there's so much else to do." He pokes his head into the custodial storeroom and looks around as if he suspects something, then continues complaining as he turns and heads to his office. "And I couldn't sneak in any work because they made me sit in the front row. The front row!"

Happy Birthday

The party of eight occupies all the couches in the lobby leading into Mireille's Maison de Cuisine Française. The brown and gray colors of their outfits are a profound contrast to the vibrant red, yellow, and gold colors decorating the restaurant. AJ is the exception. The shades of purple and pink with highlights of teal that cover her skirt, blouse, and vest are a contrast with both the restaurant's colors and her guests' apparel.

The Maître D' welcomes smaller parties into the dining area and informs AJ, "Miss, your table will be ready soon. We just need to wait for a larger table to become available."

AJ and Emily listen to the brief conversations the Maître D' has with his regular patrons and observe the many M-N 9s and 10s on their hands as they enter the restaurant.

"Welcome, Mr. and Mrs. Phillips. How is the farm holding up this winter?"

"Welcome, Dr. Cooper, Mr. Cooper. Congratulations on your appointment to the head of the surgery department!"

"Welcome, Miss Bennett. So nice to see you again. I hear you are the best housekeeper in town! I'm going to see if I can get you assigned to our house!"

Frederick whispers to Jake, "Dude! Your sister is hot! Thanks for inviting me!"

Jake, uncomfortable with the comment, responds, "Dude, EWW! She's my sister."

Emily nudges AJ and subtly points out that Frederick keeps looking at her. AJ senses they are talking about her and gives Frederick a flirtatious wave. He immediately blushes a shade of red as deep as the colors in the restaurant.

The Maître D' approaches AJ, "Right this way, Amanda. Your mother reminded me that today is your birthday. We let the staff know that you already had the reservation before the M-N 3, so you have nothing to worry about. We hope you have an absolutely wonderful time tonight at Mireille's Maison de Cuisine Française. Do you mind if I announce to the other guests in the dining area that today is your birthday?"

AJ understands why he is asking, "Sure, please do. That's so nobody gives us a hard time, right?"

The Maître D' is relieved that she understands, "Yes. We don't want any misunderstandings that might make your evening unpleasant. This way, please."

He leads the party of eight to their table and announces for all to hear, "May I have your attention please, ladies and gentlemen? Please join me in wishing Amanda Medina a very happy 18th birthday." A round of enthusiastic applause from everyone in the dining room brings a bright smile to AJ's face.

"Oh my god, AJ, this Crème Brûlée is amazing! And the Coq au Vin for dinner, unbelievable," Emily shares her excitement. "I was afraid that all these years of eating porridge may have rendered my taste buds useless."

The parents and AJ laugh at Emily's comments. Jake and Frederick are having their own conversation about video games.

Luke begins post-dinner conversation with the adults while they finish a bottle of wine, "Ward, tell me about the magnet collection on your refrigerator. Jake told me that you have magnets of all 50 States and that you visited them all. Please, I hope you don't find my question belittling, but I've got to know how you managed to do that with an M-N 3?"

Amanda smacks Luke on the shoulder, "That was rude."

June and Ward laugh.

Ward offers a very willing and long-winded answer, "No, Amanda, it's fine. I absolutely love his question! And if you don't mind, I would love to give you the long answer. But first, I think we need another bottle of wine."

"Sounds good to me!" June adds, raising her wine glass. She waves to the waiter and points to the empty glass. The waiter nods with a smile and retrieves another bottle of wine.

"Hawaii and Alaska were a challenge, but the other 48 States were a lot easier," Ward begins. "When June and I were on our first date, we talked for hours and hours until the sun came up. All our conversations were about what we wanted to do while still young. We were in awe at how similar our visions were. The biggest similarity was that we both believed we should live our adventures while we were young and able.

"What was the adventure? Simple. We both wanted to visit all 50 States in Amerita, climb all 46 Adirondack mountain peaks, and visit all 58 National Parks. But to make this happen, we needed two things: time and enough productivity to not get ourselves exiled.

"So we talked for hours, brainstorming how we could do this. And we realized the only way would be to live with M-N 3s and be very creative with lodging, meals, and transportation.

"We fell in love that first night.

"To create time, we worked hard, very hard, for a full 40 hours per week during the months of January, February, March, and April. Then we would take the next eight months and chase after our adventures! Our Productivity Calculations were so high for those first four months, that we could let them slide for the next eight months.

"But travel as an M-N 3 isn't elegant. I remember our trip to the Grand Canyon and the 57 different public transportation buses! We spent three weeks just figuring out the route.

"In the beginning, figuring out routes was almost too challenging. With only half the 50 States on board with Meritism, there was a lot of zig-zagging on our routes. This got easier as time went on and the remaining States shifted to Meritism and joined up with Amerita.

"The trick is to coordinate travel routes with available hotels. Coffin hotels that is."

"Ward," June interrupts, "Don't call them coffin hotels. They are 'Capsule' hotels."

Ward sees Luke and Amanda exchange confusing glances. "Yes, June, capsule hotels. A capsule hotel is, well, imagine a morgue. That's the best way I can describe what these are. You pull out a bed, crawl in, and slide back into the wall. They all have windows at both the head and foot of the 'capsule,' and some of them have nice views of back alleys.

"Meals are easy. All capsule hotels served breakfast, and there are plenty of grocery shops and general stores around.

"There are no M-N restrictions on hiking mountains or visiting National Parks, so that part was easy."

Luke and Amanda, now on the edge of their seats, have lots of questions, "What about Emily and Discovery School and what about Hawaii and Alaska?" Amanda asks.

Ward continues, "We actually did a lot of traveling before Emily was seven-years-old. Once she started school, we limited our travel to when Discovery School wasn't in session, June through August. Emily has been to 27 states and hiked 19 peaks.

"Regarding Alaska, we spent two months just figuring out the public transportation. That one was tough. Two months planning, five weeks travel time, and 30 different Capsule hotels just to get there. Once we arrived, we spent a couple months traveling around the State. We saw whales in their natural habitat. We met Eskimos. We hunted bear! That trip was amazing.

"Regarding Hawaii, about the same travel time to get there, but, well, let's just say, cargo ships. Yep. We traveled on cargo ships. Not very elegant and kinda smelly, but boy, what an adventure. We did Hawaii and Alaska before Emily was born."

Ward concludes, "And that's how you travel!"

Amanda is astonished, "Wow. That's the most amazing thing I've ever heard. Please don't ask us about our vacations, nothing nearly as exciting. We take a couple vacations each year, mostly to the same tropical resorts. Yeah, that's about all. But you two, I mean wow, really, WOW."

June brings Emily into the conversation, "Emily, when you graduate and meet Mr. Wonderful," June pauses and gives Ward an overly exaggerated smooch, obviously trying to embarrass her daughter, "you are going to continue the adventure, right?"

"Uh ... no, Mom. We've had this conversation more than once now. I'm going to be a Veterinarian and won't be able to take that much time off or my surgery skills will suffer," Emily answers.

Luke is quieter for the remaining conversations about kids and vocations. He is feeling dejected by Amanda's reaction to the Mill's adventurous life compared with their rather mundane family outings.

Jake and AJ go to bed as soon as they arrive back at the apartment. The long conversations kept everyone out later than expected.

"I'm going to bed too," Amanda tells Luke.

Luke decides that he is going to do some investigative work, "I'm going to stay up and watch some shows and surf the Internet for a bit."

Once assured Amanda is sound asleep, Luke plugs the micro-disk into his laptop and begins wading through the mounds of data downloaded earlier today.

Hours go by. His eyes are burning. He keeps comparing and contrasting inventory data surrounding D-phenylalanine, Levoamphetamine, Fluoride, and Acetaminophenyltrexide. Nothing stands out. He queries comparisons with previous timeframes and still nothing out of the ordinary, not like the 5,000% increase Anne claimed she saw.

He takes a break from the inventory data and switches to Damien's emails. He searches for 'New Year's Eve Employee Party' and finds the original email Ripley showed him, but no other emails were found with those search words. He tried 'NYE', 'New Year's Eve', 'NYE', '12/31/2051', '1/1/2052', but still nothing other than the original email is returned.

Luke sorts Anne's emails by date descending, looking for any that were sent on the day she died. He finds her very last email from last Thursday, December 7, at 11:59, minutes before the elevator accident. The subject line is, 'Reports for Damien.' He opens the email attachment and sees that it's an inventory report.

Not convinced he will find anything different on this report than the inventory data he has already scrubbed for the past several hours, he considers closing his laptop and going to bed. However, he decides to search the attached report for the words D-phenylalanine, Levoamphetamine, Fluoride, and Acetaminophenyltrexide.

He discovers the acquisition totals on the emailed report from December 7 are 5,000% higher than shown in the data downloaded from this afternoon, exactly as Anne had claimed.

Luke knows without a doubt that someone attempted to scrub the Pharmavast data but forgot about data contained in emails.

Monday
December 18, 2051

Poison and Explosives

Luke kisses Amanda goodbye and reminds her that he is going to meet up with some of the guys after work at a sports bar and watch the Buffalo Bills play in the Monday night football game. She gives him a playful frown, but encourages him to have fun with his new co-workers.

He gives Jake a pat on the head and lets AJ know he remembers this is her big day, "Good luck with your EQ/IQ Test today, AJ. I know you will do great."

She questions, "So, Dad, what should I expect?"

He replies, "The real EQ/IQ Test is just like the pre-test," then scoots out the door quickly before she can question his vague answer. He heads for the bus stop to pick up his newspaper and write his Monday morning note.

AJ tries her mother, "Mom, come on, tell me."

Amanda has the same answer, "Just like Dad said, the real test is just like the pre-test."

The same Elder Luke met two weeks ago is already on the bus. Luke takes a seat next to him and places his newspaper on top of the newspaper already set down next to his seat.

He sits casually, not acknowledging the Elder. Sitting across the aisle on the side-facing seats is the same man Luke saw last week with what he thought looked like a fake M-N. He questions his accusations about the man's fake M-N because in all his years he never saw a counterfeit M-N lower than a 7. *Why would anyone spend time and resources manufacturing fake M-N any lower than a 7? Maybe I'm just getting rusty,* he wonders.

Luke is extremely tempted to ask the man about his vocation to satisfy his own curiosity about his clothes, but he decides not to because he would have to make up some reason why he was curious. He feels badly for making fun of the leather pants and cowboy boots when he saw him last week.

The Elder picks up Luke's newspaper and pretends to read the Sports section.

Anne was correct about the 4 chemicals, 5,000% over average amounts on archived email report from 12/7, but normal levels in all data as of last Friday, extremely suspicious.

Nothing else conclusive.

Have my doubts about Damien. Possibly board member Millhouse in Info Tech is involved.

Need to break into vault, a Titan 1800, will happen tonight. Tell Ripley to keep two-way radio close, I may need to call during the day and will also call at 23:00 when I breach vault.

Leave supplies in backpack behind dumpster in back lot by 13:00 today:

grappling hook, 150-foot capacity

fingerprinting gloves for the Titan 1800

7 canisters of Midazolam gas for anterograde amnesia

head camera

night vision binoculars

voice modulator

stealth suit and black wrestling shoes

micro two-way radio, one for me, make sure Ripley has other

The bus stops, and the Elder exits with Luke's newspaper. The Elder does not give Luke a glance or acknowledge him in any way. At first he wonders if the Elder was not pleased with his report and his work so far. Luke must remind himself that they are covert and need to avoid all signs of being connected.

Luke picks up the Elder's newspaper and opens to the Sports section.

Joshua Campbell blood sample, positive for Caffeineeoxx.

Elevator scrapings positive for Thermite.

Great work, you must find out what they are planning.

Next contact, Tuesday 12/26, not Monday.

Video footage on micro-disk of hallway in Hospital where night watchman died.

Reminder, do not attempt any contact with Elders outside of transportation bus, population must never know we run covert operations.

Luke's worklist is complete, and unfortunately Ned already cleaned Damien's office this morning. He hopes for an opportunity to enter the boardroom and lift a fingerprint from Damien to use on the Titan 1800.

Ned has left for the remainder of the afternoon. Luke checks the time and expects the backpack is waiting for him behind the dumpster. Taking the stairs to avoid being noticed, he finds the backpack just as expected and returns to the custodial storeroom. He hangs the backpack on the coat rack, placing his winter coat over the backpack.

Next, he heads for a bathroom stall with his phone, the micro-disk from this morning, and an ear piece. He is hesitant to spend any time in the custodial storeroom after the close call with Damien on Friday.

He bends down and looks for feet in stalls. All the stalls are empty, so he takes a seat in the furthest one away from the door and starts playing the security camera footage using his phone.

Thankfully, the footage has already been clipped to show only the timeframes when someone enters or exits Willy's hospital room. The audio is miscellaneous conversations and pleasantries as people walk through the hallway. There is never video or audio recorded from inside the room for privacy reasons.

The total duration of the combined clips is four minutes, and only doctors and nurses entered and exited the room. Luke feels badly for Willy because no family or friends stopped by to check on him.

After watching the video three times, Luke is convinced there is nothing helpful to be found. He is still alone in the bathroom and decides to listen to the audio only, and not watch. This is an investigative method he was taught by his mentor, Kesuke Ripley.

Luke closes his eyes, covers his left ear with his hand, and cups his right ear with his other hand to filter outside noise from interfering with the audio from the single ear piece.

Conversations, doors opening and closing, footsteps, phones ringing and beeping, an announcement over the loudspeakers, single footsteps, clacking, no doors or conversations or phones, clack-clack-clack.

Luke opens his eyes. The video clip staring back at him is from mid-afternoon and a doctor, presumably a doctor, with a long white coat and stethoscope around his neck, walks the length of the hallway and enters Willy's room. The doctor's back is to the camera the whole time. The frame-time advances two minutes, and the doctor exits the room and continues walking in the direction where his back is still to the camera. Clack-clack-clack.

Luke feels chills when he realizes the distinct sound of this man's boots closely matches the sound he remembers of the maintenance man's boots, the maintenance man who walked into the lobby the night of the elevator accident. *Coincidence?* he contemplates.

Exiting the bathroom hastily, Luke heads for the custodial storeroom. He pulls the mini-disk from underneath his cart, hidden and secured with a few strips of duct tape. He pops the mini-disk into the other slot on his phone and queues up the segment from Thursday night.

This is a long-shot, he thinks.

Comparing the two videos side by side, he detects an identical cadence of steps, identical build and height, and identical hair color and length. The clack-clack sounds are similar but not identical probably because the flooring surfaces are not the same.

He zooms in on both videos, looking for an identifying tattoo or mark of any kind on his hands. He finds nothing definitive.

The maintenance man had an M-N 4 on his hand. There is no M-N on the right hand of the doctor. He cannot see the back of the doctor's left hand because of the camera angles. Desperate to see the M-N and determine if the numbers match, he watches the video frame by frame.

Just as the doctor turns into Willy's room, he passes a fire extinguisher door inset into the wall. The reflection from the plastic covering of the door reflects the man's left hand. No M-N.

Luke is aware that when entering a hospital as an employee, including doctors and nurses, or as a volunteer, your M-N remains visible. Enter as a patient or a visitor and your M-N number is disabled. He concludes, without a doubt, that this man is not a doctor.

He removes both mini-disks, wraps them in a small piece of paper, and duct tapes them to the bottom of his custodial cart. Then he exits the custodial storeroom, realizes he had not locked the door, and breathes a sigh of relief.

EQ/IQ Test

AJ energetically hops off the transportation bus and walks up to the entrance of the Merit Agency. She stops for a moment to read the directory and sees the EQ/IQ Testing Department is in the basement.

Nervousness sets in for the first time. She has looked forward to this day and now reels with uncertainty, wondering if she should have waited until the end of her time in Discovery School instead of being one of the first of her classmates to take the test. Her energetic jaunt slows to a purposeful slow walk.

She opts to take the stairwell to the basement instead of the elevator because she can walk as slowly down the stairs as she pleases. Eventually she reaches the basement and the EQ/IQ Testing Department.

She pushes open the heavy steel door and thinks to herself, *I could really slam this door!*

In front of her is a dimly lit hallway that stretches what seems to be the full length of the Merit Agency building. The small number of light bulbs on the ceiling flicker subtly inside their wire encasements. Judging the distance to the end of the hall is challenging because the ceiling, walls, and floor are all the same color, dim gray. She thinks the number of doors along the two sides of the hallway is very limited for such a long hallway.

The only fixture breaking up the deserted hallway is an a-frame stand with a poster-board sign. On the sign are names, numbered 1 to 10. Below the names is the verbiage, EQ/IQ Test Time: 08:00. Her name is next to number 7. She realizes there are ten doors, five on each side of the hallway, equally spaced.

AJ walks up to the first door on the left side. The door has no window, just a door knob and a sloppy hand-painted #1. The number is a slightly darker shade of gray than the door, almost not visible because the colors are so similar.

"What the heck," she mutters under her breath. "This is frigging creepy."

She closely observes each door, wondering why the numbers were painted so sloppily. Half-way down the hall, she reaches door #7 and hears a sound behind her. She looks over her shoulder and sees there is another student standing at the poster-board looking for his name, but he turns and gets back in the elevator.

AJ apprehensively turns the knob on door #7, pushes the heavy steel door open, and steps into a small reception area, cramped with chairs and a single coffee table. There are no other Discovery School students waiting in the room.

She looks around and sees a conservatively dressed woman, about her mom's age, sitting behind the glass window of a reception office. Chairs line the walls, nothing is placed on the coffee table, the monitor mounted on the wall is turned off, and the magazine racks in each corner are empty. The room, much like the hallway, is pristine, however, dreadfully plain. There is no color other than varying shades of off-white, slightly brighter than the hallway. There are no paintings on the walls. The only break in the walls is an irregularly narrow door to the left of the monitor.

The receptionist does not notice AJ walk in and is startled when she taps on the glass.

AJ speaks through the glass, "Hi, I have my EQ/IQ Test at 08:00 today."

The receptionist slides the glass open, "Oh, ha ha. So sorry, dear. I didn't hear you come in. Give me either hand, please." AJ obliges and the receptionist holds her hand firmly and swiftly wraps a black band around AJ's wrist. "Please have a seat. We'll be with you shortly. The band is just so everyone knows who you are, dear." She points to her nametag, announces "My name is Mrs. Stanfield," then slides the glass closed and returns to her administrative tasks.

AJ sits in the thinly padded chair behind the coffee table and places her coat in the seat next to her. Glancing at the black band, she sees her name prominently displayed in white lettering.

She is extremely disappointed. Her preconception of the EQ/IQ Testing Department was different in every way possible. No happy students waiting with her for their test to begin, no endless supply of snacks and drinks, no flowers, no congratulatory reception.

She waits patiently for a few minutes, watching the clock on the wall positioned directly in front of her. Just as she decides to pull some homework out of her backpack, the receptionist slides the glass open and insists, "Excuse me, dear. Could you please hand me your backpack?"

AJ obliges, hands her backpack to the receptionist through the open class, and asks, "Sure, no problem. But why?"

The receptionist gently places AJ's backpack on the floor behind her as she says "Thank you, dear. Just a little while longer before they're ready." She then slides the glass shut.

Concerned that other things might be confiscated too, AJ carefully retrieves her phone from her front pocket and props up her coat to keep it hidden. She keeps her sigh silent when she sees that there is no cell reception in the basement.

AJ looks up to the clock, 08:15, and can't believe only 15 minutes have passed. It feels to her more like an hour. Not sure if approaching the receptionist is a good idea or not, she decides to take her chances. Tap-tap ...

The receptionist slides the glass open with a scowl that forcefully flips to a smile when she begins to speak, "Yes, dear?"

"Excuse me, but I was wondering if I could connect to the Wi-Fi?" AJ asks with trepidation.

She answers, "Sorry, dear. We don't have public Wi-Fi. Security you know!" then shuts the glass before AJ has time to question further.

08:17

08:20

08:23

...

08:37

The minute hand on the clock seems to stand still.

AJ approaches the glass window and stands with a smile for a minute before the receptionist looks up and opens the glass. "Yes, dear? How long have you been standing there, silly girl? Just tap on the glass next time."

"Would I be able to turn on the monitor and watch a show?" AJ asks.

"Absolutely! Here you go," she cheerfully exclaims as she hands AJ a remote control. "Should be any time now, dear," she adds before swiftly closing the glass window.

AJ slouches in the thinly padded chair, fighting to find a comfortable position. She points the remote at the monitor and presses the On button, but nothing happens. She walks closer, presses the button again, and still nothing. She holds the remote right up to what appears to be an infrared receptor on the monitor, presses the On button one last time, and nothing. She feels the perimeter of the monitor for an on switch, but there isn't one.

Oh, come on! she thinks to herself, making sure not to vocalize the frustration.

She turns and glances at the receptionist, who is not looking up, starts walking toward the glass window, but turns at the last minute concerned about interrupting the receptionist again. She heads back to her seat and sits in silence.

08:50

08:55

09:00

AJ takes a deep cleansing breath, approaches the glass window, and taps so lightly with a single finger that the receptionist does not hear the noise. Her head is still looking intently at the tablet on her desk.

AJ takes another deep breath and taps with a little more force.

The receptionist looks up and grimaces, glaring at AJ for a few seconds before smiling and sliding the glass door open, "Yes, dear?"

"I'm sorry about bothering you again, ma'am. But if you don't mind, could you give me an idea about what time you think they will be ready for me?" Amanda asks with extreme caution.

The receptionist, without looking away from Amanda, replies, "Good news, Amanda! They are ready for you. Thank you very much for waiting, dear."

AJ expresses her appreciation, "Thank you, Mrs. Stanfield." AJ looks over her shoulder toward the door to the left of the monitor. The door opens outward to darkness. She stands still and hesitates.

"Go on, dear. They are waiting for you," Mrs. Stanfield prompts. "I'll hold on to your backpack for you. Why don't you hand me your phone too? Good luck." She leaves the glass window open and AJ hands her the phone.

AJ takes one step into the darkness and the door slams behind her. She can see nothing but hears someone pleading, "No! Please no! Let me try again." The pleading fades quickly. A voice in the darkness from several feet away, just loud enough for her to hear, whispers, "Come on, she's here. Next time keep the door shut."

She stands frozen.

Three spot lights burst into the darkness shining on three people standing on the far wall, about 20 feet in front of her. Each spotlight shines on a person, and all three are wearing the same apparel, loose-fitting gray slacks and white button-down dress shirts with the Ameritan flag above the left pocket. The woman in the middle has long silver-gray hair pulled into a single braid. The men on either side each stand in front of a door. The door on AJ's left looks like the front door of an elegant home. The door on her right looks like the entrance to a classroom.

"Hi, Amanda. Welcome to your EQ/IQ Test," the woman standing in the middle between the two doors begins. "This room is your challenge. If you choose the correct door, then we'll be assured of your commitment to doing your very best on the rest of the test. If you choose incorrectly, we'll have to conduct the rest of the test using alternative methods to ensure you are doing your very best. These alternative methods can be quite unpleasant and, unfortunately but unavoidably, sometimes painful. And AJ, we want you to know these methods are not easy for us to administer because we care about you very much. Please believe that we have your best interests in mind, as do your parents. They agreed to leave you in our care, knowing fully what could transpire today."

AJ is about to ask a flurry of questions when the woman continues without letting AJ speak, "We are not accepting questions at this time. Listen carefully." AJ stands with her mouth still half open, frozen just before trying to speak.

The woman points to both men, one on her left and one on her right, and explains, "One man will always tell the truth. One man will always lie. You can ask one of them one question. Then you must make your decision. You have as much time as you need to ask your question and make your choice."

AJ takes several deep breaths and performs a relaxation technique she learned from Muay Thai classes with her father.

Then she sits with her legs crisscrossed underneath her, closes her eyes, rests her hands in her lap, and begins thinking ...

30 minutes pass.

AJ does not move. She has no idea how much time has passed.

Another hour passes.

The woman and the two men stand stoically.

Another hour passes.

The impeccable silence is broken as AJ quietly and calmly asks her question, eyes still shut, "Sir on my left, if I ask the person on my right what door will prevent me from having to do the test using alternative methods, what door will that person tell me to use?"

She opens her eyes and the man on her left looks directly at her and answers without hesitation, "The man on your right will tell you to enter his door."

AJ jumps up from her crisscross seated position and walks briskly to the door on her left that looks like the entrance to an elegant home. The man in front of that door quickly steps to the side and AJ swings the door wide open and walks in without hesitation. Bright light from a perfectly white room floods in, and she squints from being in the dark for three hours. She accidentally slams the door shut behind her with an echoing bang that seems to shake the floor and walls.

She finds herself in a room that looks like the rooms she has seen on broadcasts of Merit Number Reviews, except the furnishings are different. The tiled floor is the same gray color as the single chair and desk placed in the center of the room; the ceiling and walls are white and void of decorations. The outline of the door she entered through, a single ventilation grate at the base of the floor next to the door, and a white loud speaker centered on the ceiling are the only items that disturb the solid-white surfaces.

AJ walks to the desk. A paper test and five sharpened pencils with erasers are the only items on the desk. Her name has already been filled in at the top.

Before pulling out the chair, she reads the first question out loud, "Why did you pick that door? Please explain in detail." She sits, picks up one of the pencils, and begins writing several sentences to explain her logic.

Flipping through the remaining pages, she sees questions very similar to the questions on the paper EQ/IQ Pre-Test. AJ begins answering the questions, taking her time to print neatly.

She takes another hour to complete the test. When complete, she places the pencil softly on the desk, folds her arms, and breathes a sigh of relief.

Without warning, another door emerges from the solid white wall in front of her and a dozen adults, all dressed in loose-fitting gray slacks and white button-down dress shirts with the Ameritan flag embroidered above the left pocket, enter the room clapping with resounding energy. They encircle AJ, still sitting in the desk, and continue clapping for what seems to be several minutes.

Mrs. Stanfield puts her arm around AJ and gives her a big hug, "Amanda, I'm so proud of you! You did great. Just great."

AJ sits around a meeting table with Mrs. Stanfield and three other Merit Agency EQ/IQ Test Moderators. The mood is very relaxed. AJ munches on endless snacks and sips from a tall glass of water.

Mrs. Stanfield begins the conversation, "Amanda, we all had such high hopes for you, and you fulfilled our hopes to a degree well beyond our expectations."

"Umm ... okay. I waited in a lobby, figured out a riddle, and took what seems to be just about the same test I took at the beginning of the school year. I'm really not sure what I did that was so amazing," she questions.

Mrs. Stanfield smiles and shows her excitement for revealing the secrets of the EQ/IQ testing, "You just sit back and listen to everything I have to tell you. I'm willing to bet you won't even have any questions, but if you do, just stop me and ask your questions.

"Let's talk about the IQ portion of the test first, that's easy to measure. The band on your wrist measures pulse rates, perspiration, and I don't know how the tech works, but it also measures brainwave patterns. That is how we can be assured someone is not intentionally trying to do poorly on the IQ test. If the IQ test score is low and brainwave patterns indicate only partial use of mental capacity, we adjust the IQ test score accordingly. Like I said, that part is easy. We also have reports from all your mentors since you started school. We easily know if someone is intentionally trying to do poorly on the test."

AJ giggles thinking back to the conversation where her classmates talked about the strategy of trying to intentionally blow the IQ portion.

"I bet I know why you are laughing. Some of your friends probably suggested you intentionally do poorly on purpose, right?" Mrs. Stanfield asks.

Through a mouth full of snacks, AJ confirms with another giggle, "Yep!"

"And now for the EQ portion of the testing," Mrs. Stanfield enthusiastically states, "Emotional Quotient Testing, my favorite part! We can't measure EQ accurately by conducting a paper test.

"We measure seven areas of Emotional Quotient: Independence, Assertiveness, Self-Actualization, Empathy, Social Responsibility, Tolerance and Impulse Control, and Adaptability and Problem Solving under Stress."

AJ interrupts with her first question, "I've got to know right away though because I'm so curious, what's up with the creepy hallway?"

"Independence, that one is always fun to watch. Yes, we watch you guys. Lots of students don't even make the walk to their assigned room. They find the hallway frightful. Oftentimes they go to the 1st floor lobby and ask if they are in the correct building, even after they see their name on the poster-board. Then they ask if someone will accompany them to their assigned room. Many times students leave and come back with their parents. All students are nervous, we know that. But throw in a creepy basement hallway and that nervousness is amplified.

"The creepy hallway thing is really minor. We mostly measure independence with input reported by those in your life. You too will be asked to report on these measures regarding the students you interact with after graduating Discovery School. I like to say, it takes a village!

"Here are a couple examples. Your Muay Thai instructors frequently boast about your independence and how you are not afraid of taking on the teachings of a male-dominated discipline. However, your Discovery School Mentors have reported on your tendency to follow, without questioning, the direction of those two friends of yours, Nora and Chloe. Overall, your independence score is above average.

"Assertiveness, like some of the other measures, comes from input. We have many examples of your demonstrated assertiveness. The most recent was reported to us from your bus driver, Mr. Sargent. He dropped off a note about your interaction with Shawn on the bus, the time you challenged him to a fight. We do not condone violence in any way, and we were happy to hear you called off the challenge. We did increase your assertiveness score after that interaction.

"Self-Actualization, that's about how much you truly want to do your very best. We love that you scored so high on your pre-test. That tells us you really do want to fulfill your full potential.

"Empathy, my favorite. This one is difficult to capture, but last week your interaction with Millie as described to us by Mrs. White was wonderful.

"We see these turning points as youth approach Discovery School graduation. We're very excited to see so much potential developing in you over just these past few weeks.

"Social Responsibility. Honestly, AJ, we didn't see much here. We are hopeful you will start to do more volunteer work and get involved with some school organizations.

"Tolerance and Impulse Control. You aced this one. Most students last about 20 minutes in my waiting room before threatening to call their parents. Many of them are rude and bang on my glass. But not you. I love the way you gently tapped on my glass. And you were so polite. Excellent job on Tolerance and Impulse Control, dear.

"Adaptability and Problem Solving under Stress. Again, aced. Only 1 in 200 students provides a sensible answer on the test regarding how they reasoned picking the correct room."

"Wow. I don't know if I should be angry or happy. I'm going with happy. I understand. Well, almost. Now my questions. What do you do with those who pick the wrong door?" AJ asks with heightened curiosity.

Mrs. Stanfield discloses, "Every door leads to the same style room, white room with a paper test on a desk. That plea you heard was staged. You should read some of the creative answers students come up with for how they were able to pick the correct door after having made a blind choice. Once in a great while a student will be honest and write down that they just guessed."

Next AJ asks with sadness in her eyes, "What about students like Millie? How can you justify giving her that riddle and putting her in that situation?"

Mrs. Stanfield discloses more secrets, "We 'adjust' the tests, Amanda. Millie will only wait briefly in the waiting room. We'll give her a riddle that we feel she'll be able to solve. We tell her nothing about having 'alternative methods' of testing.

"We gave you a tough riddle, one of the toughest we have. The true challenge is to adapt and solve a problem in a stressful situation."

AJ reflects on the EQ portion of the test and decides she needs an important clarification, "Wait, I have one more question, actually a concern I guess. How can you keep opinions out of scoring the EQ? We've all been taught that the Merit Agency relies on factual data only for everything from setting the Vocation Levels to calculating Production Calculations. But with E/Q, you can't measure Empathy or Social Responsibility or—"

Mrs. White softly interrupts, "Correct, Amanda ... sort of. You are correct that we can't measure Empathy. Empathy does not increase or decrease your E/Q test score. Maybe we'll figure that one out someday. However, we do have algorithms for measuring the other six EQ factors. I'll give you a couple examples. How many times did you tap on my glass window? And when you did tap on my window, was your heart rate elevated? Both are measurable facts. We run those numbers against our algorithms using years of data collection and billions of data points."

Mrs. White hands AJ a fairly thick book, "Here. This is your Merit Agency handbook. The book provides full transparency into how every Vocation Level, every Productivity Contribution Score, and every Merit Number is calculated. For obvious reasons, we do not include information about the EQ/IQ testing."

"When will I know my score?" AJ asks, her voice slightly trembling.

"9, Amanda. A 9," Mrs. Stanfield unveils. "I will not say congratulations. Do you understand why?"

"I think so. I'm a 9 because I'm a 9. I have the emotional and mental capacities to be productive in a Level 9 vocation. Did I work for a 9? Well, not really. The 9 represents a combination of qualities and traits about me that will apply to the productivity our society can expect from me," AJ surprises herself with the depth of her answer. "The 9 does not mean I am better than anyone else. The 9 just means I should be productive at a Level 9 vocation."

"Now I will congratulate you, Amanda. This is what we all hoped for. Not that you would achieve a 9, but that you would understand what your score represents. Congratulations, dear!" Mrs. Stanfield gives AJ another big hug.

"Do you understand why you must always say the pre-test is just like the real test?" Mrs. Stanfield questions.

"Absolutely," AJ agrees. "The pre-test is just like the real test."

Before Mrs. Stanfield concludes the meeting, she asks one last time, "Amanda, any last questions?"

"Umm, yes, actually. What happens when someone takes the test and is angered and doesn't understand the importance of what happens here?" AJ asks.

"Great question and one I hate to answer, but I'm glad you asked because we needed to tell you this anyway." Mrs. Stanfield pauses. "If the Merit Agency ever finds out that someone who took the real test tells anyone who has not taken the real test what transpires here, that person and the people they tell will be exiled permanently. How do you feel about that, Amanda?"

"Harsh." AJ pauses to contemplate the consequence. "I do understand, Mrs. Stanfield. Harsh, but I can see why exile is a necessary threat.

"You know what really worries me, Mrs. Stanfield? Many of my classmates feel they're entitled to the M-N their parents earned. I'm not sure how they will react after realizing they actually have to work for their own M-N. I guess we'll just have to wait and see how that plays out."

Logistics

"Good news, team!" Damien announces, walking confidently around the oval conference table, his team constantly shifting in their seats to follow him. "One week of production complete and one more to go. Michael, where are we with logistics to handle doubling the supply?"

Michael informs the team, "All set, Damien. We doubled the allotment of delivery trucks and doubled the scheduled staff for the first week of January. Ashley, how did you make out on securing the larger cargo plane?"

"All set. We're going to use a drone plane because of the increased onboard cargo space. Damien, are you okay with drone cargo planes?" Ashley asks.

Damien, looking slightly disappointed, approves the change, "Hmm. I suppose that will be fine. You know I get nervous about drone planes. I'm sure that will be fine, Ash. Make sure everything is in place for December 26th. I want to start transporting the canisters to the cargo plane first thing in the morning. They need to be loaded up by end of day Friday. Cargo plane departs at the stroke of Midnight on January 1st, 2052! We're the only ones who know these logistics, and let's keep it that way."

Millhouse, anxious for his contribution, arrogantly jumps into the conversation, "And good news from Info Tech, sir! We reviewed the databases after running Rashad's data-scrubbing software application, and I'm happy to report all inventory levels and acquisitions of D-phenylalanine, Levoamphetamine, Fluoride, and Acetaminophenyltrexide have all been set to normal levels."

Damien interrogates Millhouse's results, "Great job, Rashad and Millhouse. Question Rashad, you also included a spider in your application that searches email threads for attachments that may contain that inventory data too, correct?"

Rashad pauses, then answers, "Yes. Yes, we did," lying to Damien for fear of what would happen if he admitted to making such a huge oversight. He breathes a sigh of relief that Damien's back was to him when he answered. He wipes his brow before Damien turns the corner and faces his direction.

"Chemists?" Damien asks, "What do you have to report on the long-term effects of D-EERg?"

Miriam fills the board members in on her team's findings. "We underestimated another variable, the effects of the increase in Fluoride. This is likely due to the improved half-life of the solution. We implemented our time-lapse methodology with the chimpanzees and found that the Fluoride stunted their creativity by 30% more than expected over a simulated three-month period. They experienced more difficulty with creative problem solving."

"And the downside?" Damien asks rhetorically. "Actually, I think those results sound encouraging." Damien focus on Ashley, "Do you agree, Ash?"

Ashley, doing her best to hide her distress, agrees, "Absolutely." For a moment, she regrets passing the message 'LOOK IN THE VAULT' to Luke for fear of Damien. She has doubts that Luke actually picked up on the message anyway.

Damien concludes the meeting, "Great job, team. I have some news you will all like! The next meeting is Sunday, New Year's Eve, just before the party. Everything is in motion, and I'm giving you all Christmas Day off!"

Luke is headed toward the custodial storeroom to drop off his cart, purposely taking the longer route to pass by the boardroom. There is a meeting concluding at 17:00. He still has not lifted

Damien's fingerprint and is hopeful that the boardroom will have a print. He considers pushing the vault breach to later in the week, but the most difficult part would be coming up with another believable excuse and alibi.

As he passes by the boardroom, Damien is exiting wearing his pale-orange suit jacket. "Sorry about the whole 'Three' thing last Friday, but if you could, please clean my boardroom before you head out for the day."

Luke simply replies with a quick nod. Damien struts out of the dimly light boardroom, sun almost set outside the floor-to-ceiling windows.

Yes! Luke thinks to himself. He knows the time is now or never. Already having the micro two-way radio in place, the pencil eraser-sized earpiece tucked into his left ear, and the microphone under his collar, Luke calls, "Ripley come in."

"Go, Luke." Luke is relieved to hear his mentor's voice.

"I'm in the boardroom, and there's a phone in here where Damien was sitting and I need a fingerprint. Not sure the phone is his, but let's lift the prints anyway." Luke slips the snug-fitting black fingerprinting gloves onto his hands.

"Tap the phone's home button. There's always a fingerprint on the home button," Ripley instructs.

Luke thinks quickly. Damien's M-N is on his right hand, his dominant hand. He switches the phone to his right hand, and taps the home button with his right thumb. The phone turns. "Good news, the phone belongs to Damien. Do we have his thumb print now?"

"Give it a sec, the prints aren't validated immediately ...," then silence is on both ends of the radio.

"Damn! I can see that frickin orange jacket coming down the hall. He's probably looking for his phone," Luke whispers into the two-way radio.

"And ... and ... come on ... got it! Confirmed thumb print of right hand. Don't take the glove off yet! The data has to transfer back to the glove, and the thumbprint must be completely formed while your hand is still in the glove or the print won't work," Ripley warns.

Before Luke could place the phone back on the table, he felt someone touch him on the shoulder.

He turns around and sees Damien's devilish face. "I forgot my phone."

"Oh, yes. Sorry, sir." Luke is almost at his limit with having to suck up to Damien but knows he can't blow his cover. Grudgingly, he adds, "I was going to bring the phone to Tiffany so she could find out who it belongs to."

He hands Damien the phone.

"What's with the gloves?" Damien asks suspiciously.

Luke freezes and feels sick to his stomach certain his cover is blown.

Damien snickers, "Ha, never mind. You look embarrassed, Luke. I forgot about the gloves. Mr. T already warned me to not to be surprised if you start wearing gloves all the time when you clean. He told me your secret ... Germaphobe." Damien reaches out to touch Luke's cheek and withdraws just as he is about to make contact, teasing Luke about what he believes is his phobia. "Luke, you might as well head out for the day. By the way, how is your 'new' home? Is your family enjoying Village Garbage?"

Luke struggles to refrain from knocking Damien on his ass but manages to stay in character.

The Vault

Luke locks himself in the custodial storeroom. The business day is over, and he is not concerned about being interrupted. He preps another makeshift bed and lays down to think. He turns off the light to help focus his thoughts. The closet is almost totally dark except for the sliver of light from underneath the door. He is reminded of a desensitization chamber he once experienced.

He reviews the facts.

Elevator was a trap. Thermite. Conclusive. Anne worked in Acquisitions and accidentally received an email that made her suspicious. Damien took her on a date and has an alibi. He was not in the building that night. Damien asked her to run reports for him the night she died. Her laptop was not working so she had to go into the office. Millhouse supposedly fixed the laptop, but there were no work orders for that fix. Theory, Damien and Millhouse got her to the building through a cleverly masked set of consequences.

Millhouse, or someone else in Info Tech, must have had something to do with the inventory data scrubbing. No doubt that the acquisitions and inventory data were manipulated.

Willy was collateral damage. Wrong place at the wrong time asking the wrong questions. Theory, killed by the maintenance man/man posing as doctor. Theory, maintenance man rigged both elevators and detonated the thermite on the one Anne chose to use. Was he watching from a dark corner on the 8th floor? Doesn't matter how. He must have been onsite, watching. There were footprints leading to each hatch on the roof. Frick! That means he has access to this closet.

Luke scrambles to his custodial cart and pulls off the two micro-disks from underneath. He smashes them on the floor with a hammer and tosses the fragments into the cart's wastebasket.

He returns to his review of the facts.

Caffeineeoxx. Luke turns on his phone, glowing brightly in the dark closet, and searches for Caffeineeoxx. The resulting information was surprising. The drug failed Governance approval because the artificially enhanced caffeine derivative was over 100 times more potent than organic caffeine. Small dosages caused arrhythmic heart attacks in primates. The drug was never tested on human subjects. Governance approval requests were submitted by Damien Myers, Pharmavast Chemist.

Luke reviews one last thought, *And then there was Ashley. The note on the bottom of her coffee cup.* He stares at the dark for a few more minutes, then puts his plan in motion.

First, he leaves the hatch to the roof unlatched.

Next, he strips down and puts on the black stealth suit, then puts his custodial uniform back on.

With his winter coat on and backpack of spy gear slung over his shoulder, he takes the elevator to the 1st floor and leaves the Pharmavast building, headed for The Clinton Square Sports Bar to set up his alibi.

"Luke!" he hears the group of custodial staff cheer when he enters the bar. He enjoys the company of his colleagues who are assigned to the other floors at the Pharmavast building.

"Surprised you decided to join us, son! Glad to see you!" Ned, holding a frosty mug half full of beer, welcomes Luke.

Luke walks up to Ned, smirks, and shakes his head, "Germaphobe? Where do you come up with this stuff, Mr. T? Are you my guardian angel or something?"

"Something like that, Luke," Ned confesses, then retracts with laughter, "Ha, ha, ha, guardian angel. Hey guys! Do I look like a guardian angel?"

The colleagues from the 9th floor jest, "No, not a guardian angel. But you do look like our grandfather!"

Luke drops the guardian angel questioning, knowing he will never get a straight answer.

He hangs his backpack on a nearby hook and hangs his winter coat over the backpack. *Hidden in plain sight*, he tells himself.

Luke's next few hours are filled with billiards, cheering on the Buffalo Bills, and doing everything possible to avoid consuming alcohol. He enjoys watching Ned flirt with women half his age and listening in on his introduction, "Hi, I'm Ned I. Tammarin, the I is for Intoxicated!"

He checks his phone, 22:54, puts on his jacket, and slings the backpack over his shoulder. "Hey, guys, I've got to get going, need to catch the 23:00 bus. Do me a favor and make sure Mr. T sets his car to auto-navigate, he shouldn't be self-driving tonight."

"Better run or you will miss your ride! Tell your wife and my kids I said hello!" jokes his friend from the 9th floor.

Perfect Timing, Luke thinks to himself as he rounds the corner, reaching the side of the Pharmavast building. The 11:00 bus is departing, setting up the next hour of his alibi, waiting for the next bus.

He cautiously walks along the narrow alley and reaches the dumpster in the back of the building, slips behind the dumpster, takes off his coat and uniform, and pulls the black hood and face covering over his head. He opens the backpack and prepares his gear. He slides the voice modulator, his favorite piece of gear, into place inside the face covering, and seals the gas filter over the mouth and nose.

Luke straps on the grappling harness, stuffs the Midazolam gas canisters into the pockets on the back of the stealth suit, and puts on the head camera.

And last, the fingerprinting gloves.

He tests the two-way radio that is built into the stealth suit, "Ripley, you there?"

"I'm here. You sure you want to do this, Luke?" Ripley asks.

Luke reinforces to Ripley that the breach is crucial, "Yes. I have a ton of evidence, but no clue, none, about what they may be planning. The vault is my last lead. There are no cameras in the stairwells or the basement hallway. When I get to the Sub-Levels, I'll need you to disrupt the cameras. Might need some help unlocking some doors too. You all hacked in?"

"Affirmative," Ripley assures.

Luke visualizes the breach several times before pulling the trigger on the grapple gun, sending the hook ten stories high.

Grapple to roof.

Enter through custodial storeroom hatch.

Crawl on floor to stairwell to avoid tripping lights.

Take stairwell to basement.

Enter basement hallway and gain access to the Sub-Levels.

Search Sub-Levels and find the vault.

Toss Midazolam canister into hallways to induce anterograde amnesia.

Kick some ass!

Nobody dies.

Enter vault with thumbprint.

Photograph all documentation.

Take stairwell back to 10th floor.

Crawl to custodial storeroom to avoid tripping lights.

Rappel to ground.

Put clothes back on.

Catch 00:00 bus.

He reaches the steel door to the basement, the lowest level accessible by the stairwell. The door is not locked, so he opens it slowly, just enough to hear voices coming from down the hall.

He listens in on the conversation without making his presence known and can see two guards through the opening. They are wearing plain blue uniforms, with a Pharmavast logo on the front pocket and an Ameritan flag on the right shoulder. Their utility belts hold batons and mace but no lethal weapons or Tasers.

"Damien seems to think there's a traitor at Pharmavast. He said to keep on our toes," the guard warns.

The second guard has doubts, "No way, nothing ever happens down here. And why do we have all the extra security for the next couple of weeks? Maybe something is going on. Whatever. Doubt it. This job is probably the easiest M-N 10 around, so I'm just going to keep my mouth shut and do my job."

The first guard is not concerned either, "A traitor? Who would that possibly be? The new guy? Luke the janitor? Look out, I'm going to smack you with my plunger!"

The two guards laugh hysterically.

Filled with anger and fed up with playing pacifist, Luke tosses his first Midazolam gas canister into the hall. The white smoke makes a perfect cover as he runs into the hallway, and with one swift movement, he kicks the first guard in the chest and jabs the other in the throat with an open hand. The first guard drops, passed out from the blow to the chest. The other guard falls to his knees gasping for air.

Luke wraps his arms around the guard's neck and threatens, "Where is the vault?" The voice modulator creates a sinister snarl.

"I ... don't ... know ... nothing ..."

"Well, then," Luke starts to tighten his arms and the guard's neck.

He stutters, "It ... it's on Sub-Level 5."

Another voice shouts, "Hey, you!"

As Luke turns, he sees two more guards running right at him, one armed with a pistol. Using reflex, not thought, he throws a perfect roundhouse kick, sending the armed guard flying through a pane of safety glass, landing inside a laboratory. The other guard stops in his tracks, fumbling to pull his baton from the holster.

"Boo!" Luke shouts through his sinister-sounding voice modifier, then knocks the guard out with a single punch.

To ensure the encounter is forgotten, he pops off another canister of Midazolam gas.

Realizing the shattered safety glass must have echoed loudly, he stands in silence and waits for the rest of the guards in the building to come charging into the hallway.

The only guard who responds is an unarmed younger man who was locking up the laboratory doors. He looked to be fresh out of Discovery School and immediately surrenders.

Luke could not risk leaving witnesses, so he leaves the guard with a warning, "If you ever speak about what you have seen here, I'll find you." His intimidating voice and outfit were enough to make the young man wet himself.

Luke decides it's still too risky. He spins behind the young man, careful not to step in the urine, and locks his arms in a sleeper hold, and slowly lowers the young man to the floor and leaves him fast asleep in the cloud of Midazolam gas.

Adrenaline pumping, Luke thinks to himself, *If Jake could only see me now!*

Looking for access to the lower levels, Luke steps into the room across the hall and realizes he has walked into a stairwell. He descends floor by floor, opening security doors between each floor until he reaches the stairwell landing of Sub-Level 5. The door leading into the Sub-Level 5 hallway is the first locked door he encounters. The lock has a fingerprint scanner. Luke, wearing the fingerprint gloves, places his right thumb on the scanner, confident that Damien has access to all floors of Pharmavast.

The lock disengages.

Luke opens the door slightly and catches a glimpse of five more guards, all heavily armed, standing in a huddle at the far end of the hallway. He hears one of the guards, "Hey, did you see the door just open. Let's check it out."

Luke knows he has no more than ten seconds to get out of there before the guards approach and draw their handguns on him.

Ten ...

Nine ...

Eight ...

"There's a vent near the ceiling that's big enough for me, but I can't get in there fast enough."

Seven ...

Six ...

"Ripley, override and lock all doors on Sub-Level 5."

Five ...

No response from Ripley.

Four ...

No response from Ripley.

Three ...

"RIPLEY, OVERRIDE AND LOCK ALL DOORS ON SUB-LEVEL 5."

Two ...

No response from Ripley.

One ...

"All set," Ripley replies.

At the last second, the automatic door slams shut right into the face of one of the guards. Luke hears a muffled "Ugh" through the small, thickly glassed window on the door and sees blood dripping down the glass from the guard's nose. The lock engages. The door separates Luke in the stairwell landing.

After wiping the sweat from his face, Luke grabs the bars on the vent cover and pulls forcefully. The vent cover easily breaks free, sending Luke stumbling to the ground.

He hops to his feet and sees the security camera pointing right in his direction. "Ripley, the cameras! You took care of them, right?"

"Don't worry, Luke. We hacked the cameras before you even got down to the basement. We can see the feed from the cameras, but they're not being broadcast to Pharmavast security. We can see the night watchman from our van. He doesn't even notice. He's completely engaged with something on his phone. Oh yeah, one more thing ... Nice fail when pulling off that vent cover! Wish I could post that clip, I bet it would go viral."

Luke hears laughter coming from the other side of the two-way radio and scolds Ripley, "Come on, man. Stop screwing around."

He pulls himself up and into the vent. Once in, he crouches on his hands and knees. Luke has never been scared in enclosed spaces, but this vent was barely big enough for him. Cobwebs are everywhere he turns, and luckily there are no spiders.

The vent extends for a few feet then turns to the right. It starts to angle upward at a slow incline, and Luke senses this is leading to the room he saw on the schematic drawing.

Eventually, Luke crawls over a vent perched right above the five guards from the other side of the door, one of them holding an ice pack on his bloody, swollen nose. Below the vent is an open area with a grated floor. Luke needs to move cautiously, knowing that if any of the guards looked up they would see him through the section of vented duct work.

He pauses and listens to one of the guards rant, "What do we do now, guys? One break-in and our Productivity Calculation will drop dramatically. What if we don't say anything? The guy didn't get to Sub-Level 5. So maybe we just let the guys on Sub-Level 4 get in trouble."

Focused on crawling as quietly as possible, Luke didn't notice the vented duct work was breaking loose. The second he places his knee down, the section of venting gives way.

Falling, Luke feels as if he is moving in slow motion. As he falls, he grabs a Midazolam gas canister and tosses it toward the center of the room. His fall is broken by landing on one of the five guards.

Another guard charges at him, baton drawn. Luke spins to the right, escapes the swing of the baton, and lands a devastating uppercut. The guard's feet trip Luke up and he tumbles, landing on his head, briefly dazed.

The other three guards try to encircle him. The first one charges and attempts an awkward kick that reminds him of something a child might attempt when throwing a fit. Luke parries and grabs the guard's foot and flips him into another guard.

As both guards fall, Luke sees a reflection from a window of the third guard charging. Luke shatters the guard's flying knuckles with an elbow block. The scream the guard makes rings in the room as Luke crouches and punches his knee cap so hard that his leg buckles backward. The guard drops to the ground.

Luke looks around the room and spots a door that likely leads to the vault, but the door has a retinal-scanner lock.

The guard with the buckled knee staggers toward Luke with baton in hand. Luke easily dodges out of the way of the baton and grabs the guard by his hair and shoves his face up to the scanner. The guard's eye does not open the door.

One by one, Luke shoves the faces of the remaining semi-conscious guards up to the retinal scanner. On the last try, the door opens and standing in front of the Titan 1800 is another guard. This guard is nothing like the other guards Luke encountered so far.

This guard's face is covered with a black, featureless mask, likely a protective shield, and he is wearing a solid-black, one-piece skinsuit. The mask has no face, no eyes, no mouth.

A deep whisper comes from the other side of the mask, "I'm going to silence you."

Luke, stunned by the appearance, hesitates, and the masked guard throws a right hook sending Luke flying across the floor.

Spitting out blood, Luke wondered how this masked guard knew to be here, or is this thing always here? Luke slowly rises to his feet, and the masked guard charges. Luke dodges to the left and lands an elbow drop on the back of his neck.

The masked guard turns around, grasping his injured neck.

The two pause and stare each other down, neither able to see the other's eyes.

The masked guard whips out a four-inch butterfly knife and takes a swipe at Luke, but he's too slow. Luke grabs his foe's hand and turns the knife around, swiping the blade toward where the eyes would be on the faceless mask. The knife slices the mask and Luke sees one of the masked guard's eyes, and the eye immediately starts to ooze blood.

The masked guard realizes he is outmatched, screeches in pain, and disappears into the cloud of Midazolam gas lingering around the retinal scanner door entrance.

The haze clears and the other five guards remain unconscious on the floor.

Luke approaches the Titan 1800, hoping the thumbprint has not been damaged. He places the gloved thumb of his right hand on the vault's scanner. A green light glows behind the scanner glass, and gears begin to churn. He hears the sound of heavy metal rods sliding and then no more sounds. Luke grasps the handles of the six-foot-high door and swings the vault open.

He steps through the two-foot-thick steel threshold into a sterile metal room that looks to be a perfect square. The only item in the vault is a pale-yellow, four-drawer horizontal filing cabinet that's nearly eight-feet wide.

"Ripley, I'm turning on the head cam. Can you see what I see?" Luke asks.

Ripley communicates back, "Yes, crystal clear. Now remember, don't pause on each page. Just rifle through the pages you think are important and the camera will catch everything. We'll run the individual video frames through enhancement filters. So again, do not pause. Flip through the pages as fast as you can and get out of there. I'm concerned that any minute now the night watchman will notice the cameras are out."

Luke opens the lower of the four cabinets first. He sees neatly organized manila folders, each with a clearly written label on the tab and a date. All the tabs in this drawer are labeled either 'Stock Certificates' or 'Investors' with various dates.

"That's all old stuff. Move on," Ripley instructs.

The middle two drawers contain similar folders. Each folder has the name of a pharmaceutical on the tab, and the front is stamped either Approved or Not Approved. He figures these must be all the proprietary formulas Pharmavast has developed over the years. Out of curiosity, he searches the alphabetically organized folder for Caffeineeoxx, and there's the folder, stamped Not Approved.

Getting anxious, Luke slides open the top drawer hoping to find something revealing. The very first tab is labeled 'Board Meeting - 12/18/2051'. The top drawer is full of manila folders labeled 'Board Meeting' with a date, descending chronologically from right to left.

"Okay, Ripley. Here we go," Luke queues his partner, then starts flipping through each page in the Board Meeting folders starting with the one from today and working his way backward.

"You need to make the 00:00 bus or you will be stuck in downtown and your alibi could be questioned. Leave yourself enough time to get out and get on that bus! You only have 20 minutes until Midnight," Ripley warns.

Luke moves quickly, holding each sheet of paper in front of the head-camera. During the next ten minutes, he works his way back to a Board Meeting from July 2050, and decides that is far enough.

He glances at the remaining manila folders, wondering how far back the board meetings go, wondering if they precede Amerita. He finishes walking the width of the file cabinet, 2049, 2048, 2047 ... and on and on until he reaches 1998, which he realizes would be during the time of America. The last group of folders on the far left are labeled differently; these say 'THE 97 1-10', 'THE 97 11-20', 'THE 97 21-30' ... through 'THE 97 91-97.'

The 97, Luke contemplates the potential value of capturing the information in these files. Could Jake be onto something with his conspiracy theories about the tragedies that befell, in one way or another, all 97 of the original members of the Meritism party?

"LUKE, what are you doing? Get out of there," Ripley shouts through the two-way radio.

Luke snaps out of his distraction and heads for the roof, tracing his every step backward and picking up the gas canisters.

Ripley shares a few parting thoughts with his protégé before Luke removes the two-way radio, "Luke, you're doing great, great things. I'm glad you reached out to me for help tonight. The Elders almost decided against my involvement. Not that they don't care about you, you know they care, they care deeply about every Ameritan citizen. But there's no way the population can ever find out about this operation. You're on your own from here on, buddy. That decision is directly from the Elders. Black Ops, Luke, Black Ops. This will never make the papers. No medals will be awarded. We know you know, and that's what makes us all so proud."

Not ready to let Luke go, Ripley continues chatting and reflects on a time when he was running Black Ops, "Remember when terrorism was prevalent? You were just a kid. There were thousands of successful anti-terrorism Black Ops run inside America before the crash. The population only heard about the ones that were not contained. Could you imagine if the population knew that five terrorism-related attacks per week were being stopped? The fear and uncertainty would have caused mass panic and chaos. Well, Luke, things aren't as bad today, but they're still pretty bad.

"You're behind the curtain now, Luke," he concludes.

Luke arrives home at 00:30, having barely made the bus. Sprinting to the 10th floor, taking off his gear, and stashing everything back into the backpack took a lot longer than anticipated.

While on the bus, the only other passenger offered Luke his newspaper as he departed and suggested he read the Sports section. Tucked into the Sports section was a large envelope with an inch of printouts rendered from the video recorded in the vault.

Luke takes advantage of the quiet time while Amanda and the kids are sound asleep. He begins reading through the pages, starting with the board meeting notes from today and working backward.

Within minutes of reading the notes, he discovers the focus of the board meetings has been on a new drug called D-EERg, not a New Year's Eve Employee Party. Anne's suspicions are definitively confirmed.

Several sections are blacked out with thick, black marker. There seems to be extra precaution taken to hide details about what the board is planning to do with this drug. Three pages about an experiment have been blacked out too, except for the title, *Exile Region Experiments*. The amounts of the four main chemicals are so excessive, the only logical conclusion Luke can think of is population-wide distribution.

He begins researching the four chemicals to determine effects that would be considered detrimental to the Ameritan population and finds disturbing results.

Acetaminophenyltrexide, an extremely potent version of acetaminophen, causes changes in the anterior insular cortex region of the brain, leading to significant reductions in empathy.

Excessive amounts of Fluoride cause decline in creativity.

D-phenylalanine and Levoamphetamine combine to regulate chemicals in the brain responsible for mental focus.

Less empathy. Stifled creativity. Extreme, unnatural, and self-serving mental focus.

Luke envisions humanity de-evolving into what was described in the notes about the chimpanzee experiment.

He lays back on the couch, enthusiastic and scared at the same time. Enthusiastic for the challenge staring him down and his responsibilities as a Merit Agency Investigator. Scared because he is on his own. Scared because of the anonymity he must maintain. Scared that this assignment may be too big for one man.

Luke fixates on figuring out a way to interrogate Damien or Millhouse for the missing details.

Friday

December 22, 2051

Pledge of Fidelity

Guidance Counselor Mrs. White welcomes her students, "Welcome, future Amerita contributors!" and asks, "Do we have any volunteers who would like to lead our opening discussion?"

AJ shoots her hand in the air and holds her M-N 3 high as she walks to the front of the class, announcing without asking, "Mrs. White, I'll take the lead for our opening discussion."

She goes right into her commentary, "Hi, class. I have an M-N 3. Last Monday, I scored a 9 on my EQ/IQ Test and would like to talk about what that means to me."

Nora snottily scoffs, "Oh wow, a 9, that's the best you could do?" and gives AJ a slow and purposefully non-enthusiastic round of applause.

Eddie looks over at Nora, gives her a disapproving glare, and asks AJ with sincere curiosity, "AJ, congratulations on the 9, really, I mean that. I was wondering what you can tell us about the test. Is the real test just like the pre-test?"

AJ exchanges a brief glance and smile with Mrs. White, then answers Eddie, "The real test is just like the pre-test."

She continues her lecture. "Eddie, I really appreciate the congratulations, however, I can't accept it."

Eddie looks slighted and confused.

AJ addresses him directly again, "Sorry, I didn't mean it like that. What I mean is that congratulating me for something I just am, just because this random collection of atoms and genetics fashioned themselves in a certain way, and the events of my life and the impact of my environment, and the decisions I have made and decisions made by others that impacted me, have made me who I am. Was this all my doing? No. All I did was make a series of decisions spanning 18 years. Some decisions were good and some were bad. My life is what my life is. And I'll live my life striving to fulfill responsibilities expected of someone who scored a 9 on her EQ/IQ."

Eddie doesn't look slighted anymore, but instead looks confused, as do all his classmates. Mrs. White smiles, understanding the meaning behind every word AJ speaks.

AJ attempts to clarify, "Eddie, congratulate me for accepting my 9 and the responsibilities that go with taking on a Level 9 vocation."

Eddie tries again, "Congratulations, AJ. Congratulations on accepting the responsibilities that go with taking on a Level 9 vocation."

"Thank you very much, Eddie," AJ replies, then she notices Millie's hand and walks toward her desk. "Hi, Millie. Did you have a question?"

"Yes! Are you going to be a scientist, AJ?" Millie asks, enthusiastically hoping AJ will say yes.

AJ answers delicately, "Well, Millie, I've been thinking about this all week. I'm not 100 percent positive yet, but I did have another idea about something I may do instead. I'm thinking I may follow in my father's footsteps and become a Merit Agency Investigator, working my way up to Director, which is a Level 9 vocation."

Millie jumps to her feet, claps loudly, reaches to AJ for a hug, and shows her support. "AJ! That's so exciting! I'm so happy for you!" The classroom follows Millie's lead with a resounding round of applause.

Mr. Garcia calls Jake to the front of the class. "They're all yours, Jake!"

Jake takes his place at the front of the class, notices Wendy smiling, and begins. "My topic today is the Pledge of Fidelity and the Ameritan Flag. Many of you may not know that the pledge we say every morning is a variation of the pledge kids used to say before World War III."

Frederick interrupts right away, "No ... frigging ... way!"

Jake humors his best friend and continues, "Yeah ... frigging way! I'll take you through the old pledge and the new one and explain why I think different words are used. You may think these differences are small, but to me, these differences are what make Amerita great. Mr. Garcia, the overhead please?"

Mr. Garcia turns on the overhead display and Jake begins his discussion.

I pledge <u>fidelity</u>
I pledge allegiance (old pledge)

"Allegiance means loyalty to a governing body; fidelity means loyalty to obeying the rules of the society you live in. I like that Allegiance has been replaced because we need to be loyal to the rules we agree to live by, not to the people who enforce those rules.

to the United States of <u>Amerita</u>
to the flag of the United States of America (old pledge)

"Why would anyone pledge Allegiance or Fidelity to a flag? That just doesn't make sense. Let's pledge our loyalty to Amerita, not the flag of Amerita. And, of course, there's the name change from America to Amerita, which is the most significant change of all.

and to the Meritocracy, for which we stand
and to the Republic, for which it stands (old pledge)

"I really like the word Republic, but I like the use of Meritocracy better. The definition of Republic is 'a State in which the supreme power rests in the body of citizens.' But Meritocracy takes the definition one step further emphasizing that the leaders of our Country are chosen because of their abilities and dedication to the people they represent. The power rests with us, and that is why I also like the change from 'which it stands' to 'which we stand.'

one <u>Society, Under God,</u> Indivisible

one Nation, Indivisible (old pledge)

"The land where we live now was first settled by people seeking religious freedom. I'm glad the word God is part of the pledge. 'Under God' was in the old pledge at one time but they took it out, I'm not sure why. All citizens have come to agree that people don't have to say the 'under God' phrase; they can just skip that part and remain silent for those two words. I know a lot of us do, and I think that is perfectly fine and have never heard anyone complain one way or the other. Freedom of Religion also means freedom to not have a religion, and I think we're very fortunate to be able to choose whether to say those two words.

"Oh yeah, and Society versus Nation. I think that pledging fidelity to each other is important. The idea of pledging fidelity to the Nation is already covered in the first line when we pledge fidelity to the United States of Amerita.

"Indivisible is a great word to put in there too. That comes from the 1800s when America almost split into two nations over slavery. Yeah, slavery. They used to make people with black skin be slaves for people with white skin."

Frederick uncontrollably interrupts, "Dude, that's MESSED UP! I could have been your slave?"

"Yeah, REALLY MESSED UP! I totally agree, Frederick," Jake acknowledges. "So the Indivisible means all 50 States are going to stick together. All 50 States have been reunited again under Meritism for 12 years. Texas tried to hold out and use currency for a while, but the people there eventually realized Meritism was the way to go. They were the 50th State to join.

with Opportunity and Equality for all.

with liberty and justice for all. (old pledge)

"And the final line. Liberty and Justice are important, but if every person has Opportunity and Equality, liberty and justice will follow."

Frederick leads the rousing applause, quickly followed by Wendy and the remaining students.

Jake humbly accepts the accolades, "Thank you. And now just a few notes about the flag of Amerita. Mr. Garcia, the picture please?

"The 10 stars of various sizes represent the 10 Merit Numbers.

"The 10 red and white stripes of identical height and width represent the 10 Vocation Levels. The stripes are the same size to symbolize that all vocations are equally important.

"The light blue background behind the stars is the color of the sky, representing unrestricted opportunity.

"The black stripe on the bottom represents the consequence of exile if a person doesn't contribute. Notice how the smaller stars are closer to the black stripe? That represents lower productivity scores being closer to exile.

"I thought a lot about that black stripe, wondering why it was included as part of the flag. I concluded that the fear of exile needs to be a consequence that we're not afraid to admit exists as part of Meritism."

Masquerade Party

Luke quietly pushes his custodial cart past Damien's office, hoping not to be asked to clean the boardroom at the end of the day again. He promised Amanda a Date Night. Their plan is a stop at the M-N 3~4 Pizza Palace for a slice of slightly flavorful pizza followed by a movie from last year showing at the M-N 3~4 movie theater. He shakes his head at how lame tonight's entertainment will be compared to the dinners and shows they enjoyed with their M-N 8s.

He steers the cart around the corner as Damien and Millhouse exit Damien's office. Luke stops to tie his already tied shoe, ducking behind the cart. "Good night, Tiff. Hey, Millhouse is throwing a holiday costume party tonight at his house."

"She can come, right, Millhouse? Why am I even asking? Of course, she can," Damien declares. "Maybe you could dress up as a sexy nurse or sexy superhero or something like that. And what's up with your new wardrobe? You look like the women from the 8th floor."

Tiffany does not look in their direction and declines the invitation. "Sorry, I have to visit my grandmother tonight," Tiffany states, attempting to sound convincing.

Millhouse corrects Damien, "A masquerade party, not a costume party, Damien."

The two continue to the elevator. Luke slowly backs up, back around the corner, and stays hidden from their view until he hears the elevator arrive and is sure they have left.

He parks the cart in the custodial storeroom, shuts the door from the inside, turns off the light, flops down on the makeshift bed Ned left after his mid-morning nap, and starts strategizing for a Friday night covert interrogation.

He realizes step one is to get out of Date Night and the only way to get out of Date Night is to not go home first. Luke pulls out his phone and sends Amanda a text:

```
Bad news, employee party tonight for the
management, and boss asked if I would help
with setup, keeping bathrooms clean, and
cleanup after. Some guy named Millhouse, a
masquerade party. I really can't say no, only
been here a few weeks. Okay?
```

He waits anxiously for a reply.

Five minutes pass. He knows Amanda is home. She did not have a volunteer shift today.

Five more minutes pass, then 'Ding.' He closes his eyes, holds the phone in front of his face, and slowly opens his eyes to see her reply:

```
Whatever, I'll take the kids out instead.
```

The text is followed up with a series of icons, a heart, a sad face, an angry face, and then an icon of a hand with the middle finger raised followed by a broken heart. Luke puts the exchange behind him and focuses on improvising a plan.

Deep breaths and visualization keep him focused, running through scenarios over and over, anticipating the outcomes. He pieces together a plan, thanks largely to having decided to bring his backpack of investigator tools to work with him every day, just in case an opportunity presents itself.

Step two of the plan will be the most challenging and the most necessary, counterfeiting his own M-N. If he is unable to pull this off in the confines of the custodial storeroom, there is no possibility of moving forward with the outrageous plan.

Luke does not hesitate. New Year's Eve is fast approaching, and he needs to uncover the logistics of what is being planned for the D-EERg. This may be his only opportunity.

He pulls an alcohol-based cleaner from the cabinet and a razor blade from the tool kit, then douses the razor in the cleaner.

Firmly grasping the razor between the thumb and index finger of his right hand, he slowly cuts a quarter-inch incision on the back of his left hand, diagonally across the top of his M-N. He wiggles the thin, half-inch by half-inch electronic device out, stretching the small opening in his skin, careful not to tear the incision.

He is surprised at the lack of bleeding and happy he did not sever a vein. Placing a bandage over the small incision, he searches for a set of needle-nose pliers.

Holding the M-N with pliers, he wedges the razor blade in the precise location of one corner, where when twisted, the two halves separate.

He sets the two halves down onto a clean sheet of white paper. One half contains a mini-disk. The other half contains the holographic projector. Carefully extracting the mini-disk with the pliers, he maintains the hold on the mini-disk with the pliers for inserting into his phone.

With the disk inserted into the phone, he is able to open key files in a plain text editor. He searches for certain sequences of characters, knowing exactly which sequences, out of millions of characters, to manipulate. The difficulty with manipulating the files in a text viewer is that obtaining the precise shade of green is impossible. Having counterfeited M-Ns in the lab to understand the technology, he is confident the shade of green will be close enough.

However, if detected by another agent or a citizen with a keen eye, he could be asked to let an agent hold an M-N Verifier up to the back of his hand. That would lead to instant exile, no questions asked. If that happened, the Elders would not reveal his mission.

M-N reassembled and wiggled back into position, Luke seals the incision with a small bead of Super Glue.

He looks closely at the M-N 10 hovering over the back of his left hand and is pleased with how closely he replicated the shade of green.

Luke feels confident to go ahead with his plan and looks forward to the next step, acquiring the perfect outfit.

"Good evening, sir. Welcome to Mauricio's Fine Men's Clothing. How may I be of service?" the proprietor greets, his Italian accent very thick. "I'm Mauricio!"

"Hello, Mauricio. My name is ... Jack." Luke holds the back of his left hand up for a moment, making sure the proprietor sees the M-N 10. "I'm on my way home from work and need a tuxedo for a masquerade party tonight. I'm thinking a fedora would be a nice touch too. I don't need to acquire, just borrow for the evening."

"Ah! Jack. You look very athletic, and I have the perfect tuxedo for your physique." Mauricio smiles, looking forward to having a customer with a build that will complement his favorite garment.

Mauricio leads Luke to a fitting area, takes a few measurements, and returns with a garment bag.

Luke enters the changing room and tries on the tuxedo. The fit is precise, and the look is exquisite. His movements are unrestricted. The shoes have a solid grip. The fedora Mauricio selected tips nicely down the front of his face.

He opens his backpack, digs for the voice modulator, and fits the device under the collar. He then swaggers out of the changing room, his custodial apparel tucked into his backpack.

"Ah, Jack! Perfetto!" Mauricio is thrilled to see his work of art perfectly displayed on Luke.

"Thank you, Mauricio. I'm just going to look around for a bit."

"Yes, sir. I'll place the tablet here on the counter, when you're ready. If you will excuse me, I'll be in the back of the shop for a few minutes," Mauricio says as he walks away.

Luke takes the opportunity to slip out the front door without acknowledging the Merit Evaluation Tablet, which would have blown his cover. Having mentioned a borrow and not an acquisition, he is not concerned, knowing Mauricio will assume he forgot and will return the tuxedo tomorrow.

He tips the fedora sharply downward, doing his best to hide his face, and continues walking down the prestigious block of the city, lined with glass-front M-N 9~10 shops and restaurants. He pauses at a corner and searches the Internet for 'masquerade party mask' and locates a jeweler only two blocks away who has these in current inventory.

The interaction with the jeweler proceeds without incident. Just as with Mauricio, Luke borrows, not acquires, a masquerade mask, and slips out of the shop without completing the Merit Evaluation on the tablet.

Luke ducks down an alley next to the jeweler and across the street from a bus stop. He opens the backpack and confirms the tools he needs to reset his M-N back to 3 are still there. Then he makes a last-minute decision to retrieve a canister of Midazolam gas from the pack and tucks the small canister into an inside pocket of the tuxedo. He looks in all directions for any passersby, then stashes the backpack behind a dumpster. Satisfied with the hiding spot, he turns on the voice modulator and sets a tone that is a slight pitch lower than his natural voice, yet not intimidating like the setting he used during the vault breach.

Next, he uses the same tube of glue used to seal his incision to glue the top edge of the mask to the underside of the brim of the fedora. He gently snaps off the wooden dowel from the side of the mask and dons the fedora/masquerade mask. Then he stands, throws a few roundhouse kicks and jabs, and is pleased to see his mask stays perfectly placed without needing to use his hands to hold a dowel. The mask covers his face from his forehead to upper lip.

Luke walks one more block, holding the fedora/mask in his right hand, and he enters a limousine and taxi station. He flashes his M-N 10 to a driver and requests a ride to the Smee residence in Brighton, two miles away, bordering the city limits.

The velvet carpeting in the backseat of the limousine reminds Luke of the bus he frequently rode with his parents from the airport to the hotels at Disney World. He pushes thoughts of his father to the back of his mind to avoid distraction.

Luke puts on his fedora and mask.

The driver comments, interrupting the silence-filled limo, "A little old-fashioned, don't you think? I mean, a party is one thing, but a masquerade? What is this, the 16th Century?"

Luke remains silent. He removes the fedora and looks closely at the mask. The gold material glitters in the dim setting of the limo. The face is human with no exaggerated features. He feels the look is plain enough to not draw extra attention and is pleased that almost his whole face is covered.

"I wonder if there will be ballroom dancing," Luke thinks, realizing too late that he was actually speaking.

"Finally you're talking, buddy! Was not sure you could," the limousine driver jokes, attempting to make conversation.

"Yeah, I can talk," Luke replies, donning the fedora and mask, then raises the black divider cutting off the driver's view of his spacious back seat.

The driver pulls into the semicircle at the entrance of the Smee residence and waits behind a line of exotic sports cars and other limousines.

Luke realizes this is an M-N 9~10 party that Millhouse is hosting. He swiftly exits from the backseat and does a walk/jog toward the mansion, looking back at the driver with a wave of thanks. The driver steps out of the car and shouts to Luke, waving the evaluation tablet, "Jack, can you—"

Luke ignores the driver's request and continues to move swiftly toward the entrance. A quick glance over his shoulder, and he confirms the driver got back into his limousine and decided not to pursue.

At the door now, Luke steps into the party. The lights are bright, and the music is filled with heavy bass. Having expected to hear an orchestra, he is surprised by the dance music. Everyone wears a different mask, no two are the same. Some people hold their masks to their faces with wooden dowels, and others appear to have their masks adhered to their skin. His is original, the only mask held in place by a fedora. People take notice and nod with approval at the originality.

Locating Millhouse would be impossible because of the masks. He will need to wait until Millhouse reveals himself.

Luke struts to a table for two at the edge of the dance floor, takes a seat, crosses one leg, one foot resting on a knee, leans back in his seat, and subtly bobs his head with the rhythm.

His attempt to appear arrogant and unapproachable does not work. A young woman sits down at the table with Luke at the same time the D.J. switches moods with a radical change from energetic dance music to a modern remix of a classical piece.

"Hello, stranger. The music sounds familiar. Do you know what this is?" she asks flirtatiously.

"It's a dubstep remix of a waltz in A minor by Chopin," Luke answers, surprising himself with that knowledge. He does not turn toward her, hoping she will find him rude and excuse herself. He suspects she will stick around because he left his wedding ring in the backpack and he has an M-N 10 on his hand.

"Wow! You know your music. My name's Katie. And your name?" she asks, obviously not leaving his company.

"Jack," he answers void of attentiveness.

"Jack, let's dance," Katie insists.

Luke hesitates joining her but decides his refusal could attract attention. The goal, he reminds himself, is to blend in.

Katie grabs his hand and leads him to the dance floor. Luke never waltzed before but easily follows the footwork patterns of the others on the dance floor. His smile shows at the bottom edge of his mask as he realizes he is not that bad at the waltz. Then he fails in convincing himself that his smile has nothing to do with the beautiful young woman flirting with him.

The mask Katie wears resembles the face of a feline, likely modeled after a tiger. Her long, blond hair flows behind her as they move in circles. The music speeds up as the D.J. mixes into another waltz, a fast-paced dubstep remix of Blue Danube. Katie intentionally presses her body closer into Luke as they spin faster and faster. The two run right into another couple, sending Katie falling to the ground.

"Oh my god. Are you okay, Katie?" Luke asks with genuine concern.

"Yes, I'm fine. Kinda embarrassing. I suppose everyone saw that," she comments, blushing under her mask.

As she stands up with Luke's assistance, he notices that the mask she wears has broken from the collision and a large portion remained on the floor.

"Katie, your mask broke," Luke mutters, almost unable to speak. All he sees is Amanda in the half of Katie's face that is now revealed. Katie touches her mask and feels the missing portion, turns and runs into the crowd. Luke tries to chase after her but loses her in the sea of masquerades.

Luke slides into the crowd, stepping off the dance floor. He spends the next couple of hours wishing the party would wind down and that Millhouse would appear. He stands on the edges of the crowds, blending in and avoiding conversation. Katie does not reappear.

The music stops and everyone's attention shifts to the stage where the D.J. hands the microphone to Millhouse, "Everyone, settle down. Okay? Hi! Thanks for coming to my party! I'm Millhouse Smee. Welcome, everyone. I decided to host a party, not just any party, but a masquerade party. A masquerade gives us all an opportunity to be anonymous. So everyone is equal, a blank slate you could say. A blank slate as long as you're a 9 or a 10, that is!"

The arrogant crowd cheers.

Millhouse continues, "Party on, my Capitalist friends!"

Luke's stomach drops. He realizes for the first time tonight this is a party of devotees to the Capitalist Party. He speculates what would transpire if he grabbed the microphone and announced his loyalty to the Meritism Party.

Millhouse excuses himself from the stage. His mask is pale white, no color, shaped like a bird face with a long pointy nose. Luke wonders where Damien may be or if he is even here. There is no way to tell.

Luke follows Millhouse inconspicuously down a hallway leading away from the D.J stage. There appears to be bedrooms off this hallway and likely a bathroom. Luke is hopeful that is where Millhouse is headed. The intoxication of the party goers will work to his advantage. They will be less likely to notice his moves.

Gradually closing the space between he and Millhouse, Luke is right on his heels, still unnoticed, as Millhouse turns into a bathroom. The door is just about shut when Luke stomps his foot between the door and the threshold. He forces the door open, knocking Millhouse to the ground, landing on the bathroom tile.

With one swift motion, Luke shuts and locks the door, throws the canister of Midazolam gas to the ground, lunges at Millhouse, and wraps him in a sleeper hold with one hand firmly over his mouth.

"Shh," Luke whispers, then takes a huge breath. "Where is the D-EERg headed? Tell me or I'll snap your neck like a frickin twig."

Luke holds his breath, determined to not breath in the anterograde amnesia-inducing gas.

Millhouse breathes heavily underneath Luke's hand. Luke tightens his grip and lifts his hand from Millhouse's mouth just enough so he can move his lips and speak.

Fear for his life, and intoxication, loosen his lips, "New Year's Eve, stroke of midnight, cargo plane leaves, municipal water supply, everywhere. You can't stop us ... everything is already in motion ... you're too late."

Luke increases pressure, cutting off the circulation, and lays Millhouse down gently forward onto the toilet, positioning his head in the bowl as if he was vomiting.

He opens the bathroom window, confirms the opening leads to the backyard, and tosses the gas canister and his fedora and mask into the dark. Then he slides out the window into the snow, leaving Millhouse passed out, exposed to the gas. Luke takes a deep breath of fresh air, then jumps up to shut the window behind him.

Luke cuts through adjacent backyards until he is clear of Millhouse's neighborhood. He begins the two-mile walk back to the city center. As he walks, he thinks back to a phrase he loved to use as a teenager, *Did I have Plot Armor on back there?*

Back at the dumpster, he is relieved to find his backpack. He tosses the empty canister and the fedora and mask into the dumpster, but he takes extra care with the tuxedo and shoes. Looking in both directions, up and down the alley, he confirms nobody is around and changes from the tuxedo to his custodial uniform. He neatly packs the tuxedo and shoes into his backpack, planning to return them to Mauricio anonymously using mail delivery.

Luke enters a restroom in the back of a nearby shop, locks the door, and extracts and resets his M-N to a 3. He manages to board the 00:00 bus and heads for home.

Sunday
December 24, 2051

Christmas Eve

"Come on, everyone. We've got to get going. I told my mom we would get there early," Luke shouts. "And Jake, put down your presents. You might break something."

"Dad, I know you got me what I wanted. I'm just anxious to open it! Do we really have to wait until after church?" Jake pleads.

Luke denies Jake's request, "Yes, we do have to wait. I promised Mamie we would not open them until tonight when we're all here for dinner."

Amanda begins to worry about the guests, "Don't forget we still need to pick up Sofia and her parents at the airport after church. I just don't understand why everyone wants to gather here. We're going to have a big crowd tonight. Your cousins, Alina, Noah, and Marin and their families, and my sister and her family, and your mother will all be here. Did you say Uncle Rico is coming too? They all have beautiful houses. Your mother's apartment is bigger than this place!"

"They insisted. I suspect they're all just doing this to try and make us not feel any different about the M-N 3," Luke suggests and notices Jake shaking all three of his presents again. "Jake!"

"Dad! This is huge! Do you realize this is the first Christmas with the new 'gifting' policy? I know you have authorization as my parent, as does every parent, to choose up to three Christmas presents for their kids, any present, ANY! Regardless of M-N! That means this one," he points to the largest of the three boxes, "could be a Play Station X2!"

"You all look beautiful in your church clothes. Now can we get going, please? You know how Mamie is when we don't get there early enough and miss the choir's caroling hour," Luke begs.

The family arrives early enough and selects a pew two rows from the front, on the right side where Mamie will see them from her seat with the choir.

Mass has not begun, and there is a short pause between songs. AJ and Jake sneak out of the pew and go up to Mamie and give her a big hug. Luke gazes upon his mother, appreciating what an amazing woman she is, and for a moment thinks that maybe she and Ned would make a cute couple. He chuckles to himself a little too loudly and Amanda gives him an elbow to the ribs.

The music is beautiful. Everyone is dressed in their church outfits. No M-Ns are visible among the congregation. Luke reflects on how much he loves the feeling of equality under the eyes of God.

Father Sergio begins his homily, "Merry Christmas!"

"Merry Christmas, Father!" the congregation cheers.

He walks among his fellow Christians, up and down the aisles, speaking personally with them, "Merry Christmas. Gifts. Gifts. And more gifts. Christmas is about gifts and that's fine because the greatest gift God gave us is his Son.

"His Son did not *tell* us how to love. His Son *showed* us how to love.

"His Son did not *tell* us about freewill. His Son *showed* us freewill. How you ask? We had the freewill to choose his fate. We chose crucifixion for his fate. Yet, we choose with our freewill to be here today, knowing we are all sinners, all of us, including me. With our freewill, we have the choice to choose between good and evil. And we don't always choose good.

"And that's why His Son did not *tell* us how to forgive. His Son *showed* us how to forgive.

"His Son did not *tell* us we all have talents. His Son *showed* us we all have talents. The greatest living example of our talent is this gathering right here, right now. Look all around. Everyone here contributes something to our congregation. We have singers, musicians, friendly greeters at the door, fantastic liturgical ministers, Sunday School instructors for our children, and on and on. Just look around at the immense amount of talent we have around us. You, being here, with us, gathered on this glorious eve, listening from your pew, you being here is as important a contribution as any contribution.

"Love, Forgiveness, Talent, and Freewill. Four amazing gifts God bestowed on all of us, and demonstrated to us by his Son.

"We all have potential.

"We can all contribute.

"Now children, please join me up here on the alter for this year's Christmas story, *The Three Trees*."

The children gather near Father Sergio's feet while he reads the story, taking time to turn the book outward for them to see the pictures.

"Would anyone like to tell us what you think the story means?" Father Sergio asks the children.

Almost every arm is raised high. A young boy wearing a beautiful, colorful Christmas outfit is called upon. He stands and shares, "The sad tree didn't think he could do anything as important as the other trees around him and he was wrong. He did something very, very, very special."

Tuesday

December 26, 2051

Boots

Luke sits on the bus, headed for his vocation. His note is written and ready to pass to his contact. His note includes details about D-EERg, the effects, and the logistics regarding the release into the population. Luke also briefly explains his intentions to find the cargo plane and destroy the payload. He suggests that the Protect and Serve Agency closely watch future Pharmavast chemical acquisitions to help prevent this from happening again. He leans back into the bus seat and daydreams about sitting in the contoured leather seats of the Charger again.

The man with the flat-brimmed cowboy hat sits directly across from Luke, loosely holding a newspaper. The man's hat is tipped sharply forward, shielding his eyes from the morning sun. He appears to be napping.

A couple more stops come and go, but no Elder boards the bus. He rolls up his paper and looks out the window toward the next stop. Again, no Elder boards the bus. He begins nervously tapping the rolled-up paper against his leg.

The bus reaches the last stop before the Pharmavast drop off.

No Elder boards. Nobody sits on either side of Luke. Nobody introduces themselves with the now familiar greeting, "Sir, good morning."

The doors begin to close as the bus prepares to depart. The man with the flat-brimmed cowboy hat jumps to his feet, flicks back his hat, and tosses his newspaper into Luke's lap. Luke looks up at the man. The area above and below his left eye has a fresh scar, and the white of his eye is not visible, just a black pupil surrounded by a sea of red.

Luke freezes, and before he can react, the man jumps through the closing door. The clack-clack-clack of the cowboy boots against the steel deck of the bus floor sends Luke into a frenzy.

He lunges for the door but is too late. The man has already disappeared into the crowded sidewalk filled with people hustling to their vocations.

Distraught and still in shock, Luke slowly opens the newspaper thrown into his lap. He flips page by page until he reaches the Sports section. His rage ignites when he sees the paper is covered with thick black marker scribblings of the letter J crossed out with an X, and the letter A crossed out with an X, covering both sides of the paper. The taunting haunts him. The symbolism is obvious. The man is boasting about the murders of Joshua Campbell and Anne Gonzales.

Sunday

December 31, 2051

Decoy

"Settle down, people. What's all the laughter?" Damien asks lightheartedly. "Tonight's party doesn't start for another four hours."

Michael fills him in, "Ann was just telling us about how you found Millhouse passed out in his bathroom, puking his guts out."

Damien confirms the story and joins in the laughter, "Oh my god, that was hilarious! Funniest thing ever. I was a little drunk too and when I walked in and saw a man-sized, bird-faced creature with his head in the toilet, I laughed so hard I almost started hyperventilating."

Millhouse smirks, happy to be the center of attention. "Yeah, glad you found me. I remember stepping into the bathroom and next thing I know my head is in the toilet. I must have been puking pretty good."

"All right, team. Down to business," Damien announces as he begins circling the conference table. "Production went well and the drone cargo plane is loaded and programmed for departure at midnight tonight. That's all folks! I know we could have cancelled this meeting, but I wanted to confirm first-hand that you all arrived. Head home or to your hotels and get ready for the greatest Pharmavast Employee Party ever!"

"And the theme?" Ann asks. "What's the theme? We know 'Capitalism Reborn' isn't actually this year's theme!" she laughs, and everyone joins in.

Damien announces, "The theme is ... ready for this? ... There is no damn theme!" Damien, extremely annoyed by the question, begins to rant, "Do you think I had time to pull together an actual theme? Have you not been paying attention this past month? A theme? Really, Ann? Yeah, there's a theme. Pharmavast Employees.

How's that for a theme? Everyone out. Everyone except Millhouse and Ashley."

The room vacates quickly. Millhouse moves seats, sitting next to Ashley. Damien sits across from the two.

"Ash, is the second cargo plane secured?" Damien inquires.

"Yes, all set," she answers with certainty.

"Excellent, Ashley. I'm so glad we had that little chat, so glad we're on the same team. I admire the courage you've shown, coming directly to me about the whole vault thing. We all make mistakes. We can all own up to them with honesty and move on."

Damien checks in with Millhouse, "How about you, Millhouse? Are the flight routes of both drones pre-programmed? And did you disable remote access so the onboard servers can't be messed with from outside the planes?"

"Yes, all set," he answers with certainty.

Damien stands up and heads toward the door, "Excellent. I'll see you both at the party. Remember, these last few modifications are on a need-to-know basis and nobody needs to know except us."

In his office, door securely locked, he removes the *Community Effort* painting from the wall, retrieves the phone, and calls his contact.

"What?" the man with the flat-brimmed cowboy hat answers.

"Lawrence, brother, how's the eye? Can you see okay yet?" Damien asks his half-brother with concern.

"I can see just fine! And don't call me Lawrence!"

Damien apologizes, "Sorry. I forgot you're going by Cyrus Lance now. I do admit that's a pretty cool name you came up with this time."

After a brief silence, Damien continues, "Hey, listen. I've gotten past your vault fail—"

Cyrus interrupts, "My fail? MY FAIL? I had to sit in that vault every night for a week! How did you expect me to be on my A-game?"

Damien is angered, "Yes, your fail! I'm not the one who ran away!"

"Look, I still think we should have killed him days ago. Why did you make me wait? Lots of accidents could have happened between then and now. A mugging, a car accident—" Cyrus argues before being interrupted.

"Patience brother," Damien attempts to calm Cyrus. "Three accidental deaths of Pharmavast employees in three weeks were enough. One more and the Protect and Serve Agency would have been all over this place. I don't want anything to interfere with the plan, and that's why you must wait until things are in motion. He doesn't know the logistics anyways."

Damien hears an agreeable sigh from Cyrus and ensures he is engaged, "You're lucky we made sure there was nothing incriminating in those vault files and nothing about our distribution plans either. I'm giving you this one last chance. Don't mess up again or I'll rip that M-N I had made for you right out of the back of your hand and see to it that you end up back in exile. Luke will show up, likely intoxicated from being at our employee party, so that should make your job easy this time. Take your revenge, little brother."

Damien ends the call before Cyrus can respond. He returns the phone, hangs the painting, and gazes at the artwork longing for the future he craves.

New Year's Eve

"Do we have to go? Look at me, Luke! I can't go to a party dressed like this," Amanda complains.

Luke acknowledges her feelings, "I do understand. I know this sucks. And I'm working really hard. This break from the pressures of being an investigator is helping. Honestly, only three weeks and I'm not feeling burnt out like I used to. I may be ready to go back when my Merit Review comes around in another 337 days. But who's counting?"

He goes to hug Amanda, but she dodges the affection and heads for the door. "Fine, come on. I suppose we should go."

The couple enters the lobby. Amanda is impressed with the lavish furnishings and extravagance. The lobby is decorated with silver and gold streamers and silver and gold balloons. Tables draped with black table cloths and decorated with silver and gold centerpieces are placed throughout the lobby.

Amanda offers her input, "Beautiful place but those decorations are gaudy. Looks like a guy picked them out."

They step into the reception line for employees to meet the board members. As they progress through the line of 19, Luke hesitates when he reaches Ashley. He forces an introduction, "Hi, Luke Medina, and this is my wife, Amanda."

Ashley replies perfectly, "Hi, I'm Ashley Haynes. I think we've run into each other before, Luke. Nice to formally meet you."

They continue down the line, Amanda holding Luke's hand. She leans into him and whispers, "What's up with the orange suit jacket at the end of the line?"

Luke answers, "Damien Myers, head of Pharmavast."

When they reach the end of the reception line, Amanda greets Damien warmly, "Hello, Mr. Myers. Luke has told me so much about Pharmavast. Thank you for welcoming him to the organization. And by the way, I love the decorations."

Damien is pleased with her introduction, "Hello, Mrs. Medina. Nice to meet you too. And as for the decorations, I chose them myself this year. Our Board of Directors put the party together to let the employees know how much we appreciate them."

Amanda smiles tightly and nods, holding back her laughter.

The reception counter where Willy once worked is converted into a bar for the evening. The elevator has been repaired, and there is no sign of the accident having occurred. A dance floor consumes a large area of the lobby toward the back corner.

Luke introduces Amanda to his colleagues. They mention how fun Luke was to hang out with on Monday night. Luke is relieved, confident that Amanda will never know he was also breaking into Pharmavast that night.

A small group of women from the 10th floor, including Tiffany and Amber, stop and say "Hi" to Luke. When they move on, Amanda whispers to Luke, "Really, Luke? They *all* know your name and work on your floor? Really? Do they also have poles in their offices they dance around on their breaks?"

Luke and Amanda approach the bar. Amanda orders a gin and tonic. Luke orders a Jack Daniels, double, on the rocks. Amanda flashes him a glare that Luke interprets as, *Don't you dare get drunk tonight!*

They take a seat at a table on the edge of the dance floor. A few minutes pass, then Amanda feels a tap on her shoulder. She turns and sees an elderly man, long, scraggly, white beard covering most of his face, and tinted glasses. He is dressed in a tuxedo that fits perfectly. She notices the M-N 9 on the hand. She also notices Luke watching Tiffany, Amber, and their girlfriends dancing.

Amanda greets the gentleman, "Hello, sir."

"You must be Amanda. More beautiful than I imagined. Hi, I'm Ned I. Tammarin, the I is for Irresistible." He shakes her hand and helps himself to a seat at their table.

Luke finally notices Ned. "Mr. T! Great to see you! Amanda, this is my guardian angel, Mr. T."

Amanda speaks softly to Luke, not worried that Ned will hear, "Luke, easy on the drinks. Please." She turns to Ned. "You work with Luke, right? Keeping him out of trouble, I hear," she says while laughing.

Ned does not laugh and replies with a stern face, "Yes, I'm keeping him out of trouble." He breaks the stern face and laughs off the statement.

"Mr. T, who are you here with? Would they like to join us?" Amanda pries.

Ned answers, not minding the question, "I'm stag tonight so if you know any single ladies interested in an 81-year-old man, send them my way. I'm single, have a really good M-N, and keep myself in good shape. But no family to mention. I've been on my own for quite a long time now, but that's a story for a different day."

"You two get to know each other, I have to visit the men's room," Luke announces as he walks to the bathroom with a slight stumble.

He is alone in the bathroom and continues to build tonight's alibi. Taking a large swig of the Jack Daniels, he swishes it around in his mouth for several seconds, then spits it into the sink, swallowing none. He dumps most of the remaining drink into the sink after repeatedly dabbing an ample amount on his shirt. He fills the cup to three-quarters full with water and what remains of the whiskey, leaving just enough caramel color to look like a strong drink. He runs his fingers through his hair, looks in the mirror, takes a whiff of himself, and is satisfied with his drunken appearance.

He returns to the table with what looks like a fresh drink. Amanda pays no attention to him and chats with Ned instead. They take turns filling dessert plates with sweets. Ned and Amanda dance a waltz, and Luke cuts in as the waltz winds down.

He holds Amanda close and starts slow dancing, moving in small circles.

"Oh my god, you smell disgusting. Really, Luke? That's just embarrassing. Please, enough of the booze." Amanda pushes him several inches away, hoping to alleviate the smell of alcohol.

A few other men from the custodial staff join their table with their wives. Amanda enjoys the conversations and the glimpse into Luke's vocational day.

Luke catches the orange suit jacket out of the corner of his eye, moving toward their table. He stands up and intentionally intercepts Damien's path, bumping slightly. With his best drunken drawl, he invites him to join them, making sure he moves in close enough for Damien to smell the booze, "Damien! Hey, buddy. Good to see you. Sit down, join us!"

"Hi, hi. Hello all. I'll stop back in a little while. Save me a seat." He continues moving, not attempting to hide his lack of desire to join them.

"I'll be right back," Luke tells Amanda. She continues conversation with the other wives and ignores her drunk, embarrassing husband.

On his way to the men's restroom, Ashley bumps into Luke, and asks, "Would your wife mind if I steal you for a dance?"

Again with the drunken drawl and hoping the stench will change her mind, he accepts, "Sure! What the hell. She's all mad at me anyway."

Ashley grabs his hand and leads him to the far corner of the dance floor, hidden from most of the tables in the lobby area. The song playing is an upbeat dance song, but she puts her arms up on his shoulders and insists they slow dance.

Luke is taken by how closely she pulls him in.

"Listen," she whispers, "I'm positive that they're on to me. I told Damien about how I told you about the vault because I was so scared and I begged him to let my mistake go. I pledged to him that I would be onboard with his plan and never waiver again. But I realized I need to protect my children's future and that means protecting Meritism. I'm not even sure you saw my note on the coffee cup. I hope I didn't get you in trouble with that. But listen, I only have a minute or two before Damien makes a lap around the corner. I don't want him to see us together. There are two cargo planes at Rochester International Airport. One is a decoy. I don't know how you will be able to tell which is which. They both look like they're loaded with cargo, but the decoy is just empty boxes. They take off at midnight, and the real cargo plane is loaded with a new drug that could destroy everything Meritism has accomplished. You must stop that plane. I'm so sorry about everything. I should have just gone to the Protect and Serve Agency, I know, but I'm just so scared for my life. I don't know what my little angels would do if something happened to me. I'm terrified they may try and hurt my girls too."

She abruptly pushes him away just as Damien turns the corner. Luke leans up against the wall, doing his best to look drunk and alone in a corner. Damien glances in his direction and continues his lap around the lobby, making small talk with all the employees.

Luke returns to his table after another trip to the bar and then the bathroom to further his drunken performance.

He sits next to Amanda, and she stands up immediately and walks away. One of the other wives follows her to the women's restroom.

Luke holds his glass on the table, arms stretched out in front of him, and lowers his head, looking drowsy. He stays in that position while his colleagues continue chatting and laughing.

When Amanda finally returns, Luke tells her, "Hey, I'm really sorry. I just don't like this place or the people. Except Mr. T. I like him. I'm going to walk around and see if that sobers me up a little. I'll be back for the countdown to midnight. Hey, Mr. T! If I don't return in time ... kiss my beautiful wife for me."

Amanda mutters softly but loud enough for Luke to hear, "Asshole."

"I'll keep a good eye on her for you, Luke. Why don't you go walk off some of that booze? Countdown to 2052 starts in 120 minutes, son."

Luke excuses himself and stumbles out of view. He heads for the back of the dance floor, exits into the stairwell, and sprints up ten flights of stairs.

He enters the custodial storeroom, puts on his stealth suit, places his alcohol-smelling clothes in a plastic bag, and then into the backpack. He slings on the backpack, adjusting the straps tightly. With grappling gun in hand, he exits to the roof through the hatch and runs to the back edge of the roof. He secures the grappling hook, attaches the harness, and lowers himself ten floors.

Looking at every vehicle in the back parking lot, he knows the importance of selecting an inconspicuous one. If he were to be stopped by Protect and Serve, everything he has worked for over the past three weeks would be ruined. He picks a dark blue sedan with slightly tinted windows. A hack using the wireless connection between his phone and the vehicle's computer gets him in. Ignition engaged.

Being cautious to adhere to all traffic lights, signs, and speed limits, he sets the car to auto-navigate and arrives at the airport without trouble at 23:07.

Luke parks the car off the road in an empty field. He exits, puts on his backpack, pulls down the stealth suit face shield, and sprints for the chain-link fence that encloses the airport runways.

Using the night vision binoculars, he spots two drone cargo planes, exact same size, parked side by side. Then he runs a half mile along the chain-link fence, bringing him within 100 yards of the two planes. He snips several links of the fence and crawls through.

Now within range to remotely connect to the planes' onboard systems, he checks the time, 23:32. He quickly assembles the micro-laptop and uses his phone's Internet connection to access the dark web.

Through the binoculars, he can see the tail numbers on the planes. Entering the tail numbers into an aviation application he acquired last week after a few all-nighters on the dark web, he can now reprogram the flight routes and access the onboard cameras of both planes.

Luke plans to reprogram the flight routes, causing both planes to crash into an open field. The D-EERg will be destroyed and the anti-Meritism conspiracy will remain unknown to the citizens of Amerita.

He starts with tail number FBR-2010 and follows the exact steps in the simulation he ran last night. *Connecting* ... He watches the indicator, no change, *Connecting* ... He checks the time, 23:43.

Next, he attempts connecting to tail number LTM-0910. Same, stuck on *Connecting* ... He lets this one go for another minute without success.

Time passes insanely fast, 23:47.

He quits trying to connect and devises an alternate plan, one that must include crashing the plane while onboard.

First, determine which plane is loaded with the cargo and which is the decoy. Next, board the plane with the cargo. Finally, crash the plane while onboard. Thoughts of the personal consequences don't immediately enter his mind.

He decides to attempt connecting to the onboard cameras. That could reveal which plane has the real cargo.

Success.

Time check: 23:55.

The onboard cameras of FBR-2010 appear instantly. He sees a long corridor stacked with boxes. Zooming in, he can read the labels, *Municipal Water Supply Supplement Concentrate (100 canisters per box)*.

The onboard camera of LMT-0910 appears next. In the middle of the aisle, between identical stacks of water supply supplement, the man from the vault, the maintenance man, Cyrus Lance, the man with the flat-brimmed cowboy hat, the man who posed as the doctor, stands unmasked. He has one arm around the neck of Ashley Haynes. The other hand holds a butterfly knife up to her throat.

Luke starts visualizing scenarios and quickly realizes there are too many variables without knowing which plane has the real cargo. *Is Cyrus protecting the real cargo or is Cyrus tempting me to board the decoy and attempt to save Ashley's life, letting the real cargo head for distribution centers?*

Which plane has the cargo? Which plane has the cargo? Which plane has the cargo?

Time check: 23:58.

Luke throws the micro-laptop and phone into the backpack and sprints the 100 yards to the planes. He crouches between the two of them.

The loading ramps on both planes are slowly rising in preparation for takeoff.

He hears Ashley's desperate screams for help coming from the top of the plane's loading ramp.

He looks to the left at FBR-2010 and to the right at LMT-0910, knowing there is only enough time to board one plane.

Looks left. Looks right. Tires are considerably higher on LMT-0910. FBR-2010 must be weighted down, that one has the real cargo. The boxes on LMT-9010 must be empty. Cyrus holds Ashley hostage on the decoy.

Board the decoy and rescue Ashley, D-EERg is distributed throughout the population.

Board the plane with the cargo and crash the plane, Ashley dies.

Luke runs through the interactions he had with Ashley.

Note on coffee cup.

Reception line.

Conversation on dance floor.

He runs the conversations through his head, searching for something, anything to help decide between Ashley and the mission.

Time check: 23:59

Time seems to have slowed. Luke feels his heart beating through his chest. How could Ashley have been captured? Why her? The questions race through his mind over and over.

Then he decides.

Luke darts to FBR-2010, jumps onto the closing loading ramp, and enters the cargo hold.

Immediately he pulls out the micro-laptop and views the video on LMT-0910. He plugs in his earpiece and can hear the audio.

He witnesses Cyrus' infuriation. "Son of a bitch! Arghhh!" Cyrus yells, then throws the butterfly knife down the cargo hold, clanking on the steel grates.

"Hey, I did my part," Ashley yells, throwing Cyrus's arm from around her neck. As she turns to walk away from Cyrus, Luke makes out the shape of a handgun taped to her back, likely intended for Cyrus to use on him.

Luke continues to watch as Cyrus desperately scrambles for the loading ramp and successfully slides out of the decoy plane before the ramp fully closes.

Luke runs to the loading ramp of his plane and watches it close as Cyrus' frenzied shouts approach. They make eye contact one last time through three inches of opening just before the ramp completely closes, leaving Cyrus on the runway.

"Mr. T, have you seen Luke?" Amanda asks with worry.

Ned has an answer for Amanda, "Yes, I actually did. He's passed out cold upstairs on the 10th floor in our custodial storeroom. I'm sorry tonight didn't go as planned. Your husband is an amazing man, Amanda. I think he's still struggling with the changes. Come here."

Ned gives Amanda a fatherly hug.

Ten...

Nine...

Eight...

Seven...

Six...

Five...

Four...

Three...

Two...

One...

"Happy New Year, Amanda." Ned gives her a kiss on the forehead.

Amanda hugs him back, appreciative of his understanding.

"You head home," Ned suggests. "I'll stop by in the morning and kick him out of there and send him on his way. I think letting him sleep this off may be a good idea. Then when he wakes up, he'll be afraid of coming home and having to face you, and that will teach him good, right?"

Amanda laughs at Ned's idea and agrees, "I think that's a great idea. Thanks, Mr. T. Let him wake up on his own though, you shouldn't have to come here in the morning. Why don't you come over to our house for breakfast in the morning? Say around 09:00?"

"I would love that very much. I'll be there," Ned gives Amanda another fatherly hug.

The drone cargo plane turns toward the runway and begins takeoff.

Luke scrambles to the front of the plane where the onboard servers are housed. He patches his micro-laptop directly into the server and attempts to change the flight route again.

Connecting ... Connected!

In the simulations, he crashed the plane in an open field. Being in the plane, he needs another option.

Luke takes several deep breaths and performs a relaxation technique he perfected at Muay Thai practice with AJ. He sits with his legs crisscrossed underneath him, closes his eyes, rests his hands in his lap, and begins thinking ...

Thinking ...

Thinking ...

Thinking ...

SULLY! From the far recesses of his mind, he recalls a movie about a pilot who successfully completed a water landing on the Hudson River with a large aircraft. *Lake Ontario!*

Luke starts keying in coordinates for a location two miles north of the Lake Ontario shore. He programs a landing sequence for 74 meters above sea level, the average elevation of the lake. The time to landing calculates at four minutes.

He straps on his backpack and sits at the front of the plane, back against the foremost surface, hoping the backpack will absorb some shock. Being this is a drone plane, there are no seats or harnesses to shield him from the impact.

The next few minutes are spent visualizing the remaining steps of his plan:

Survive the water landing.

Sink the plane.

Swim two miles with backpack. Fortunately, stealth suits are waterproof, retain body heat in water down to 0 degrees Celsius, and provide buoyancy up to two hundred pounds.

Put clothes back on, good thing they are wrapped up in plastic.

Walk to the nearest bus stop and catch a bus home.

Face Amanda's wrath.

One minute ...

He considers leaving a voicemail message or sending a text message to his family, but he decides to avoid pessimistic thoughts.

Bam! He braces helplessly as the plane shakes violently, grasping everything around him in an attempt to not be thrown from floor to ceiling.

He feels a wave of deceleration and is thrust backward into the front of the plane. The backpack cushions the blow.

A split second after the deceleration, the fuselage cracks in the middle. The moon provides enough light for him to see the tail section spinning off in a different direction.

He jumps up and runs for the middle of the plane, banging from side to side into the boxes of cargo.

He reaches the opening half-way down the fuselage and dives into the freezing water.

The stealth suit's buoyancy keeps him afloat and he feels no cold.

He turns on his back and watches the tail section and the nose section sink into the lake.

He closes his eyes and says a prayer of thanks.

Luke is thrilled to see the waves are rather small tonight. He pulls his face shield down, tucks the openings of his fingerprint gloves tightly into the cuffs of the stealth suit, and begins his long swim.

Monday
January 1, 2052

New Year's Day

"I really appreciate you inviting me over for breakfast. What time do you think Jake will be home? I would love to meet that young man. He sounds like such an interesting kid." Ned is enjoying Luke's family's company very much. For the first time in 30 years, he does not feel alone in this world.

Amanda hears the clack-clack of footsteps coming down the hallway, "Hear that? That's probably Luke coming down the hall now."

She snickers as the footsteps get closer. "I love your thinking, Mr. T. I bet he feels like a total schmuck."

Knock-knock.

She whispers across the dining room table to Ned, "Ha, I bet he doesn't have his key." Amanda covers her mouth so Luke will not hear her laughter. "Who is it?" she asks playfully as she walks to the door.

Amanda opens the door just slightly, prepared to make Luke beg for entrance.

Cyrus kicks in the door, sending Amanda flying into the table. He steps inside and kicks the door shut behind him. Cyrus grabs Amanda by the neck and choke-slams her into the table. The table cracks, and she falls to the floor.

Ned lunges at Cyrus, and Cyrus knocks him down with one punch to the chest.

AJ comes flying down the hallway with her softball bat raised over her head and runs fearlessly at Cyrus. He throws a punch at her face as she closes in, but in one motion she slides to the floor in a split and follows through with her bat across the outside of Cyrus' right knee. He falls to the floor screaming in pain.

She straddles over Cyrus, bat raised above her head, ready to swing a fatal blow. As her bat comes down, Cyrus pulls a handgun from the back of his belt, pulls the trigger, and strikes Ned in the back as he lunges between Cyrus and AJ. Ned lands limp on the floor to the side of Cyrus.

AJ swings at Cyrus' hand and knocks the handgun to the wall, out of his reach. Without hesitation, she swings across his jaw. Adrenaline heightening her senses and the world around her moving in slow motion, she can see seven individual teeth fly from Cyrus' mouth, each tooth making a 'ting' sound as it hits the ceramic tiles on the kitchen floor.

She continues with another blow to the side of his head, sending blood spatter across the walls and up to the ceiling. Three more blows downward to his face, then she stands above him resting the end of her bat on the ground.

Luke tries to open the door to the apartment but has to shove his shoulder into the door, sliding Cyrus' body to the side enough for him to enter.

Seeing the carnage, Luke is unable to move.

AJ drops the bat and jumps into Luke's arms and begins bawling.

Amanda slowly gets up, rubbing the back of her head.

She puts her arms around AJ and Luke.

Friday

January 5, 2052

Ned

Luke, Amanda, AJ, and Jake are the last four standing by the gravestone following the ceremony. Many of Ned's coworkers and several Elders, made known to Luke covertly, were in attendance.

They pray solemnly.

Ned I. Tammarin's headstone is set next to the headstone of Martin Thomas Medina. Luke insisted Ned's coffin be buried where his father's body would never be.

As Luke and his family gradually make their way out of the cemetery, Luke attempts to change the mood by asking Jake a lighthearted question, "Son, speaking hypothetically, if someone dumped a million liters of, oh, say, liquid vitamins, into Lake Ontario, would that have an effect on the water supply?"

"Okay, well first, that's a really weird question, Dad. Second, that would be like taking a single drop of beer and dropping that into an Olympic-size pool, going for a swim and being worried about getting drunk." Jake's answer puts Luke's mind at ease.

Luke's phone rings. Ripley is calling, so he asks for a moment alone, "You guys head to the bus stop, I've got to take this call."

"Hang on a sec," he pauses, waiting for the three to be farther ahead. "What's up?"

"Hey, bud. How's the family doing?" Ripley asks with great concern.

"We're doing all right. I appreciate the Protect and Serve Agency asking Pharmavast to give me the week off. Being home with them, especially AJ, was really good. As far as my family knows, the incident was a random home invasion by a crazy man. So what's next?"

"Well," Ripley begins, "you're a hero. Unfortunate though that nobody will know except us Elders. Here's the deal. The public bought the story that a cargo plane's server glitched out and it crashed into the lake, so we're in the clear there. We believe Cyrus was Damien's only hitman, and with Cyrus dead we're confident you guys are safe. There's no way Damien is going to go after you or your family himself.

"And now for the bad news. We have nothing to pin on the Pharmavast Board of Directors. We have all that information from the vault about D-EERg, but Myers is good. He blacked out all incriminating information. All we can do is keep a really close eye on him and the Capitalists.

"And now for one more piece of good news! On Monday, the Merit Agency is going to announce that there was an error with determining your Productivity Calculation. Effective immediately, you are welcomed back to the agency. Of course, the offer to vocation jump and go to Hollywood still stands!"

Luke is silent.

Ripley waits patiently.

"I'll see you Monday morning, Ripley. We need to stay here for AJ and Jake. Maybe when they're both out of Discovery School I'll give Hollywood a shot. But for now, family first."

Luke catches up with his family and Jake shares a discovery with him, "Dad, I have a question for you. Not really a question, more of a, well, I don't know, but I guess this is just something I noticed. The letters in Ned's name can be rearranged to spell your father's name. Weird, right?"

Postface

In the summer of 2014, while on a Disney World vacation, Luke, his cousin CJ, and I were walking to a bus stop at the Old Key West Resort. A thought occurred to me out of the blue that I shared with Luke and CJ. I proposed, "What if the opportunity to vacation at Disney World was based on how hard someone worked instead of how much money they were able to set aside?"

Over the next week, the three of us went round and round, sharing ideas of how a community could be fashioned where the population's consumption (food, clothing, transportation, vacations, etc.) was based on how hard they worked at their job instead of how much they were paid.

For the next two years, Luke and I talked at length about the futuristic society, discussing theories, plot lines, and endings. We kept sketching out chapters and developed characters, and in the Summer of 2016, the storyline started coming together. Luke focused on writing the action sequences: Apprehension, The Underground, Vault, Masquerade Party. I focused on "World-Building" and "Filler," two writing phrases Luke introduced me to.

I am an entrepreneur and have learned the importance of partnering with the right person on the right endeavor. Thank you, Luke for partnering with me on this one! *AMERITA* would never have been completed without you keeping me motivated and excited.

Thank you, Tina, my wonderful wife, for never discouraging my many endeavors no matter how crazy they may have sounded.

Thank you, Dianne for your extreme patients with the editing (that was a joke, patients, patience, are you laughing?), your admirable diligence, and helping plug the many plot-holes.

Thank you, Mia for the amazing artwork.

Thank you, CJ for the conversations regarding the topics in this book during that week at Disney.

Thank you, Jesse for suggesting the title Amerita at Mia's house that Saturday afternoon.

Thank you, Dad for teaching me the importance of hard work. You would have an M-N 10 glowing brightly on the back of your hand if we lived in Amerita.

Thank you, Mom for the hour-long conversation on the way home from Uncle Joe's funeral where I told you all about the book, the characters, and the plot. Your perspective on students, formed by first-hand experience in school systems, led to equality for Discovery School students: school uniforms, the same nutritional lunches for everyone, and equal opportunity and socioeconomic status upon graduation.

Thank you, Nick for the software development work you have brought my way. Through Nick's technology-providing company, I have written productivity software for three companies in the Cortland, N.Y. area. These companies use the factual statistics derived from the software to measure their employee's productivity for determining pay increases and promotions. Productivity Calculations are not a theory. Productivity Calculations are a reality.

AMERITA

Rise of Meritism

Martin passes through the doorway into the review room, walking past the administrator. She raises her left arm after perceiving there would not be any physical contact and motions him into the review room with the palm of her hand. Martin takes a seat in the gray metal chair. He knows the next phrase spoken by the administrator once she is seated will be "Martin, your Merit Number for the next year will begin at the conclusion of your Merit Review," followed by announcing his score.

During the moments taken for the administrator to take her seat, Martin makes his final decision. He decides he will accept exile and go along with the plan he knows is forthcoming. The Elders explained, and he agrees, that this is the only way he can keep Luke and Tina safe.

Martin prepares to act surprised and ensure the plan is convincing. He vows to survive exile and see Luke and Tina again, if only from afar.

The administrator looks directly into Martin's eyes. Martin can see that her eyes are filled with sadness and welling with tears. She announces, "Martin, your Merit Number for the next year will begin at the conclusion of your Merit Review. 0, Exile."

The administrator brought the Merit Review to a close asking, "Martin, would you like to ask one question or make a statement?"

Martin asks his question, right on cue. "Yes. Why did my score drop so dramatically?"

The answer is delivered as planned, "Martin, your qualitative score was negative, and even with the positive quantitative and days worked scores, your overall Merit Number was still below zero. The reason for the poor qualitative score is because 73 hospital deaths were found to be attributed to a poorly manufactured pharmaceutical, Nyxthonate, which was manufactured using your programmable logic controller software algorithms."

Martin's eyes dimmed. There is a slight smile on his face as his lips move with no sound, exaggerating the words, "I love you, Tina. I love you, Luke." Then he says another six-word phrase, but this time with extremely minimal movement of his lips, "I am doing this for us."

His slight smile turns into an expression of terror knowing exile is immediate.

Justin Time Movie Trailer

(from chapter Hacker)

youtube.com/watch?v=su6XytDJ9Go

The real **Luke I Am Your Daddy** book

(from chapter Apartment)

LukeIAmYourDaddy.com